SEDUCING LOLA

A SEXY ROMANCE

JESSICA PRINCE

Stay Sassy!

♡
- Jess Prince

DISCOVER OTHER BOOKS BY JESSICA

THE PICKING UP THE PIECES SERIES:

Picking up the Pieces

Rising from the Ashes

Pushing the Boundaries

Worth the Wait

THE COLORS NOVELS:

Scattered Colors

Shrinking Violet

Love Hate Relationship

Wildflower

THE LOCKLAINE BOYS (a LOVE HATE RELATIONSHIP spinoff):

Fire & Ice

Opposites Attract

Almost Perfect

THE PEMBROOKE SERIES (a WILDFLOWER spinoff):

Sweet Sunshine

Coming Full Circle

A Broken Soul

PROLOGUE

LOLA

IF YOU'D HAVE ASKED my twenty-year-old self what I saw in my future ten years down the road, I probably would've answered the same way as every other naïve co-ed living the college dream on Sorority Row.

I'd be married to the love of my life, raising our two perfect children in the suburbs—because the city is no place to bring up a family, obviously—and driving a top-of-the-line SUV that all the minivan moms would envy because I had *way* too much style to ever be caught dead driving a minivan.

Clearly, my twenty-year-old self was an idiot.

It was she who forgave—then was subsequently dumped by —my college sweetheart after finding him pile-driving my sorority sister from behind on the handmade quilt I'd spent countless hours creating out of his old high school football T-shirts as a birthday present. His brilliant excuse? "You're just not adventurous enough, Lola. She's willing to try things in bed that you aren't."

Apparently refusing to allow him to film us having sex and entering it into a contest on a porn site was just too *vanilla* for him. Last I heard, he was making a killing on the amateur scene.

Unfortunately, my twenty-one and twenty-two-year-old selves weren't all that smart either.

It was my twenty-one-year-old self who discovered I'd unwittingly been made a beard by Brad, the guy I had dated for six months, because his evangelical parents just "wouldn't understand."

BTW, Brad and Phillip's wedding was a really lovely affair. He asked me to stand as his best *woman*—since he considered our relationship the reason he finally made his way out of the closet—but I turned down the honor, choosing instead to get annihilated on mojitos at the open bar.

My twenty-two-year-old self thought I had finally found a decent guy. That was until I came home to find him doing something I'll never be able to unsee to a pair of Louboutins I'd spent the better part of a year saving up for.

The saddest part? I hadn't even had a chance to wear them before his defilement. I didn't have the heart to throw them in the trash, so I let him take them with him when I kicked his ass out.

I should've known better, honestly. It wasn't like I'd grown up in a home with my very own personal June and Ward Cleaver. Oh no, my parents split when I was only six years old. And it was anything but amicable. My mom never kept her hatred for my father secret. And dear old Dad never hid the string of women he kept on tap, one for whatever mood he may've been in. It was shocking that I hadn't grown bitter at an even younger age, having to deal with their drama, but I was in my early twenties and still a believer in happily ever afters.

Like I said, I was an idiot.

Now I know what you're thinking. After three miserable failures, I was probably a jaded cynic who was convinced true love didn't exist.

Well, you'd only be half right. See, I believed in love, sure... as long as it was happening to anyone other than me. I'd been the fateful target of that bastard Cupid's stupid-ass arrow three times already; I had no desire to go for a fourth. I wasn't anti-relationship when it came to *other people*. To each their own and all that jazz. And I didn't *hate* men. I just didn't believe they were of any use to me for anything other than a few hours of fun that eventually led to a—hopeful—mutual release before I sent them on their way.

I learned from my mistakes, grown wise as the years passed. I knew exactly what I wanted out of my life, and believe me, there wasn't a shitty picket fence in sight. If the suburbs were for families, then the city was exactly where I was meant to be. I was a successful, accomplished thirty-two-year-old woman who'd gotten where I was in life by hard work, perseverance, and the cluelessness of women all around the world.

My name was known in households all throughout Washington State. I, along with my two best friends, hosted Seattle's most successful female-based talk radio show, aptly titled *Girl Talk*. I'd managed to make more money in the past ten years by offering relationship advice to helpless women than I'd ever know what to do with.

It was safe to say the rose-colored glasses were off. I lived in the real world where men cheated and women drowned their sorrows in vats of Ben & Jerry's.

Sure, I wasn't living the future I saw for myself when I was twenty, but then again, at twenty, I still thought Brad Pitt and Jennifer Aniston were *meant to be*, that *Wedding Crashers* was cinematic brilliance, and that the whole Tom Cruise/Oprah couch jumping "I'm in love with Katie Holmes" thing was actually romantic. What the hell did I know back then?

A lot had changed over the years. And as I gazed out the

floor-to-ceiling windows of my penthouse apartment, over-looking the Puget Sound, I could honestly say without a shred of doubt that I wouldn't have it any other way.

CHAPTER ONE

LOLA

"AND YOU WON'T *BELIEVE* what that asshole you call a father did this time!" My mother's voice echoed through the receiver, drowning out the honking cars and the clicking of my five-inch Gucci heels on the pavement as I crossed 7th Avenue. The typical bustling city sounds were lost as Elise Abbatelli ranted and raved through my cell phone.

"No telling, Ma," I answered with a roll of my eyes.

"Well I'll tell you!" she continued. "He showed up at The Met with that... that... *woman*! It was like he wasn't the slightest bit embarrassed to have a *call girl* on his arm during the mayor's birthday celebration! I tell you, Lola, that man has no shame whatsoever. It's humiliating to know we run in the same circles."

I let out a deep sigh as I shoved open the glass door of the Starbucks near my building and joined the line of customers, all of us in desperate need of a morning pick-me-up. I inhaled the rich scent of brewing coffee and the sweetness of the pastries as I searched for my calm. Talking to my mother had a tendency to drive me a little batshit. Then again, I came by it honestly, seeing as my own mother was more than just a little crazy.

"For the last time, Ma, Chelsea isn't a call girl. She's a gold digger. Contrary to popular belief, there really is a difference. And you wouldn't run in the same circles if you'd just stop attending all the events you know Dad's going to be at. The only one you're torturing is yourself. Hell, no one would even know you two had been married once if you'd quit going around and announcing it to all of Manhattan."

"Don't you sass me, Lola Arianna Abbatelli!"

The irony that my father's surname stood for "little priest" in Italian wasn't lost on me. The last thing Roberto Abbatelli could ever be compared to was a priest. The man was toeing the line of sixty and *still* couldn't keep his dick in his pants. But then again, why would he? He built his investment firm from the ground up, eventually earning so much success he'd been listed in *Forbes* more times than I could count. With money and power like his, fidelity and commitment were a joke.

"I'm not sassing you, Ma." I sighed again, moving up another step as the long line shuffled forward. "I'm just stating facts. You've been divorced for over two decades. With the money you got from that settlement, you could go anywhere, yet you *insist* on staying in Manhattan where you know you'll run into Dad constantly. What's the point? Move to the Caribbean or something! Find a smokin' hot cabana boy to fill your free time." I heard a masculine snort of laughter come from behind me but was too entrenched in my mother's rantings to give it any thought.

"I *have* a life," she insisted haughtily. If I'd been standing in front of her, I had no doubt her chin would have been tilted up, nose in the air. "I have friends—"

"You have acquaintances. And I've met most of them, Ma. Believe me, you wouldn't be missing out by shirking them off first chance you get."

She didn't argue with that, knowing good and well most of

those so-called friends were nothing but bloodsucking leeches. "I have my work."

I let out an indelicate snort. "You don't work!"

"I'll have you know I'm on the boards of many very influential charities."

Another eye roll. "You can write a check from the beaches of Barbados."

"Well... I have your brother!"

There was no way I could suppress my eye roll just then. "That's just sad, Ma. Dom's a grown man. You should've cut the cord a long time ago. You're making excuses."

"I am not!"

I lowered my voice, making sure to keep my tone soft as I said, "I get it, Ma. I do. Dad was the love of your life and it sucks having to let him go, but you're never going to move on if you're constantly bumping into each other. And I'm tired of seeing you get your heart broken. You deserve better than anything he could ever give you."

The line was silent for several seconds before she finally declared, "I'm happy with my life, thank you very much."

My shoulders slumped ever so slightly. It wasn't the first time we'd had that particular conversation, but it didn't hurt any less. My mother was in pain and refused to do anything about it. I tried to be understanding, but it was just so damned frustrating. It was like beating a dead horse, then turning around and banging my head against a brick wall. Trying to make her see reason was pointless.

"If you say so," I told her as the line shuffled again. "But it's your loss. There's probably a young guy named Marco on one of those islands just waiting for you to come and show him what it means to be a *real* man."

"So scandalous," she chided, but I could hear the smile in her voice. "If you're really concerned with making me happy, you'd quit this nonsense and give me the grandbabies I've been dying for."

I finally reached the front of the line, holding my phone to my chest and placing my order before moving to the side and lifting the receiver back to my ear.

"Hate to break it to you, Ma, but if you want grandbabies, you need to start annoying Dom about it. Odds are he's got at least one illegitimate kid out there anyway. He is his father's son, after all."

Mom gasped loudly, the very definition of scandalized. She was probably clutching her pearls just then. "You watch your mouth, young lady!"

I ignored her chastisement. It had always been like that. As far as she was concerned, Dominic would always be her "perfect little boy," philandering man-whore and all.

"As it stands, if some guy's spunk manages to break through the condom I'll definitely be making him wear *and* my birth control pills, we have some serious problems of the biblical variety."

"Language, Lola!" my mother admonished at the same time someone let out a choked cough from behind me.

I chanced a quick glance over my shoulder, my face drawing in the "sorry, didn't mean for you to hear me" look I seemed to have to paste on my face every time I was out in public. That filter most people were born with, you know, the one that kept them from spewing totally inappropriate things when in crowded places? Yeah, I so didn't have that. And it wasn't something that had ever embarrassed me. Maybe it was the Italian in me, but I'd always said exactly what was on my mind right when I thought it, eavesdroppers be damned. I mainly apologized because it was the politically correct thing to do.

The man who'd just heard me trying to convince my mom to get her groove back *Stella* style while shooting down her hope for future grandbabies all in the same conversation was standing two feet away, hands in his front pockets and a knowing smile stretched across his picture-worthy face.

"Sorry," I mouthed as I did a quick scan of his body. In just those few moments, I was able to tell his suit was high quality, no doubt designer. And judging from the broad expanse of his shoulders, tailored to fit his body. And what a body it was. Slightly disheveled chocolate brown hair, amazing green eyes, a square, chiseled jaw, and a nose that was just crooked enough to make him appear rugged without going Owen Wilson over-board wrapped up the insanely hot package. The dude was most definitely spank bank material.

I'd made an art out of reading men over the past decade, and this guy, with his expensive suit and casual confidence, screamed money and power. Both of those attributes, while hot as hell, were something I stayed far, *far* away from when it came to the opposite sex.

I tended to go for middle-of-the-line good guys who didn't take life too seriously. I found they were the easiest to scrape off whenever the sex became monotonous or I just got bored and wanted to move on. Men who wielded power in their professional lives had a tendency to think they could carry that over into the personal side—including the bedroom. And when it came to sex, I *always* had the power. I didn't allow it any other way. Losing power only led to heartbreak, and despite what my career would lead people to believe, I was of the firm opinion that heartbreak was for suckers.

So, despite the fact that the man behind me was the type to rev my engine, sadly, it wasn't meant to be.

"Lola? Lola, you there?"

I spun back around at my mother's voice, determined to put Mr. Power Suit out of my mind. "I'm here."

"You know, there's nothing wrong with settling down," she told me, the same line she used every single time we talked.

I snorted—*loudly*. "There's nothing right with it either."

"Lola Arianna—"

"Abbatelli, I raised you better than that," I interrupted, imitating her nasally, put-out tone as I finished her trademark sentence for her.

"I do *not* sound like that," she harrumphed, causing me to smile.

"How about this. You don't push me for marriage and babies, and I won't push you for hot, sweaty island sex. Deal?"

"What did I do," she started, undoubtedly looking at her ceiling as she spoke to God—yet another thing I'd grown accustomed to seeing during my life, "to deserve such a crass, uncouth daughter?"

"Just lucky, I guess," I answered snidely as the barista called my name and sat my drink on the counter. "Now I have to go," I told her as I pushed through the morning crowd, trying to get to that big cup of caffeinated goodness. "I need to get to the station and I haven't had coffee. I'll call you back tonight and we can talk shit about Dad for your allotted thirty minutes."

"I do not talk *shit*, Lola," she said, as if the very thought were beneath her. "I simply express my exasperation at his childish antics."

"Tomato, to-mah-to." I shrugged, even though she couldn't see. "Gotta go. Love you, Ma."

"Love you too, sweet pea. Talk soon."

I disconnected the call and slid my cell back into my red Kate Spade bag before reaching for my venti white mocha. "Mmm," I hummed, eyes closed in delight as I sucked down that first necessary sip. That first hit was always the best. And yes, I was aware that comparison made me sound like a crack addict, but whatevs. I was a hardcore coffee addict and wasn't the slightest bit repentant.

"If that conversation I heard a few minutes ago wasn't intriguing enough to catch my attention, that noise you just made certainly would've done it."

I opened my eyes and landed on a pair of slightly familiar grassy green ones. "And if a lame attempt at a pickup line like that were enough to catch my attention, I'd have to shoot myself," I replied with a sweet smile as I blatantly looked Mr. Power Suit up and down. *Damn, what a shame.*

"Grayson!" the barista called, setting a drink on the counter behind me. "I have a venti Americano at the counter for Grayson Lockhart!"

"I take it you're Grayson Lockhart?" I asked, quirking an eyebrow as he stepped closer and reached past me to grab his coffee, paying extra attention to brush the sleeve of his jacket against my arm as he kept his stare focused on mine. I had to give it to him—he was good. His eyes never once deviated past my chin, and I was rocking some pretty sweet cleavage if I did say so myself. Not slutty cleavage, mind you. Classy cleavage. I was a professional woman, after all, but I'd also been blessed with the Abbatelli curves. I might've only been five feet, two inches tall, but I rocked a full C-cup, had a teeny waist, a J-Lo booty, and what my nonna lovingly referred to as "child-bearing hips."

Even if I wanted to cover up what God gave me, I wouldn't have been able to. At present, the short-sleeve, boatneck red and black Versace dress I was wearing hugged my curves and bared a modest half inch of décolletage. It wasn't too much, just enough to hint at the more that lay beneath, but Mr. Power Suit made a conscious effort not to look. I was impressed.

"And you're venti nonfat, no-whip white mocha for Lola,"

he said with a devastatingly handsome smile. A smile that would make any woman—other than me—shudder with need.

"You got it, Suit." I sidestepped, prepared to go around him when he spoke up again.

"I'm clearly at a disadvantage here. See, you have my full name, but I only have your first name and drink preference."

I scrunched my face in mock speculation as I tapped my chin. "That's quite the conundrum you got there, Grayson Lockhart. Hope you get it straightened out." I patted his chest and moved around him, heading for the door.

"You're really not going to give me your name?" he asked, a bewildered smile on his face that said with his good looks he was used to getting what he wanted. Unfortunately for him, so was I, and he wasn't currently on my list of wants.

"I'm really not. Stings, I know. But I have no doubt your pride will bounce back, someone as handsome as you and all."

"So you think I'm handsome?" he called out, shamelessly watching my hips as I sauntered toward the exit, his lips turned up in a seductive grin.

"I might not be interested, but I'm not blind," I scoffed, one corner of my mouth tilting into a smirk as I turned and walked backward to continue our banter.

"Not interested, huh?"

I shrugged nonchalantly as I pushed the glass door open with my shoulder. "I've made it a habit never to date someone prettier than me. See ya around, Lockhart."

The door closed on his hearty laugh as I headed back out into the gray Seattle morning.

Nothing like a little harmless flirting to brighten a girl's day.

CHAPTER TWO

LOLA

PUSHING through the doors of Hart Tower—a large, imposing skyscraper in the heart of downtown Seattle that housed Bandwidth Communications, the company that owned KTSW and their sister stations—I had a smile on my face as I scrolled through the e-mails on my phone and sucked back another sip of my coffee. Most people worked to live, burning eight hours a day behind a desk where they watched the clock and prayed for quitting time. Fortunately, I was one of the lucky few. I got to work with my two best friends doing something I enjoyed the hell out of every single day. Other than a handful of public events, charity functions the station supported, and the occasional promotional photo shoots here and there, I never had to take my work home with me. Bonus: I got paid a shitload of money doling out relationship advice to women at the end of their rope.

I liked to think of what we did as community service. We helped women who refused to help themselves. We gave them the push they needed to shit or get off the pot when it came to relationships that were circling the drain, just waiting to be flushed.

Now don't get me wrong—we weren't *always* against the guy. If a woman was a raging harpy who needed to be told to pull the stick out of her ass and stop being such a cow, we didn't hesitate. But let's be honest, the brunt of our calls was from heartbroken women done wrong, not the other way around. If my own personal experience, coupled with watching my jackass of a father stomp on my mom's heart all my life, wasn't enough to turn me off commitment, my job certainly was. And before you start thinking I'm one of those raging harpies, rest assured, Sophia and Daphne felt the same way. They both had their own reasons for their anti-relationship stance, but we all agreed on one thing:

Why buy the car when you can take it out for a twenty-four-hour test drive and return it to the lot without the hassle of greasy salesmen and a shitload of paperwork?

Hell, guys did it all the time. And we were nothing if not equal opportunity women in today's modern society.

"Morning, boys," I called, shooting a smile to the security guards who manned the front desk in the building lobby.

"Morning, beautiful," Bob, the oldest and longest-running guard, returned, giving me a cheeky wink. Bob was one of the good ones—the exception to the rule. He was faithful to his wife of thirty years, a dedicated employee who'd been working security in the building for twenty-three years, and a doting father and grandfather who just so happened to be a shameless flirt. "Break any hearts today?"

"It's only 7:00." I winked back. "I'm good, but not *that* good. Give me a little while longer."

"Usually there'd be a line out the door by now. Must be slacking, girl."

I turned to look at him over my shoulder as I headed toward my elevator bank, not missing the lustful gazes of the two younger guards zeroed in on my ass as I walked. "Or maybe I'm just waiting for the opportunity to snatch you away from Loretta. Ever think about you? You're a total catch, Bob."

He let out a rich, hearty laugh. "Don't I know it? You have a good day now, sweetheart."

"You too!" I called back as one of the elevators dinged and I climbed in with the rest of the morning rush. I took one last peek at the desk just in time to catch Bob smacking one of the younger guys in the back of the head. See what I mean? One of the good ones.

My eyes returned to my phone, scanning through the e-mail I'd received earlier that morning from Jerry, our show's producer. I smiled just as the screen cut off with a text notification.

Sophia: *You see what's on the schedule for today?*

My smile grew even wider as I typed back.

Lola: *Yep. Getting off the elevator now. Meet you at my desk in three. Bring Daph.*

The elevator doors opened and I squeezed through the remaining people, stepping onto the floor for KTSW. I gave Jodi, the receptionist, a wave as I pushed through the glass doors and wound my way through the pods of cubicles before finally coming to my own on the other side of the floor, closest to the studio.

I'd barely had time to drop my purse into my desk drawer and boot up my computer before Sophia and Daphne came scurrying around the corner, equal expressions of "oh hell yeah" written all over their faces.

"Ooh, today's going to be fun," Daphne giggled, propping her skirt-clad behind on the edge of my desk as Sophia took the only other chair available in my small work space. "We haven't done 'In the Act' in months!"

"In the Act" was an idea I came up with back in college when the three of us hosted a show for our campus radio station.

We carried it over when we came on to do *Girl Talk* for KTSW. A listener would e-mail us about their spouse or significant other who they suspected was cheating and I would call up the asshole in question, posing as some sort of vendor, offering up everything from flowers to weekend getaways in the hopes of, well, catching them *in the act*.

Because our entire show was live, we had to be careful not to overdo it. If we called unsuspecting cheaters every single week, offering hotel stays or spa packages for them and one other person, eventually people would start catching on and the ruse wouldn't work.

The three of us enjoyed the segment, not because we liked ruining relationships and breaking hearts, but because we liked being able to help a woman walk away from a terrible situation she might not have had the strength to if we hadn't been able to provide definitive proof of the man's affair.

And, I was willing to admit, it was always a little fun hanging assholes out to dry for everyone to hear. Public humiliation was revenge at its finest, after all.

"Jerry already picked the e-mail," Sophia said. "Have you had a chance to read through it?"

"I skimmed," I answered as I brought up my e-mail on my desktop, opening the one I'd been reading on the elevator ride up. "Sounds like your typical dimwit/douchebag scenario," I stated as I read through the woman's ranting. "They've been dating for a year and a half, no sex in the past six months, late nights at the office and constant business trips...." I kept going until I reached the line that gave me pause. "Wow. He hasn't even taken her to meet his parents yet? And this chick doesn't get it yet?" I scoffed. The warning signs were flashing bright red and could be seen from miles away, but she was still holding out hope. It was a little sad, really.

"Probably why Jerry picked the e-mail," Daphne voiced as

she crossed her ankles and began swinging them back and forth. "Honestly, you have to pity the poor girl. From the sounds of it, this entire relationship is one big-ass red flag and she's too naive to see it."

"That's not naivety," I snorted. "That's a chick whose head is buried so deep in the sand, it's going to take a freaking backhoe to get it out."

Sophia stood and propped her hands on her hips. "Well, if there's anyone who can shove a dose of reality down someone's throat it's you, Lola." She grinned.

I leaned back in my chair and fiddled with a pen between my fingers. "This is going to be like strapping a pack of C4 to a relationship and lighting the fuse." I sighed. "I almost feel bad for her."

Daphne hopped off my desk, giddy with anticipation. "Well, time to get ready for an explosion."

THE "ON AIR" light clicked on and I leaned closer to the mic. "You're back with Lola, Sophia, and Daphne." I spoke clearly and concisely, relishing the high I got every time I reached out to our listening audience. "And you're listening to *Girl Talk* on 95.6, KTSW. If you're just tuning in, we've been talking to Brooke, who e-mailed the show because she suspects her boyfriend of a year and a half,"—I looked down at my notes —"Gray, has been cheating on her."

"Now, Brooke," Daphne chimed in with a soft voice, the motherly one in our little trio. "Are you sure you're ready to do this? You know, with everything you've told us, there's a possibility you might not like what you hear."

"I-I'm ready," she sobbed through the line. The woman had been inconsolable through almost the entire phone call.

I looked through the glass into the booth at Jerry, getting the thumbs-up just seconds before the sound of a phone ringing cut through our headsets. A moment later a deep, intoxicating voice came on the line.

"Hello?"

If I had to guess, the man the voice belonged to was hot as sin. It would be too cruel a joke for God to give such a rich voice like that to some scrawny, balding accountant type with a belly that hung over his pants. Jeez, just one word and women's panties all over Washington were probably melting.

"Hi," I said in a tone that was just seductive enough to catch his attention without risk of sounding slutty. "May I speak with Gray, please?"

"Speaking," Mr. Sexy-Voiced Gray rumbled. "Who's calling?"

"My name's Rebecca. You don't know me, sir, but I'm the manager of guest relations for"—another quick look at my notes, scanning for the hotel chain Brooke claimed he frequented —"Icon Hotels. I'm calling today because we're running a new promotion for our reward holders and I see that you've stayed at several of our properties throughout the States. Now, I know you're a busy man," I added, padding his ego ever so slightly in order to keep him on the line, "so I won't keep you too long, but as a thank-you for all your loyal business, we'd like to offer you a free weekend stay at our Seattle location for you and one guest, complete with a couples massage and spa package, on the house."

"Oh, well, that's very nice, thank you. But I'm afraid I'll have to pass."

"Are you sure?" I pushed, needing to find an in so I could nail the guy's balls to the wall. "It really is a lovely spa. I'm sure your wife or girlfriend would enjoy it, and bonus! You get all the credit for being so thoughtful."

Sophia gave me a thumbs-up, clearly pleased with my improvisation.

I could hear the smile in his voice as he spoke. "While I appreciate your quick thinking, sadly, there's no wife or girl-friend in the picture. But I'm sure there is another rewards member who'd be more than happy to receive such a lovely package."

No girlfriend? He wouldn't even claim Brooke to a complete stranger! "What an asshole," I mouthed to my girls before jerking my index finger across my throat at Sophia, our sign for "finish the fucker off."

She opened her mouth to jump in just as a loud banshee scream broke through each of our headphones, threatening to burst our ear drums.

"You sorry son of a bitch!" Brooke screamed on the other line. "You piece-of-shit *motherfucker!*"

"Jesus," Daphne put her hand over her mic. "Thank God we're on a ten-second delay. Poor Jerry's probably sweating bullets trying to beep those out."

We turned to look in the booth, and sure enough, Jerry's entire face was red as he hurried to cover every curse word spewing from Brooke's mouth.

"What the hell!" Gray barked. "What is this?"

"Well, Gray," Sophie finally joined in, "that wasn't Rebecca from guest relations. That was Lola, and you're currently on *Girl Talk* on 95.6, KTSW. Your *girlfriend*, Brooke, called in because she had a suspicion that you've been cheating on her. And based on your refusal to even admit she's in the picture, I'd say her concerns are valid, wouldn't you?"

"Are you fucking *kidding!*" Gray yelled. "Brooke isn't my girlfriend! She's a psychopath I went on one date with a year and a half ago who's been stalking me ever since! I can't believe this!"

"Wait, wait, wait," I said into my mic, trying desperately to get a word in edgewise between our two irate callers. "Brooke informed us you've been together for over a year. Was that a lie?"

"Of *course* it was a lie! I have a restraining order on her crazy ass!"

"Who is she, Gray?" Brooke shrieked. "Who the hell is the bitch you're screwing? I want to know!"

I shot wide eyes at Sophia and Daphne as they both struggled to maintain their composure. All three of us were at risk of bursting into laughter at any moment.

"Brooke," Daphne spoke over the screaming couple. "Is that true? Have you been stalking him?"

"Well I wouldn't *have* to if he'd quit moving and changing his locks!"

"I change them because you're certifiably insane!" Gray shouted in return. "Brooke, calling a radio station to have them set me up for some sick prank is a violation of the RO! I should have your ass thrown in jail!"

"Wow," I chuckled before adding sarcastically, "It's so hard to believe you two didn't work out."

Movement out of the corner of my eye caught my attention. I glanced toward the booth to see Sam, the station's programming director, had just barged in, waving his hands at Jerry like a madman.

What the hell?

Jerry's red face had turned an uncomfortable shade of purple as the two men shouted and waved their hands around in a frenzy. Poor Andrew, our board operator, had attempted to take over covering the bad language, but based on his wide, panicked eyes, I was afraid he might have let a couple F-bombs slip through.

Yay, we get to pay penalties.

"Ladies of Washington State!" Brooke yelled through her phone. "Do *not* date Grayson Lockhart! He's a douchebag asshole!"

"Whoa, hey!" Sophia broke into the fold. "No last names, Brooke. Not cool."

Grayson Lockhart? Where have I heard that name? I needed time to go through my memory bank, but unfortunately, I was too busy trying to settle down the two people on the line who had just gone completely ape-shit to bother with figuring out what was so familiar about that name.

"*Grayson Lockhart!*" Brooke shouted.

"Have you lost your *goddamned mind!*" Grayson bellowed.

"*GraysonLockhartGraysonLockhartGraysonLockhart!*" she screamed over and over again.

I spun back to the booth. Sam was losing his ever-loving mind, and as Jerry shoved Andrew out of the way I knew, I just *knew* the man on the phone's full name had managed to slip through the sound waves, delay or not. The "In the Act" segment had just turned into a clusterfuck.

"Drop her, Jerry," I demanded, my gaze on the men in the booth. Sam looked ready to commit murder. Jerry was about two seconds away from having a heart attack, and Andrew more than likely had a concussion from Jerry shoving him into the filing cabinet. Brooke's voice was suddenly gone, leaving only a seething Grayson Lockhart on the line.

"Uh, Gray?" I hesitated, trying to slip back into professional mode. All eyes were on me, and Daphne and Sophia looked just as shell-shocked as I felt. "We've dropped Brooke and we sincerely apologize for the confusion. Her e-mail clearly stated—"

His deep tone, once hypnotic, now sounded menacing as he declared, "You'll be hearing from my attorney," right before disconnecting.

"Well," I laughed uncomfortably. "That was certainly interesting, ladies."

"Understatement of the year," Sophia added just as someone knocked on the glass of the booth, pulling my attention back.

Oh shit.

Sam's finger was pointed straight at me as he mouthed, "Get your ass in my office," clear as day.

I gave him a thumbs-up, then pointed at the clock so he could see there were about fifteen minutes left of our show. I thought the vein protruding from his neck was going to burst as he bellowed "*Now!*" so loud Jerry and Andrew flinched.

Well okay then.

CHAPTER THREE

LOLA

THIS IS NOT GOOD. This is so *not good.* I paced the length of the conference room. Of *course* the stupid thing had to be all glass. Everything at KTSW was glass. There wasn't an ounce of privacy anywhere. So I got the luxury of pacing while Sam took his sweet-ass time starting the meeting *he* demanded we have, everyone in the office watching me with rapt fascination.

Assholes.

"What the hell's taking him so long?" I grumbled to myself as I chewed on my thumbnail, a nasty habit I'd had since childhood. A quick glance at the clock on the wall showed I'd been stewing for a good thirty minutes. If he was going to make me wait, the least he could've done was have some muffins or scones catered in, for Christ's sake. Was a carafe of coffee asking too much? Really. After the ass chewing I'd received the day before and the late-night e-mail from the boss man himself, demanding an early morning meeting, I'd gotten no sleep whatsoever.

As I continued to pace, I thought back to what had taken place in Sam's office after I'd been all but forced out of the studio.

"Jesus Christ, Lola! Do you have any idea who that was on

the phone?" He didn't wait for an answer, just continued yelling and gesticulating like a madman. "Of course you don't! Even you couldn't be stupid enough to prank call Grayson fucking Lockhart!"

"Uh"—I raised my hand like a child in school—"just saying, it wasn't really a prank call."

"Not the time," Jerry hissed between clenched teeth. I lowered my arm at Sam's furious glare.

"Look," I huffed. "It's not like we could control what that psycho was going to do. If you hadn't come in and ranted at Jerry, he'd have been able to catch her spouting his name off during the delay. So really"—I shrugged—"this is technically all your fault, if you think about it."

I'd never seen a look like the one he gave me on another human being's face before. I was truly afraid he was having an aneurysm and was contemplating calling an ambulance when he closed his eyes and sucked in a long breath.

When Sam opened his mouth again, he spoke slowly, as though he was talking to a four-year-old.

"Grayson Lockhart is the CEO of Bandwidth Communications."

Uh-oh.

"Son of Nolan Lockhart. The fucking president of the company! For Christ's sake, Lola! Their name is on the goddamned building!"

"Uh, pretty sure it says Hart *Tower outside. Not Lockhart."*

Jerry smacked his forehead as soon as I finished my sentence.

"Hart *Tower... owned by Lock*hart!"

Oh okay. I got it now.

And shit.

I shot to my feet and threw my arms wide. "Well how the hell was I supposed to know!" I pointed my finger at my red-faced producer. "Jerry's the one who sent the e-mail this morning! I didn't even know we were going to do the 'In the Act' segment until I was on my way in!"

That's right, buddy. If I'm going down, I'm taking your ass with me.

A true gentleman would've gladly thrown himself under the bus so I didn't have to push him myself and risk screwing up my manicure. But was Jerry chivalrous like that? Nooooo. Of course not.

"It doesn't matter whose fault it was," Sam continued to blather. "Now we need to think about damage control. As it is, it's going to take an act of God to save both of your jobs. Since Grayson's name was released during the segment to Lord only knows how many fucking people, he might not be feeling all that gracious."

"But-but," I sputtered, then ended with a very eloquent—if I do say so myself—"It's not my fault!" Because I was super mature like that.

Sam sliced his hand through the air. "Doesn't matter! Just be prepared to grovel like your life depends on it."

I groaned at the memory. Groveling was *so* not my thing. I sucked at it. You know that saying, "Fake it 'til you make it?" Yeah, well, I'd never mastered the art of faking it. Hell, I couldn't even fake an orgasm believably—just ask Billy Jefferson from my senior year in high school. He'll tell you. Anytime I had to kiss ass, my face did this weird scrunchie thing that made it look like I'd just sucked on a lemon.

After another five minutes, my heels began to pinch my toes so I decided to sit in the plush chair at the head of the table. Another five minutes passed and worry for my job was pushed from my mind, replaced with boredom so acute I was convinced I just might die from it. So I did what any sane, reasonable woman would do while waiting for her boss to come tear her a new asshole.

I watched YouTube videos on my phone of cats doing funny shit.

I'd kicked my uncomfortable shoes off, propped my feet on the wooden conference table, and settled in for some laughs. I was on my fourth video when the door swung open, followed by a sarcastic "Oh please, Lola, make yourself comfortable. Can I get you anything? Grapes? A palm frond, maybe?"

I stood from the chair, my back to the door as I slipped my heels back on. "Well if you hadn't taken so damn long I wouldn't ha—" The words died in my throat as I turned around to face Sam and was greeted by... well, *more* than just Sam.

Sweet merciful hell. I suddenly recalled where I knew the name Grayson Lockhart from. "Venti Americano Grayson!" I shouted, snapping my fingers as those familiar glittering green eyes hit me. "*That's* where I know you from! Damn it, that's been bugging me since yesterday!"

"Venti nonfat, no-whip white mocha Lola," he spoke in that low, velvety voice. It would've been enough to induce shivers had he not been staring at me like he was trying to light me on fire with the powers of his mind.

Well if that was how he was going to play it, I'd just take my ball and go home.

"You two know each other?" another man asked. That was when I realized we had more company. A *lot* more company. As in Jerry, Sophia, and Daphne—they both waved and gave me supportive smiles—Sam, Carmen from the PR department, and some man in his late fifties to early sixties, if I had to guess by the fit build under his suit and attractive salt-and-pepper hair. Seeing as he had the exact same piercing green eyes and square jaw as Americano Grayson—yup, I'd nicknamed him—I could only venture a guess that the one who'd just spoken was Nolan Lockhart.

"No," I answered at the same time Grayson said, "We met at

Starbucks yesterday before she decided to try and emasculate me for all of Washington and God knows what other states to hear."

"In my defense," I spoke unwisely, despite the wide eyes and head shakes I was getting from my girls, "I wasn't really the one trying to emasculate you. That was all Brooke. And if we'd known she was going to turn out to be a bunny-boiling psycho, we never would've let her on the show. I swear!"

Sam pinched the bridge of his nose and sighed. The man had a tendency to do that a lot around me. "Lola, please just... stop talking." He turned to address the rest of the people standing in the doorway. "Please, everyone, take a seat. My assistant should be down here with coffee and pastries in just a few moments."

"*Now* you offer sustenance?" I grumbled to myself. Unfortunately, Grayson was close enough to have heard me and gave me a funny look that caused my cheeks to flush in embarrassment.

I moved to take a seat next to Daphne, only to pause when Grayson spoke up. "Oh no, please, take this one." He pulled out the chair at the head of the table, the one I'd been so comfortably kicked back in, sans shoes, when he walked into the conference room. I gave an uncomfortable laugh and slid onto the chair. He took the one to my left, his father on his other side, and Sam took the one to my right, next to Carmen.

"Okay, so let's get started." He clapped like it was just your typical, everyday budget meeting and not something that could land both Jerry and me on the unemployment line.

I shot a glance at Jerry; poor guy was seriously going to keel over any day now if he didn't eliminate some stress from his life. I really needed to e-mail his wife about putting him on a heart-healthy diet.

Carmen cleared her throat and shuffled some papers

around, the picture of professionalism. "Well, we got the numbers in for the show yesterday after the... unfortunate incident...."

Well played, Carmen. Well played indeed.

"An unfortunate incident that millions were audience to," Grayson cut in. "I'll have you know I was approached on the street yesterday and cussed out by a total stranger for leading that, and this is a direct quote, 'poor mentally unstable girl on.' It hasn't even been twenty-four hours and the tabloids are having a goddamned field day," he growled. "I'm being crucified."

"We understand, sir," Carmen continued. "And although we understand Mr. Lockhart's embarrassment due to the... debacle—"

"Debacle?" Lockhart Sr. snapped. "My wife called me, hysterical! She's terrified that psychopath is going to find him again and murder him in his sleep! I had to give her an Ambien just to get her to calm down last night."

Yikes. Who knew Brooke was of the *Snapped* variety of crazy.

"It's okay, Dad. Just calm down." Grayson patted his father on the arm. I actually thought it was kind of sweet. "I've got a state-of-the-art security system and a privacy fence. There's no way she's getting in."

"Well explain that to your mother after the last time."

"Uh," I cut in, "the last time?"

Grayson shot me a murderous look. "That's not relevant to this discussion."

"Got it." I sat back and clamped my lips shut, shooting a "WTF" look in Sophia and Daphne's direction.

"Yes, well, as I was saying," Carmen continued, "while we're all extremely sorry for what transpired yesterday morning, our listenership actually skyrocketed. We've had more feedback than ever before, and the interest in *Girl Talk* seems to be bleeding over into both the midday and evening shows. Now I know it's probably not what you want to hear, all things considered, but yesterday's segment took KTSW to a whole new level."

She slid the papers forward and Nolan scooped them up, his eyes scanning furiously as Grayson leaned over his shoulder and did the same. I looked at Jerry and mouthed "For real?" He nodded, looking a little less red at the good—well, better than expected—news.

"Are these accurate?" Nolan asked Sam.

"They are. And while we understand you'd like us to take action"—he gave me a look and I barely managed to suppress my eye roll—"we think it would be a mistake to release any parties involved with *Girl Talk*."

Carmen held up a finger. "But we think we've come up with a solution that will placate you both."

"And what is that?" Grayson asked, leaning back in his chair, one ankle resting on the opposite knee as he propped his chin in his hand. Even in his relaxed state, he still reeked of power... and sex. A *lot* of sex. Even *I* couldn't deny how attractive he was when he was in business-mode. And he wasn't even my type!

Just then I totally understood why Brooke went all nutty.

"Well, as you know, the show tends to lean towards being more...." Carmen tapped her chin. "How to put this...."

"Anti-male?" Grayson offered snidely.

"That's not true!" I smacked my palm against the table in outrage.

Sam, Jerry—hell, even Daph and Soph—looked at me with equal expressions of "Bitch, *puh-lease*." My indignation quickly melted away and I slumped back. "Well, not *totally* anti-guy."

"Anyway," Carmen continued, ignoring my outburst, "we're thinking that the best way to get in front of this is for you two to be seen out together. Miss Abbatelli would offer a public apology, and then we'd set it up for you to attend a few events as each others plus one. One of the faces of *Girl Talk* with the CEO of Bandwidth Communications," she said like it was a freaking headline. "The speculation around whether you two are together or not will not only boost ratings, but it would also repair any damage your reputation might've faced."

Grayson hummed. He actually hummed! Meanwhile, I thought my head might explode.

"Are you kidding me!?" I shouted. "You *actually* expect me to parade around Seattle like some playboy's piece of ass, all so he can look good to the public? You're out of your mind! My credibility will be shot to hell if our listeners get wind that this is just some PR stunt! Those women call in for honest advice. What kind of hypocrite would I be if I told them to do one thing, then turned around and did something that went against everything I stood for?"

"You'd be the employed kind," Sam replied dryly.

"Oh, For fu—dge's sake, he's not even my type!"

"I think it's a brilliant idea," Grayson stated, tapping his fingertips on the table. My head shot sideways to gape at him, only to find both him and his father looking *way* too pleased with themselves.

Crossing my arms over my chest, I harrumphed. "Well I won't do it. I won't! I'm fine with a public apology, but I'm not going to be some... some... billionaire's arm candy! Nope, nuh-uh, not happening."

"I'm sorry," Sam said with false contrition. "Were you under the impression that this was a request? You'll do it, or not only will you face termination, but also a lawsuit if Mr. Lockhart feels so inclined."

I glanced back at Grayson. The bastard was actually smiling as he said, "Oh, I'm looking forward to this."

I shot to my feet, trying my best to melt the skin off Grayson's pretty face with my eyes. "Fine," I ground out. "But let the record show I think this is absolute bullshit!" So much for professionalism.

"So noted," Sam deadpanned.

I glared at him and crossed my arms over my chest. "I don't see you letting the record show."

Sam sighed at my ridiculousness and picked up his pen, scribbling on the notepad in front of him as he spoke the words he was writing. "Ms. Abbatelli thinks this is bullshit." He made a flourish of ending the sentence with a bold period and dropped the pen back down before looking up at me. "Happy now?"

"That'll do." Then I pointed at Grayson and threatened, "But if you expect me to play the doting little girlfriend, you've got another thing coming, sir."

I spun around on my gorgeous but painful Manolos and stomped toward the door, giving one last parting shot over my shoulder. "I'm going to make Brooke look like a freaking Disney princess!"

I'd just finished thinking, *Ha! That'll show him*, when I suddenly smacked face first into a wall of glass.

"Sonofabitch, that hurt!" I shouted, cupping my nose as I looked to see I was off the mark and missed the door by a good foot.

Most definitely not the exit I had planned.

CHAPTER FOUR

GRAYSON

I SHOT to my feet the moment her face made contact with the glass, ready to rush to assistance if necessary, despite my serious aversion to blood. If the rattling sound the glass made was any indication, she smacked into that thing like a linebacker.

"Sonofabitch, that hurt!" she shouted.

I took a step in her direction just as the hand not cupping her nose came up. With her back still to everyone, she announced loudly, "I'm okay. I'm okay. I'm just... going to go now." She took two small side steps, to where the actual doorway was, and mumbled, "Good day to you," before high-tailing it out of there like her ass was on fire.

I heard the squeak of chairs and turned to see the two women Lola had attempted to sit next to at the start of the meeting stand and point in the direction she'd just scurried off in. "We'd better...." the tall one with the jet-black hair and thick bangs started to say.

"Yeah, Sophia," Sam sighed, squeezing the bridge of his nose. "Go make sure she didn't break anything."

"I'm sure she's fine," the somewhat shorter blonde next to

the Amazon announced. "She hasn't managed to break anything yet."

"This isn't the first time she's walked into a wall?" I asked, aghast. "Is this a daily thing or something?"

"More like monthly," the tall woman, known as Sophia, answered. "She's been complaining about all the glass for years. Poor thing's been a bit of a klutz for as long as we've known her."

I pointed a finger between the two women. "So I take it you're the other two members of the *Girl Talk* trio?"

"Uh...." The blonde's cheeks started growing pink as she looked anywhere but at me. "Gotta go! You know, make sure Lola's all right and all that. Don't want any worker's comp claims. Nasty business." She laughed uncomfortably and the duo began to move.

Before I could get another word out, they bolted from the conference room.

I turned back to Sam and the woman from PR—I couldn't remember her name—and spoke in my most commanding voice. "I'll be expecting an e-mail with all of Miss Abbatelli's personal contact information by the end of the day."

The PR lady's eyes went wide. "Oh, Mr. Lockhart, I'm not sure that's—"

"It wasn't a request," I interrupted, looking up to find Sam tugging at the collar of his shirt in discomfort. "Do we have an understanding?"

"By the end of the day," he answered quickly. "Yes, sir, you got it."

Neither my father nor I uttered another word as we made our way out of the conference room and to the elevator. I jabbed the Down button and stood tall, my arms clasped behind my back as I watched the red digital numbers descend with each floor until my father's chuckle pulled at my attention.

"What's so funny?"

"Oh nothing." He grinned in amusement. "Just wondering if our employees would be nearly as scared of you if they had any clue what a pushover you actually are."

I turned back toward the doors. "I'm not a pushover."

His voice was still laced with humor as he asked, "You're not? So it *wasn't* you who spent three hours out in the freezing cold last Christmas because Nana's beloved Fifi got loose and she was so distraught she just couldn't imagine celebrating a holiday without that damn dog?"

It was my turn to tug at my collar uncomfortably. The damn dog in question was an overweight Great Dane who'd been sleeping comfortably in the laundry room the entire time. Seriously, a Great Dane named Fifi. My grandmother was a bit... eccentric, to put it politely.

"Well, I come by it honestly," I defended. "Need I remind you of the soap opera fiasco?"

The elevator dinged and the doors opened. "Your mother loved that character!" he insisted as we stepped in and began our journey down. "She was devastated when they killed her off. Cried for two whole days."

I chuckled. "You realize it's not a normal reaction to use your connections to get a damned soap opera character 'brought back to life' just because your wife misses them, right?"

He waved me off. "Happy wife, happy life, son. Besides, I work hard for my money and connections. What kind of man would I be if I didn't take advantage of them every once in a while?"

It was true that my father worked hard. He had for as long as I could remember. He'd started Bandwidth from the ground up, turning it into a multimillion-dollar company through nothing but blood and sweat. It was a legacy I was happy to have passed down to me when he finally decided to retire. But unlike all the other rich assholes we had to deal with on a daily basis, Dad had always taught me that all those luxuries could disappear in the blink of an eye. My brother and I had been raised to be humble, never expecting things to just be handed to us because of our wealth.

We might have been rich, but my parents were two of the most down-to-earth people I'd ever come across. Hell, my old man could waltz into Seattle's dingiest bar and make friends with everyone there just as easily as he could command attention in a boardroom. It was a trait I strived to embody.

"I'm curious," Dad started once we exited the elevator on the floor that housed the epicenter of Bandwidth Communications. "You seemed familiar with that woman in the conference room. Have you two met before? What was with the 'Venti Americano' thing?"

A small grin worked its way across my face as I thought about the feisty woman I'd just had the pleasure of dealing with. "I ran into her at Starbucks yesterday morning. She was having an... interesting phone conversation. It caught my attention."

Dad gave me a knowing grin. "If she was as passionate during that call as she was in that meeting, I have no doubt it caught your attention."

"She refused to give me her last name when I asked. Blew me off, then walked out like it was nothing."

He let out a loud bark of laughter and clapped me on the shoulder. "I *knew* I liked that girl! Oh, this is going to be fun to watch, son. So much fun. A woman like that, she'll keep you on your toes."

My mouth gaped open. "Have you forgotten that this is the very same woman who publicly humiliated me just yesterday morning?"

He brushed that off like it was nothing. "What have I always told you, son? First impressions aren't everything."

My face fell flat. "It's because of her that that psychopath has probably revitalized her efforts to track me down and filet me to make her very own Grayson skin suit."

He simply shrugged. "People make mistakes. Besides, you like her. I can see it written all over your face. That's why you jumped at the chance to spend time with her... whether she was a willing participant or not."

"I—" I had no argument because, honestly, it was true. When I walked into the room and saw her sitting there, bare feet propped on the table like she was in her own home, I'd been drawn in. Just like when I'd eavesdropped on her conversation at Starbucks. She interested me. She was a ball of fire wrapped up in a tiny, sexy-as-hell package.

"It's all right," Dad offered. "You're a Lockhart, after all. We aren't easily intrigued, so when someone catches our attention it's hard to let it go. It was the same way with your mother and me. And it'll be the same with Deacon when he finally finds a woman." He got a faraway look in his eyes as a small grin formed on his lips. "Damned woman had me tied up in knots," he said in a tone that belied just how much he'd enjoyed it.

My phone pinged and I pulled it out of my pants pocket, smiling the moment I opened the e-mail.

"Ah," Dad chuckled, looking over my shoulder, "looks like Sam's on the ball. That tough guy façade back there must have really scared the piss out of him if it only took—" He looked at his watch. "—six minutes to get you that girl's personal info. Hell, I'm surprised he didn't include her social security number and blood type."

Everything I needed on Lola Abbatelli was right there at my fingertips. The day before I couldn't even get her to tell me her last name; now I had a home address, personal *and* work e-mail, along with her phone number. I closed out of my e-mail and shoved my phone back in my pocket before looking back over at my father.

"Yep." He laughed again when he saw the pleased expression on my face. "This is going to be fun to watch."

AS I LAY SPREAD out on the large sectional in my living room, ESPN creating white noise in the background, I flipped my phone with one hand, lifting my beer bottle to my lips with the other and taking a long swig. I'd given it a few hours after getting home before reaching out, not wanting to come off too eager or anything. But the urge to shoot Lola a text was no longer going to be ignored.

Grayson: *Dinner at The Warf tomorrow at 7. I'll pick you up.*

Her response was almost instant.

Lola: *Who is this?*

I grinned as I typed, knowing my response would undoubtedly set her off.

Grayson: *The billionaire who plans to use you as arm candy for the foreseeable future.*

Lola: *How'd you get my number?*

Grayson: *I have my ways. Be ready at 7.*

I watched the tiny bubbles flutter on the screen as she typed, looking forward to whatever snarky reply she was working up. She didn't disappoint.

Lola: *Can't. I'll be busy trying to find a way to solve world hunger. I expect it'll take hours. Sorry.*

Grayson: *While your work is admirable, I still expect you to be ready at 7. Even humanitarians need to break for dinner.*

Lola: *Not this one.*

Man, she was lively. I'd have been lying if I said it wasn't a bit of a turn-on.

Grayson: *We have an agreement.*

Lola: *If I recall, I didn't agree to anything.* She even added an angry-face emoji at the end of that text before my phone pinged with another one.

Lola: *I'm sure you have enough money to pay a woman to fake enjoyment while in your company. I've heard if the price is right, you can even get a happy ending.*

At that, I full-on laughed.

Grayson: *It would be such a shame if unemployment pushed you into that particular line of work... wouldn't it?*

The bubbles on the screen popped up, then disappeared, then popped up again. I'd just started to question if I'd pushed too hard when my notification went off.

Lola: *You're a dickhead!*

My assumption was right. She wasn't the type of woman content with not having the last word. As long as I kept this game up, she'd play along.

Grayson: *Why do I suddenly feel like I'm having a conversation with a middle schooler?*

Lola: *I'm rubber and you're glue, asshole.*

I just couldn't help myself; something about the fire in that woman set me off. I typed out another message.

Grayson: *Just so you know, I've never had to pay for sex. And I've never had a single complaint.*

Lola: *Just because it wasn't said to your face doesn't mean it wasn't said behind your back. Not all women are as vocal as I am.*

I was still smiling like crazy as I shot off one last text.

Grayson: *We'll just have to see, then, won't we? I look forward to hearing just how "vocal" you can be.*

Lola: *What's that supposed to mean?*

Lola: *Did you just proposition me?*

Lola: *That was innuendo, wasn't it?*

Lola: *You should be ashamed of yourself.*

Lola: *Damn it, Lockhart! Where'd you go!*

Lola: *You're a real pain in the ass, you know that?*

With that, I closed out of my text screen, allowing her to have the last word she was so desperate to have.

My father was right. This was going to be *a lot* of fun.

CHAPTER FIVE

LOLA

WITH A GRUNT, I tossed my phone to my feet at the other end of the couch and fell back on one of the toss pillows that littered my fluffy couch, returning the bag of frozen peas to my nose. After the abuse from that stupid glass wall earlier that morning it *still* hurt like a mother.

"Who are you texting?" Sophia asked, pushing my feet off the couch so she could sit down. I lifted the frozen peas just long enough to shoot her a killing look and prop my legs across her lap.

"Nobody," I answered sullenly.

She hummed. "Doesn't look like nobody to me. Who's Lord Voldemort?"

Okay... yes, I was a total nerd who was in love with Harry Potter—so sue me. I was a hot chick with enough boobs and ass to guarantee my obsession with fantasy novels wouldn't hinder my chances of getting laid. I was golden. "So, there are these books about a boy wizard who travels to a place he never knew existed by way of a hidden portal in a train station so he can attend this magic school called Hogwarts, all the while never knowing he's being hunted by an evil, sinister—"

She smacked my leg to shut me up. "I know *who* Lord Voldemort is, you ass. I've seen the movies."

I shrugged and tossed the bag of peas onto the coffee table. "The books were better."

"Wouldn't know," she said casually, lifting one of *my* wineglasses full of *my* wine to her lips—the bitch. "Only reason I saw any of them was because someone said that hot dude from the *Twilight* movies was in one of them."

I sucked in a gasp of outrage as I shot up, snatching the wineglass from her hand. "Blasphemy! This is mine and you can't have any." I chugged the rest of the wine and held it out for a refill, waving it around haughtily like Sophia was my servant and she needed to fetch me more.

"Get your own damn wine," she laughed, slapping my hand away. "I meant who's the person you have saved in your phone under Lord Voldemort?"

I let out a frustrated sigh as I stood from the couch, walked over to my kitchen island, and refilled my wine. "He's our bastard of a boss who conned me into dating him at the threat of losing my job. Remember?" I spouted off as I pulled a second wineglass from the built-in rack next to my state-of-the-art wine fridge beneath the marble countertop of the island. I filled it to the rim for Sophia—because I was a good friend like that—and made my way back to the couch, handing one of the glasses to her before sitting back down.

"You really think it's smart to call your boss an asshole?" she asked with a quirk of her perfectly sculpted ebony eyebrow.

Tucking my legs beneath me, I turned my body to face Sophia straight on. "I gave it serious consideration, then decided to go with my gut, and my gut said, 'Call the bastard an asshole, Lola!'"

"I don't know." She shrugged casually. "This might not be

such a bad thing. I mean, he's really hot. You could do a lot worse."

I let out an indignant snort. "You're kidding me, right? The man's the devil! He forced my hand! I was under duress."

Sophia rolled her eyes at my dramatics. "This isn't a court and I'm not a judge. You don't have to try and defend yourself to me. All I'm saying is that it doesn't hurt that he's pleasant to look at. Better than being stuck on the arm of an uggo. Oh, don't give me that look," she chided when my face scrunched in anger. "I know you, and I know you think the guy is gorgeous. That's why you're so pissed about this whole thing."

"You... I can't even... that's so not...." She gave me a smug look when I couldn't form a proper argument. "Ugh! You're *such* a bitch. You know that, right?"

"I do. That's why you love me. Besides—" She took a long sip of wine. "—I saw the way he was looking at you. He's totally interested."

I paused. I actually *paused*. I hated myself for feeling a twinge of pleasure at what Sophia had just said. "You think? Really? Wait... *no!* I don't care. I don't. He's stupid and a jerk and... yeah, he might be totally gorgeous, but he's... he's...."

Sophia had the nerve to laugh at me. "An asshole?"

"Yep!" I gulped down my wine in a very unladylike fashion.

She laughed again just as I lowered the glass from my lips and let out a satisfied "Ahhh." She'd just opened her mouth to say something else—undoubtedly something that would piss me off for her own amusement—when the sharp trill of my cell phone sounded from its place on the coffee table. Sophia's eyes darted to the screen, her lips curling like she got an awful whiff of poo or something. It made her look positively feral as she let out a curse at the name on the display.

"That's my cue to leave," she snapped as she set her glass on the coffee table and stood.

"I'm sorry," I said softly, understanding how even seeing his name was enough to hurt her, but hating that I'd spent years stuck in the middle of two people I loved, all because my brother was an epic prick.

Sophia leaned in and pressed a quick kiss to my forehead. "Don't worry about it, babe. I'll see you tomorrow, okay?"

"'Kay. Good night," I called just as she opened the door to my apartment, pulling the strap of her purse higher onto her shoulder.

"You too, sweets." Then she was gone.

I let out a huff and slid my thumb across the screen of my phone. "Dominic," I answered smartly. "To what do I owe the pleasure? Bail money? Need help finding the name of a good attorney who can fight your latest paternity suit? No, wait... I know. You're calling to tell me someone gave you syphilis and it's slowly deteriorating your brain."

"Always so colorful, little sister," his deep voice reverberated through the line. "I've missed you too."

A twinge of guilt pierced at my chest. No matter how angry I was at Dom for having broken Sophia's heart years before—and no matter that I'd sided with her because Dominic had been wrong, so very, very *wrong*—I still loved the bastard. It was a curse to love the men in my family, even though I didn't necessarily *like* them because of the shitty choices they'd made.

"I have missed you," I sighed. "Sorry for being a bitch. It's been a rough day."

"No worries, I'm used to it," he chuckled. "Let me guess, Sophia's with you?"

My eyebrows shot up. "She was... until she saw your name on my phone. How did you know?"

"You have a tendency to be short with me when she's around."

I hadn't realized he'd ever caught on to that. Not that I

should've been all that surprised. For someone who could be extremely selfish when it came to other people's feelings, Dominic had always been good at reading moods. He just had a nasty habit of not caring enough.

"Can you really blame me?" I asked, a hint a venom in my voice.

"No, I haven't blamed you for years. Why start now?" He went silent for a few seconds before asking, "So how is she? Sophia, I mean. Is she... good?"

"Oh no, you don't. Nuh-uh. We don't talk about her, remember? That was the deal to keep my sanity intact. I don't discuss you with her, and I don't discuss her with you."

He let out a weary sigh that floated through the receiver and had my back stiffening in discomfort. It wasn't normal for Dom to sound so melancholy. "Fine. I won't ask about her."

"Thank you," I replied, still on edge at the tone of his voice. "What's going on with you? What's wrong? You don't sound like yourself."

He sighed again. "Nothing. I'm good, just...."

"Just what?" I pushed when he stopped talking.

"It's nothing. Don't worry about me. Tell me what's new with you. Mom already got on my ass today about bearing her grandbabies. I'm guessing that means you already got the lecture from her first?"

I laughed and reclined into the plush cushions of the sofa, resting my head on the arm. "Oh yeah, I got that call yesterday. Not sorry at all to admit I threw you under the bus, big brother. After I stomped all over her dreams of me popping out little baby Abbatellis." Dom's full-blown laughter rang down the line when I admitted I might have hinted that he was her only chance.

"Poor Mom," he chuckled after a few seconds of uncontrollable laughter. "Between you and me, the likelihood of her ever holding a grandbaby is slim to none. Think she knows that?"

"Oh, I'm sure somewhere deep, *deep* down she does. She just refuses to accept it."

"True."

I found myself smiling at the humor in my brother's voice, though there was an undercurrent of something I couldn't quite read in him as we continued to talk. I couldn't remember the last time we'd just *talked*, had a conversation that had no purpose other than to fill the other in on our lives. He told me of the stress he was feeling at the office. Apparently, working for our father wasn't all it was cracked up to be, and he found himself running around, cleaning up after Dad and preventing potential sexual harassment suits rather than doing his job. He talked about desperately needing a vacation and how he'd been thinking of coming to Seattle to visit me.

I told him about the show and the fiasco with the "In the Act" segment. He laughed his ass off when I told him all about the deal with the devil I'd been forced into with Grayson Lockhart.

"Grayson Lockhart, Lola? Seriously?" Another round of raucous laughter.

"You know him?"

"I know the name," Dominic replied. "Hell, most people around the *country* know his name. His father is only the founder of one of the country's largest broadcasting companies *ever*. They have stations in almost every state, New York and Seattle being two of their biggest. What I can't believe is that *you* didn't know any of this. What, have you been living under a fucking rock? The guy's your *boss*! Grayson Lockhart and his father make Dad's company look like nothing more than a lemonade stand."

"Well how was I supposed to know?" I defended. "It's not

like I pay attention to this shit. You know my attention span's always been small."

"Oh, baby sis," Dom snickered. "Congratulations. You just landed yourself one of the country's most eligible bachelors. And all you had to do was publicly humiliate him."

"Don't be a prick," I snapped.

"Who knows, maybe Mom's hope for grandkids isn't dead in the water after all."

I was going to murder my brother. As I had a nasty tendency of doing when I felt backed into a corner, I spoke without thinking. "The likelihood of that ever happening is lower than Sophia forgiving you." I instantly regretted the words as soon as they left my mouth.

Dominic remained silent for so long I began to worry that I'd truly offended him. When he spoke, it was with a question I certainly hadn't expected.

"You really think she'll never forgive me?"

I closed my eyes with a heavy sigh, reaching up to rub the spot between my eyes. "I honestly don't know, Dom. Could you blame her if she didn't? I mean, you cheat—"

"I know what I did," he interrupted, his voice short. "You don't have to remind me."

"Look." I let out a guilt-riddled breath. "I don't want to fight with you, okay? It was wrong of me to even say that. I'm sorry."

"Don't worry about it, shorty. You know I can't stay mad at you."

Usually, his nickname for me grated on my nerves. I was aware I was height-challenged. It was why I lived in high heels. But I didn't mind it so much just then.

Trying to change the subject to something safer, I asked, "Are you serious about coming to Seattle?"

"I...." He paused, seemingly giving my question serious

thought. "Yeah, I am. I need a break, a change of scenery. You think you could put me up for a bit?"

I found myself smiling at the thought of some quality time with my brother. Truth was, when he was out from under our father's thumb, he wasn't so bad. Where I'd spent my life subjected to my mother's dramas, Dominic had always felt the pressure to follow in our father's footsteps... even in the worst ways. "I think I have an old sleeping bag and air mattress around here somewhere," I joked.

"Good to know." He chuckled, and I could tell by his lighter tone that all was forgiven. "It's getting late, and I'm beat. We'll talk about it more later, yeah?"

"Yeah. Love you, bro."

"Love you too, shorty."

We hung up and I went about my nighttime ritual of getting ready for bed. I turned out all the lights in the living area and headed for my room, stripping out of my dress in exchange for one of my soft, silky nighties. I twisted my mass of long dark hair into a knot on the top of my head, washed and moisturized my face, and brushed my teeth before turning out the bedroom light and slipping between my sheets.

I snuggled down into my cozy bed, ready for the Sandman to take over, but just as I started to doze, Grayson's tantalizing smile and twinkling greens popped up behind my eyelids, and I felt my skin break out into goose bumps.

Damn it. That sexy, sinful jerk was even screwing with my REM. All the more reason to hate him.

CHAPTER SIX

LOLA

THE FACT that I woke up an hour early the following morning to get ready for work had nothing to do with stupid Grayson Lockhart. *Nothing at all.*

Or at least that's what I kept telling myself as I took extra care and effort on my makeup and hair. I'd worked at KTSW for ten years—ever since graduating from college—and had never once crossed paths with the man... at least not that I'd noticed. But when my alarm went off that morning, all I could think about was how I could potentially run into him, and how, after the embarrassment of walking into a plate-glass wall, I wanted—no, *needed* to make an impression. Well, a *different* impression.

I would not be the woman known for walking into walls. That wouldn't be my legacy, damn it.

I parted my brown hair down the middle and curled it so it hung in wide, glossy curls past my bra strap. My eye shadow was slightly darker than what I did for work, and the contrasting pale lipstick made the smokiness pop. I'd tucked my white satin blouse into a high-waisted black pencil skirt that hugged my curves just enough, but not too much. Four-inch peep-toe

Jimmy Choos on my feet completed my armor, and as I studied my somewhat sultry reflection in the mirror of my master bathroom, I felt ready for battle.

I took the elevator down to the lobby of my building and smiled at Maury, the doorman, as I made my way to the exit.

"Morning, Ms. Abbatelli. Would you like me to me hail a cab for you?"

I looked through the glass front of the building and saw that Seattle was having a rare dry morning. The sun was peeking through the clouds, adding to my already cheerful disposition.

"No, thanks, Maury." I placed a kiss on his weathered cheek, causing the adorable old man to blush. "It's actually kind of nice outside. I think I'll walk."

He looked down at my shoes and lifted a skeptical brow. "You sure about that?"

I laughed as he held the door open for me. "It's only a few blocks. Believe me, I grew up in heels. That walk in these babies is nothing." I pointed at my feet. "Have a good day," I called over my shoulder as I made my way down the steps toward the sidewalk. "Don't work too hard."

"You as well, Ms. Abbatelli," he replied.

The smile was firmly planted on my lips as I made my way the few blocks to my regular Starbucks near Hart Tower. Visions of maiming Grayson Lockhart during our "date" that night had been dancing through my head all morning long. As I joined the line of waiting customers, the grin stretched further while I pictured him being run over by an out-of-control bus that just so happened to have an advertisement for *Girl Talk* posted across the side of it.

"You know, you really are quite stunning when you smile," a familiar smooth, velvety voice said into my ear from behind me. "Even if it's a smile of pure evil."

I spun around, ready to lay into the cocky bastard, when my breath froze in my lungs.

Sweet Mother of Mary.

Side note: It should be said that I totally flunked out of Catholic school, so most all of my "Sweet Insert-Saint-or-Holy-Deity-Name-Heres" were totally off base. But moving on....

Did the jerk have to be so freaking good-looking?

"Let me guess," he continued when I remained silent, words having completely failed me at my very first glance, "you were plotting my demise as you waited in line for coffee?"

My brain finally rebooted a few seconds later, after the system failure it received at the sight of Grayson's purposely mussed hair and the faint stubble that painted his square, masculine jaw. And my God, could the man where the hell out of a suit!

I gave him a side-eye look, one corner of my mouth hitching up in a smirk. "A bus might have been involved," I admitted, batting my eyelashes coyly.

He placed on large hand on his chest in feigned hurt. Geez, the man was so ripped I could make out the muscle definition through his shirt. "You wound me, Ms. Abbatelli. I expected more creativity from you. A bus? It's like you're not even trying."

The smile vanished from my face at his quick-witted comeback. I couldn't remember the last time my acid tongue held no effect on the opposite sex. And I didn't like it.

"Yes, well. It's still early," I muttered.

"Ah, I see," he chuckled, the stupid sound far too appealing for my liking. "I'm sure you'll come up with something better once you've had your coffee."

I didn't respond. Not because I preferred giving him the silent treatment, oh no. That would have been understandable. But because the sheer presence of him had me tongue-tied and tangled in knots. The effect he had on me was completely unwelcomed.

Maybe it was because I hadn't been laid in an embarrassing number of months.

That had to be the reason. That was the only logical excuse for why a man who wasn't even close to being my type seemed to fry my brain cells. I made a vow to myself to scroll through my little black book as soon as time permitted.

We shuffled further up the line, coming closer to the register, and from the corner of my eye I caught him giving my body a long, sweeping perusal.

"You look quite lovely today, Lola." His voice was close. So close I felt his breath whisper across my neck.

I told myself that the tremor that shot up my spine was from disgust, not pleasure, as I took a step away and sneered at him. "Careful, Mr. Lockhart. I get the feeling you're close to treading into sexual harassment territory."

He actually had the audacity to smile. The handsome jerk-face.

"I assure you, I meant the compliment with the utmost sincerity. There was nothing lascivious about it."

I frowned as I took in his features, looking closely for any hint of dishonesty but coming up empty.

"Next," the girl at the register called out, pulling me from my stupor. I stepped up and opened my mouth to relay my order, only to be cut off by the egotistical stupid-head behind me.

Great, he's fried my brain so badly even my internal insults are embarrassingly adolescent.

"The lady will have a venti nonfat, no-whip white mocha, and I'll take a grande Americano." He slapped a twenty on the counter and offered the poor girl a smile that had her swooning on the spot. "Thank you so much,"—I caught his eyes dart to her name tag before landing back on her face—"Cathy."

"S-sure thing," she stuttered with a sigh as she grabbed two cups and wrote our orders down. The whole time she pushed buttons on the register to make his change, she gazed at Grayson as if she wanted nothing more in life than for him to put a baby in her.

"I can pay for my own coffee, thank you very much," I grumbled as we moved out of the way for the next customer.

"I'm very aware of that, Lola," he said flatly. "Independent woman that you are. But I'm also a gentleman."

I snorted. Yes, an actual snort, so help me God. "A real gentleman wouldn't have tried to impregnate that teenage girl behind the counter with his smile."

Grayson stepped close, the woodsy, spicy scent of his cologne invading my senses and suddenly rendering me speechless. "First of all, I was just offering the girl a smile and a thank-you. It's called being polite. You really should try it sometime." I opened my mouth to spit out something nasty but he cut me off. "And secondly, I'm truly flattered you find my smile *that* disarming." To prove his point, he grinned at me, and my ovary popped out an egg. Just like that. Smile and *pop*!

A grin. Just a simple grin and I could feel my nipples hardening behind my bra, my breasts growing heavy as a heady desire I hadn't felt in... well, ever flooded through me. It took every ounce of willpower I had to keep my breathing under control as he inched even closer.

I don't know how long we stood there in a silent battle of wills, as if each of us was daring the other to cave first. I couldn't explain why, but some part of me felt that Grayson knew exactly how he affected me even though I'd done everything I could to hide it.

"Uh... excuse me." Our heads shot to the side to find a wide-eyed barista staring at us. "Your drinks are ready."

"Oh...." Grayson gave a small, almost discernable shake of his head, and a tiny voice inside mine cheered at the fact that he seemed just as flustered as I was. It was good to know I still held that kind of power even on mornings when I was feeling off my game. "Thank you," he said, clearing his throat. Taking the coffees off the ledge, he handed me mine, and I had no choice but to offer him a thank-you as we both wound through the crowd toward the door.

I needed fresh air. I needed to get the hell away from Grayson Lockhart and whatever weird voodoo he had going on that was throwing my entire world off-kilter.

Unfortunately, we were heading in the exact same direction. And he didn't appear to be nearly as eager to escape as I was.

"Looks like it's going to rain," he said conversationally. "I have an umbrella if you'd like to share."

I gave him a look that said "Poor dumb man thinks he knows everything. How sweet." "The sun was shining just a few minutes ago, Grayson. I think your meteorology skills are a little off." I walked a few feet ahead of him just as the sky above miraculously opened up, as though God had dumped a bucket of water on me just to be spiteful.

"You were saying?" Grayson yelled over the thunder crackling across the sky, his voice chock-full of humor as I stood there, being soaked to the bone.

I turned to look back at him, umbrella opened and protecting him from the sudden downpour. "It's just a little drizzle," I argued bitterly, never having been one to admit defeat.

"You have many admirable qualities, Ms. Abbatelli," he started as he closed the distance between us, "but your pride is not one of them. Please, spare us both the unnecessary drama and just get under the damn umbrella. Mother Nature has already proven her point. No use in trying to piss her off further just because you're feeling a little butthurt."

My mouth dropped open to argue that I wasn't feeling "butthurt," as he so eloquently put it, but the rational side of my brain kicked in, telling me it was pointless. I moved in, only inches apart from Grayson's warm body as I accepted the protection the umbrella had to offer. We made the rest of the journey to Hart Tower in complete and blessed silence. I'd started the morning on such a positive note, and there I was, not a half hour after leaving my apartment, already wishing for a do-over.

"Morning, Mr. Lockhart," Bob's chipper voice echoed off the marble floors of the pristine lobby. "Skies really opened up this morning, didn't they, sir?"

"That they did, Bob," Grayson answered, a laugh in his voice that made me want to reach down and yank a chunk of his leg hair out just to hear him scream.

"Ms. Lola?" Bob asked once I was no longer blocked from view by Grayson's massive body. "Why, you look like a drowned rat, sweetheart. You know better than to leave home without an umbrella, girl. Lucky for you Mr. Lockhart was there."

"Shut it, Bob," I bit out sharply, not sounding the least bit pleasant as my unwelcome companion led the way to the elevator banks. To his credit, Grayson was kind enough to hold in his laughter until the door closed, leaving us alone... utterly alone. *Where the hell are the rest of the employees? Damn slackers!*

"Well," he said as we started our ascent, "I have to say, I can't remember when I started a morning off in such a good mood."

My only response was a low, threatening growl as I watched the red digital numbers begin to climb.

The *ding* sounded as we grew closer to Grayson's floor, and it couldn't have come soon enough, because the bastard who smelled too delicious for words chose that moment to say, "I'm looking forward to listening to your apology later this morning. Make sure you sound genuine. Wouldn't want Sam to lose his mind."

I was contemplating punching the smug look right off his pretty face just as the doors slid open to his floor.

"And I'm looking forward to tonight even more," he leaned in and whispered into my ear in a low, sultry voice before stepping off the elevator. "Have a good day, Ms. Abbatelli."

He offered me a wink moments before the doors slid closed.

CHAPTER SEVEN

GRAYSON

I COULDN'T STOP PICTURING what her tits looked like in that soaking-wet white blouse. I prided myself on being a professional, a grown-ass man who could control his libido, but *Christ*, that woman was something else altogether.

And that attitude of hers did nothing but make me crave her more.

"I don't know if I should be concerned that you've been sitting there staring at your dick for the past minute and a half, or proud that you finally found the little guy after thirty-five years."

I looked up at Caleb McMannus, best friend, CFO of Bandwidth Communications, and all around pain in my ass since we met in elementary school. I'd have gotten rid of him before high school had he not conned my mother into thinking he was the greatest thing since skinny margaritas were invented. Despite already having two of her own, he was like another son to her.

A son who the tabloids loved to follow around, photographing his latest sexual exploits. Side note: There might have been a time or two when he'd been caught very publicly in some very private positions. But Mom always forgave him, claiming it was "just a phase." I didn't have the heart to tell her that a man in his midthirties didn't go through phases anymore —he was just a dog.

"I don't know whether to be concerned by the fact that you've been standing there mooning at me in silence for the past minute and a half, or flattered."

"Flattered," he chuckled as he made his way into my office and sat in one of the chairs across from me. "Definitely flattered. I *am* a catch, after all. Most women and men alike would kill for my attention."

I laughed. "What are you doing back from the New York office? I thought you weren't scheduled to return until next week."

"I figured you missed me too much and decided to cut the trip short."

I sat back in my chair, twirling a pen between my fingers. "You're like a ringworm. Just when I think I've gotten rid of you, you come back."

"That might be the nicest thing you've ever said to me." He rested an ankle on one knee and threw his arm along the back of the chair. "Honestly, we got the business meeting part of the trip wrapped up fairly quickly, and there's only so much ass kissing I can take. If I had to sit through one more dinner with that fucking brownnoser Peter Wilkinson and his human pin cushion of a wife, I was going to hang myself."

I chuckled at the thought of Wilamena Wilkinson. The woman had been nipped, tucked, and sucked so many times it should be illegal for a plastic surgeon to touch her. The last time I saw her was when I traveled to New York for a conference over a year back. Peter brought her to one of the happy hours and I'd spent most of the night worrying that if she so much as sneezed, her entire body would rip at the seams.

"She try to corner you in the men's room and suck you off?"

Caleb's eyes went wide. "How'd you know!"

I shrugged, internally cringing at the memory of my own personal run-in with the life-sized Barbie doll. "I might have had to suffer through the same thing a time or two before I finally told Peter to keep his trophy wife in check."

He shivered in the chair. "Man, just the thought of those talons she calls nails anywhere near my junk makes me want to lose my breakfast."

I clicked on a link on my computer and spun the monitor around for him to see. It was a picture of him with his face buried between some exotic-looking chick's boobs in the middle of the city's hottest nightclub. "Well I'm glad to see the terror didn't have any lasting effects."

A wide smile split his lips as he sat back in the chair and let out a sigh. "Ah, Tatiana. That one had the power to make everything better," he announced with a dreamy, glazed-over look on his face.

"Victoria's Secret model?" I guessed.

"*Sport's Illustrated* swimsuit edition." He winked. "The cover."

I gave a low whistle, my eyebrows rising. "How'd this one take your standard morning-after brush-off?"

"Wouldn't know," he said with a yawn. "Didn't hang around long enough to find out. She sucked me dry and I bolted before she woke up."

"Jesus, man," I snapped. "One of these days that shit's going to get you stabbed, and the last headline about you will be how you were found dead in a ditch with your dick severed from your body."

"Please," he scoffed. "Any woman who wanted to kill me would have to get through Mama Lockhart first, and that woman adores me. She'd never let any harm come to her favorite son."

I scowled at him. "You know you aren't *actually* her son, right?"

He let out an exaggerated gasp and jerked back. "You shut your lying bastard mouth! Just wait until I tell her you said that."

Rolling my eyes at Caleb's dramatics, I turned the monitor back around to face me and closed out of the celebrity gossip site.

"So...," he drawled, drawing my attention back to him. "What's new with you?" The shit-eating grin on his face told me he already knew exactly what had gone down while he was in New York.

"I take it you heard?"

"Oh I heard all right." He rubbed his hands together, clearly getting too much joy out of my humiliation. "I listened to the podcast and everything. I have to ask, dude." He sat forward and lowered his voice conspiratorially. "That Brooke chick, was she a fireball in bed? The crazy ones usually are."

I picked up my stapler and chucked it at his head. Only reason I missed was because he had quicker reflexes, honed from years of dodging scorned women.

Standing from the chair, I pulled my suit jacket from the back and slid my arms in. "If you're done being an asshole, there's somewhere I have to be," I told him, giving him a look that said "Get the hell out of my office, fucker."

He stood and followed me to the door. "And what's so important you don't have time to catch up with your BFF?"

I gave him a side-eyed glare as we walked through the offices toward the elevator. "Well, if you're so up to date on all the gossip that's been happening here while you were off motor-boating swimsuit models, I'm sure you heard about a little public apology that's going to be taking place."

"Wait!" he shouted, drawing undue attention. "That's happening today? No shit?"

"No shit." I hit the Up button and waited for the elevator doors to open. "And I'd like a front row seat while it happens. Trust me, if you met this girl you'd understand just how painful this is going to be for her."

"It's a little sadistic how pleased you look about it," he said. I hadn't even realized I'd been smiling until he pointed it out. "I'm so proud." He hit me on the back and wiped an invisible tear from his cheek as the doors opened. "Go get 'em, tiger."

"M-MR. LOCKHART," the red-faced man—I think I heard him being called Jerry during our conference—sputtered the moment I walked through the sound booth's door. Good Lord, if the man didn't reduce his stress and lose a good forty pounds, he was liable to keel over from a heart attack any day now.

"Good morning." I gave him and the scrawny kid sitting beside him a pleasant smile.

"Uh...." The kid seemed dumbfounded to see me. "Hi?"

"I'm—"

"Grayson Lockhart. Yeah, I know. I think half the country knows who you are. And probably some other countries too. Is it true you turned Taylor Swift down when she hit on you during a party in LA last year?"

I stared him down and quirked an eyebrow as he visibly swallowed under my unrelenting gaze. Jesus, where did people come up with shit like that? I was seen at *one* function that she just so happened to be at, and the gossip rags went crazy. We hadn't crossed paths the entire night. "No," I answered dryly, leaving out the fact that it had actually been a *different* Top Forty pop princess I'd spent the night fighting off. I won't name names—being a gentleman and all—but let's just say the woman was still as crazy as she'd been when she shaved her head and went berserk on a car with an umbrella.

Jerry hit the kid in the back of the head. "Will you shut the hell up, Andrew?" he hissed before looking back at me, his face turning a frightening purple color. "Sorry about that, Mr. Lockhart."

"That's quite all right." I smiled, showing there were no hard feelings. "I hope I'm not too late." I turned to face the glass that led into the studio. Lola and her co-hosts hadn't noticed I was standing there so I got the chance to take her in, unencumbered. She had somehow managed to clean up just fine after her trudge through the rain, and I felt myself getting hard at just the sight of her once again.

Baseball, CNN, Larry King, Nana after her Zumba class. Yeah, that last one did the trick; my stupid dick quickly deflated. I breathed a sigh of relief.

"Late for what?" Andrew asked.

"The show." I knew the smile that passed over my lips was downright wicked, but I couldn't seem to care. If there was anyone in that room who would understand the pleasure I'd get at someone else's expense, it was Lola. No doubt that if roles were reversed, she'd be standing right where I was, videotaping the whole damn thing.

Jerry looked at me. Looked at the glass. Looked back at me. I could see the understanding cross his ruddy features before it was replaced with genuine fear. "Uh... I'm not so sure that's a good idea, sir. Maybe you'd be better off just... listening?"

A sinister chuckle rumbled up my throat. "And miss this? No way in hell." Just as I finished speaking, the "On Air" light in the studio lit up and the three women slid their headphones into place. Lola's seductive voice reverberated through our little room.

"Good morning, lovely listeners. You're back on with Lola, Sophia, and Daphne, and you're listening to *Girl Talk* on 95.6, KTSW."

Fuck me, just two sentences in that voice of hers and I understood why *Girl Talk* was one of our highest-rated shows.

"Now, if you were listening the other day, I'm sure you heard the 'In the Act' segment." Something from the corner of my eye caught my attention, and I looked over just in time to see the black-haired one—Sophia—lift a legal pad, the words "Pucker up, bitch! Time to kiss ass" written in big bold letters. Jerry smacked his forehead. Andrew choked. Lola, she and her friends still oblivious to my presence, held her middle fingers up in the air as she spoke clearly into the mic.

"Before we start taking callers, I just want to take a moment to issue a heartfelt apology." The blonde lifted a notepad. "You'd have to have a heart, whore," it read. It wasn't until just then that I noticed Lola had her own legal pad and was quickly scribbling something down as she continued to talk. "Eat shit and die, twat faces." "Because of that segment, our *kindhearted* CEO"—she held up another sign that said "with a little dick"—"was humiliated by a vindictive woman who used *Girl Talk* as a platform to exact retribution on a blameless, unsuspecting pillar of our community." I could've sworn she gagged on those last words.

I could see Sophia and Daphne were both close to dying with laughter as the shorter one of the duo held her notepad up. "A little dick you want to lick like a lollipop."

I thought I heard Jerry mutter at least thirty different curses, but I was too busy watching the interaction between the three women—and finding it utterly hilarious—to care.

"Mr. Lockhart," Lola continued as she threw her marker at them from across the room, "on behalf of myself, *Girl Talk,* and KTSW, I want to sincerely apologize for the events that occurred during our show. I am so sorry for any discomfort we might have caused you." She covered the mic and leaned away, mumbling, "You pretentious prick," to her friends. "Now we're going to take a short commercial break and return with our first caller. Today's topic: Is the G-spot real, or is your man just lazy?"

The "On Air" sign clicked off and all three women removed their headsets. I took that as my opportunity to get her attention. I knocked on the glass and chuckled as all three of their heads shot over to look in my direction. Once their eyes landed on me, three identical expressions of "Oh hell, what the fuck just happened?" crossed their faces. I leaned over Jerry and clicked the button that would allow them to hear what was being said inside the booth.

"Apology accepted." I gave her a menacing smile. "This pretentious prick is looking forward to tonight." Knowing it would push her buttons, I finished with, "Wear a dress." I clicked the button again before she could form a response, then turned to Jerry and Andrew as they looked up at me, mouths hanging open in shock. "Gentlemen." I nodded. Then I left the booth and headed for the elevators, smiling the entire time.

After that performance, I knew one thing for sure about Lola Abbatelli.

The woman did not disappoint.

CHAPTER EIGHT

LOLA

SHIT.

Shit. Hell. Damn. Fuck.

As I studied my reflection in the mirror, I tried my best to keep my freak-out at bay.

I breathed out through my mouth and bounced from foot to foot, shaking my hands at my side like a boxer gearing up for a televised fight. "You got this," I mumbled to myself. "You got this. You got this." I inhaled through my nose and stretched my neck from side to side. "So what if he heard you call him a pretentious prick?" I asked my reflection. "So what if he's your boss? Your insanely gorgeous, rock-hard boss." I gave my head a violent shake and squeezed my eyes closed. "No! No! He's *not* hot. He's... boring... and his nose is kinda funny-looking." Lies. All lies. His nose was adorable and I wanted to poke it.

"Jeez! Get your shit together, Lola!" I pointed at the mirror. I'd officially lost my mind. If anyone had seen me standing in the bathroom, having a full-blown conversation with myself, they would've had me locked up in a padded room. Which, I wasn't going to lie, didn't sound too bad at the moment. Anything would've been better than going on a date with

Grayson Lockhart. Padded rooms could be fun, right? All that bouncing from wall to wall without the threat of breaking a bone. Plus, straightjackets probably felt like hugs.

My cell phone rang from my bedroom, scaring the absolute shit out of me. My heart palpitated as I picked it up off the nightstand and answered with a hesitant "Hello?"

"Ms. Abbatelli, it's Maury from the front desk. There's a Mr. Lockhart here for you."

Damn it, he beat the padded room people! Now I was stuck. I let out a slow breath. "Tell me something, Maury—how does he look?"

"I'm... not sure I'm following you, ma'am," he answered in confusion.

"His face. Does it look angry? Bored? Excited? Maybe a little constipated?"

I thought I heard Maury choke. "Constipated?"

I stomped my foot even though no one was around to see. "I'm trying to gauge his mood here, Maury. Help a woman out, will you?"

"Well...." He paused for a few seconds. "Right now he looks a little confused, and maybe even a bit scared. I don't think he's comfortable, and I have to tell you, Ms. Abbatelli, I'm not all that comfortable right now either." The volume of Maury's voice softened, like he'd pulled the phone from his ear. "Oh no, sir, I didn't mean that *she's* constipated." *Oh sweet hell.* "I'm not sure, Mr. Lockhart. Hey, how would you describe your face right now?"

This was God punishing me for the sins of my past. I just knew it. Sister Agnes *told* me I'd be punished for stealing that bottle of communion wine and getting drunk behind the gymnasium of the school with my friends. *It was* one time, *God! Why have your forsaken me?*

Maury's voice interrupted my silent pleading with God.

"Oh yes, sir. Ms. Abbatelli?"

"Yeah?"

"Mr. Lockhart for you." Then he passed the phone to Grayson and his deep voice trickled down the line, sending a shiver down my back. *Stupid back.*

"It's 7:05, Lola. You're officially late. If it's constipation I'd be happy to have the driver stop at the pharmacy on the way to dinner. I'm nothing if not accommodating." I could hear the smile in his voice.

My fingers curled tightly around the phone like it was his neck and I was giving it a good long choke. Despite the way my body reacted to him, there was still a *very* intense need deep inside of me to physically maim him in some way. "I'll be right down," I growled through clenched teeth, disconnecting the call as soon as his low baritone laugh came through.

Stuffing the phone in the beaded navy blue clutch lying on my bed, I slipped my feet into my tan heels and headed out the door, cursing Grayson Lockhart the entire trip down to the lobby.

"Do not be charmed. Do not be charmed," I repeated over the god-awful light jazz coming from the elevator's speaker. "Remember, he's a prick."

The doors opened with a *ding* once I reached the lobby, revealing the bane of my existence in all his *GQ*-esque glory. My lady parts all but shouted out the "Hallelujah" chorus at the sight of him. *Stupid lady parts.*

I knew he rocked the hell out a suit, but there was something particularly intoxicating about how he looked without the tie. I don't know why, but that small expanse of skin at the base of his throat being exposed was practically calling out to me, screaming "Lick me, lick me. You know you want to. I taste as good as I smell."

And sweet merciful baby Jesus, when he smiled? Well, a

lesser woman would've melted into a quivering puddle on the floor. But I steeled my spine and squared my shoulders as I walked toward him with a borderline vicious smile.

"You look possessed" were the first words out of his mouth. How charming.

I widened my eyes and gave him an exaggerated gasp. "What a coincidence! Seeing as you're Lucifer and all."

He chuckled as his eyes scanned my body. Not in a creepy, leering way but in a "I'm a hot-blooded male who appreciates a good-looking woman" kind of way. I'd never admit it out loud, but when I chose the dark blue jersey knit dress that ended midthigh, came down in a V-neck that showed *just* enough cleavage to make the girls look good, and hugged my curves like it loved them, I'd done it with the hopes of wowing Grayson to the point where he'd hopefully choke on one of his steamed clams—or whatever he ate—and keeled over dead.

And oh darn. Wouldn't you know it, I failed my CPR certification back in college. But in my defense, it was college and I was *really* hung over.

But as those green eyes of his shone with genuine interest, I found myself unwittingly wanting him *not* to choke to death, because... well, I kind of liked the attention. *Stupid attention whore!*

So to brush off the icky feeling of enjoyment that I did *not* want to feel, I did what any smart woman would do—I went into bitch mode. I snapped my fingers in front of his face to catch his attention. "Eyes up, bub, or your crotch is going to meet the business end of my friend Christian Louboutin." I pointed to my pumps. "You might be my boss, but I'm not on the clock and I'll cut a bitch."

He just laughed.

Okay, so maybe I took bitch mode a little over the top, but I couldn't think straight when he was around! Do you have any clue how confusing it is to hate someone when *your* bits are begging to become besties with *his* bits? I'll tell you, it's a pickle.

Shit, now I'm thinking about giant pickles.

"You look beautiful," he told me with a sincere smile. *Son of a bitch, this guy's good.* Bitch mode went into system failure.

"Uh... thanks," I relented quietly, finally willing to admit I was fighting a losing battle. "You look really nice too."

"See?" His grin widened. "That wasn't so hard, was it?"

I rolled my eyes and stepped past him, heading for the door. "You should've quit while you were ahead."

Maury gave me a grin as I walked out the door he was holding open. "If I don't come back tonight, call the police and tell them this guy did it," I said, hitching a thumb over my shoulder in Grayson's direction.

He laughed good-naturedly and tipped his head. "Have a good evening, ma'am." Then he tipped his chin at Grayson, who reached out to shake his hand. "Mr. Lockhart."

"Maury. It was a pleasure meeting you. I promise I'll return her. And you have nothing to fear. If anyone's well-being is in danger, it's mine."

"I don't know, sir." Maury looked back and forth between the two of us. "I've never seen a man give this one a run for her money. Might just be time."

"Someone's off my Christmas list," I singsonged loudly as I made my way down the steps towards the waiting town car, faking a bravado I most certainly wasn't feeling. As I climbed into the car and moved across the luxurious leather seat to the other side, I could smell Grayson's cologne lingering in the interior. I chanced a brief sniff, closing my eyes to take it in before he finally joined me inside and closed the door.

One thought bounced around the inside of my head as his overwhelming presence suddenly filled the small space.

What the hell have I just gotten myself into?

CHAPTER NINE

AS THE SILENCE stretched around us, I found it harder and harder to keep my gaze from wandering in her direction. I was convinced that dress had been made with the sole purpose of driving me out of my mind. I watched from the corner of my eye as she crossed her legs, the soft fabric riding up and revealing a creamy expanse of olive skin that made my mouth water.

Turning my focus to the passing landscape outside of the window, I breathed deeply, trying to get the semi in my pants to cooperate and go the hell down.

"So...." Lola's seductive voice echoed through the back seat, doing nothing to help my twitching dick. "How is this supposed to work? We play nice, smile, and act polite for a few hours at a couple events until this blows over?"

A bewildered laugh worked its way up my throat. "Is it really so difficult to be civil with me? You make it sound positively painful."

Even though it sounded somewhat spiteful, her laughter shot pleasure right through me. Despite my best efforts, I found myself wondering what noises she'd make while I was inside of her.

Not what you want to be thinking about while trying to control an erection.

"Please, Grayson—"

"Gray."

She paused at my interruption. "What?"

"Gray. My friends all call me Gray. I'd like you to, as well."

I watched as surprise flashed in her gorgeous amber eyes. She hadn't been expecting that; I could see it written all over her face. Dealing with me when I was an asshole was so much easier for her, but she was off-kilter when I wasn't living up to her expectations.

"Gray," she whispered, more to herself than to me, as if testing how it sounded. Hearing the way my name rolled off her tongue had me biting my cheek to stop from moaning. She cleared her throat and fidgeted in her seat. "Uh, o-okay."

"You were saying?" I asked with a smile. If I got hard on Lola's attitude, then seeing her frazzled was almost enough to get me *off*.

She gave her head a tiny shake. "What?"

"Before I cut you off, I believe you were going to say something about how easy it was to be nice to me."

The confusion disappeared from her face, replaced by a knowing smile.

"Really? Was that what I was about to do?"

I leaned in, closing some of the distance between us. Just an inch more and I'd breach the line between what was appropriate and what wasn't between a boss and his employee. But damn if I cared. Lola's job was secure. Bandwidth never maintained a strict interoffice relationship policy, so it wasn't like being with her would break any rules.

"W-what are you doing?" She pulled back, but not before I saw her pupils dilate and her chest rise with a stuttered breath.

Her lips parted as her tongue peeked out to run across her bottom lip.

I broke through that last inch, delving right into her personal space as I said, "You know, I don't think you hate me as much as you'd like to claim."

Her eyes narrowed as the fight poured back into them. "Y-yes I do. And could you move back please? Your cologne is giving me a headache. One spritz is more than sufficient, Gray. There's no need to bathe in the stuff."

"Should I take that to mean you don't like the way I smell, Lola?" I asked quietly, keeping the space between us at a minimum.

Her gaze landed on my mouth and I could've sworn I heard her sigh softly. "No. I mean yes! Damn it!" She shook her head again. "Would you please move? I can't think when you're so... close."

I pulled away with a laugh just as the car came to a stop in front of the restaurant.

"Remember," I started as my driver, Thomas, came around to open my door, "you have to pretend to like me. Shouldn't be hard considering you're picturing me naked right now." I winked and climbed out of the car, smiling at her mumbled "Jackass" as I reached back in to help her out.

As we made our way into the crowded restaurant, I kept my palm firmly in place at the small of her back, resting just inches from the tempting swell of her ass.

A gorgeous smile was plastered across her lips as she whispered through her teeth, "Your hand moves down any lower, I'll cut it off."

"Ah, ah, ah." I returned her grin. "There are people watching. You're supposed to find me irresistible, remember?"

She looked up at me adoringly. Had it not been for her next

words, I might have been fooled. "After tonight, someone should give me a freaking Academy Award."

I drew her closer to my side, wrapping my arm around her waist. "That's the spirit."

I was pretty sure she growled as I gave my name to the hostess.

The walk to our table was made in silence. As I let go of Lola to pull out her chair, the tips of my fingers slid along her back. It was just a whisper of a touch, but I felt her shiver softly before I removed my hand completely. That was all the reassurance I needed.

She could claim to hate me all she wanted—her body said something completely different. She wanted me. The more she fought it, the sweeter the reward would be when I finally got what I wanted.

I made my decision right then and there.

I was going to seduce the hell out of Lola Abbatelli.

LOLA

IT WAS BAFFLING the number of women who stopped what they were doing to stare at Grayson with big moon eyes as we made our way to our table. Even the hostess looked like she was seconds away from throwing herself at him so she could climb him like a tree.

Did these women have no pride? For Christ's sake, some of them appeared to be with their spouses or boyfriends. I mean, don't get me wrong, I understood the appeal. He was a hot guy... a *really* hot guy. Even *I* wasn't immune to his charm and good looks, but the air was suddenly clogged with excitement and desperation so thick I almost choked on it.

Ridiculous.

I chanced a sideways look in his direction to find he didn't seem the slightest bit fazed as we moved through the room. His hand stayed firmly on my back the entire way. When we finally reached the table, he trailed his fingertips along my spine in a slow, seductive move that had my traitorous body trembling with pleasure.

"If there's anything I can get you, anything at all, don't hesitate to let me know," the hostess crooned, bending close to Grayson's chair in order to put her cleavage on full display. I didn't even bother to suppress my eye roll as he gave her a quick and polite, yet dismissive grin before turning his attention back to me. I watched with a sick sense of enjoyment as her smile fell, her expression crestfallen as she stood and walked back to her post.

"Must be great being you," I said sarcastically as I began scanning the dinner options.

"What do you mean?"

I lifted my head to look at him when I heard the genuine confusion in his tone. His dark brows were furrowed over those glinting green eyes. I looked around at all the women still gawking before answering, "All the pathetic, swooning women?" I waved a hand in the air.

A deep frown marred his face, somehow increasing the handsomeness of his masculine features. *Stupid men and their ability to age well!* "What are you talking about?" His gaze darted around the dining area before coming back to me.

I let out a derisive snort. "You must be joking." There wasn't a single trace of humor on his face. My laughter dried up and I frowned in return. "Jesus, you really don't notice, do you?"

"I'm afraid you're going to have to spell it out for me, Lola."

I set my menu down and folded my hands together on top of the table. "This room is full of women who would gladly mow me over to be where I am right now. They started salivating the minute we walked in, Gray. Hell, I'm pretty sure the poor hostess ruptured an ovary!"

At that, his head fell back with a deep, rumbling laugh that caused my belly to quiver. Man, that sounded nice. "You have a fun imagination, Lola, I'll give you that."

"It's not my imagination. It's a fact." I looked around for proof, finding a woman who still seemed to be under his spell. "There, see?" I pointed and he turned to look. "That's basically the face every woman in here got when you walked in."

He turned his attention from the now horribly embarrassed woman and leaned his elbows on the table, talking in a low, intoxicating tone. "I don't recall seeing that look on *your* face."

I scoffed, desperately trying to sound indifferent. "Because I'm immune to you," I lied. I really freaking hoped God didn't strike me down with lightning for that one.

"Is that so?" He smiled and lifted one arm to rest his chin on his hand.

"Yes," I answered in a snooty voice.

"Hmm, then I guess I just imagined the way you shivered when my fingers brushed across your waist, huh?" I snorted and rolled my eyes, all the while thinking, *Shit, he felt that?* "Or how about when your pupils dilated when I leaned over you in the car? Or the way you struggled to breathe the closer I got?"

Damn it, I was having trouble breathing *again*! How was it possible that I could hate a man and want him so badly at the same time? I picked up my glass of water and sucked some down, my mouth suddenly as dry as a used-up, sixty-year-old porn star.

How's that for a visual? You're welcome.

"I don't know what you're talking about." Another lie. "That wasn't lust if that's what you're thinking. That cologne of yours was suffocating. If anything, I was having an allergic reaction. What you witnessed was probably closer to anaphylaxis than lust."

He chuckled and it was a direct shot to my lady parts. Luckily, the server took that moment to interrupt before I could do something crazy, like climb across the table and mount him.

I gave the menu another look as Grayson spoke with the server, ordering what was undoubtedly an insanely expensive bottle of wine, when brilliance struck.

"And have you had a chance to look at the menu?" the man asked.

I looked up at him with a shit-eating grin before turning that grin on Grayson. "I'm ready to order if you are." He nodded and lifted his hand in an indication for me to go first. "Hmm," I hummed, studying the menu like I was struggling to decide. "I'd really like to try the lobster, I've heard it's fabulous here." I smiled kindly to the server. "But I've also been craving a steak. And I see you have a Kobe filet. What a difficult decision." I tapped my chin in faux contemplation for a few seconds, then finally snapped the menu closed. "You know what? I'll just have both. You only live once, right? Oh, and I saw you have grilled oysters with shaved black truffle and caviar. I'd like that as an appetizer, please."

I handed the baffled server my menu and turned to smirk at Grayson. "I'm hungry." I shrugged like I hadn't just ordered myself a two-hundred-dollar meal.

If I'd expected him to get pissed about the exorbitant amount of money I'd just spent on a meal that I probably wouldn't even be able to eat a quarter of—which I did—I'd have been sorely disappointed at his reaction—which I was.

Closing his menu as well, he handed it over and said, "I'll have the same, minus the appetizer. And I think we'll try the raspberry mousse crème brûlée with the chocolate truffles for dessert, as well." He leveled me with a look that screamed "I know what game you're playing," then said, "What can I say? I'm hungry too." *Damn! Foiled again!* "You know," he started once the server hustled away to put in our *ridiculous* order, "I find a woman with an appetite *extremely* attractive."

I was losing ground. I was floundering. I was in serious danger of turning into one of the women around me and swooning at just the sight of his beautiful eyes. I needed to do something—stat! "So you're calling me fat?"

That's the best you can come up with? Really?

He sat back, his smile never wavering. "You know damn good and well that's not what I meant, but you're welcome to keep up the charade if it'll make you feel better."

The server returned with our wine, uncorking and pouring as I scowled at Grayson the entire time. Once he left again, I picked up my glass and took a *looooong* sip. Damn it, it was good. He had really great taste in wine—not that I'd ever tell him that.

"You're making it really hard to pretend to like you."

As if reading my mind, he answered, "You might not like me, but I'd be willing to lay money you want to fuck me right now."

And there went my panties. Up. In. Flames. "*Pfft*. As if." Yep, I really said it. When I got home, I was going to shove my head right in the oven. "You're not even my type."

He regarded me as he took a drink of wine. "And why is that? I've been curious ever since that day in the conference room. What is it about me that isn't your type? I have a mirror so I know I'm attractive. I have a stable, well-paying job with excellent medical benefits and a 401k, I'm disease-free, and I don't live in my parents' basement. I know how to do my own laundry, I can cook and iron, and I'm a nonsmoker. To most women, I'd be a catch."

"You might be all of that, Gray, but you're also a playboy. I've made it a rule in life to stay far, *far* away from playboys."

It was his turn to scoff. "And what could possibly make you think I'm a playboy?"

I opened my mouth to reply, only to come up empty. *Shit!* There had to be *something*, some reason for my assumption, right? "Uh...." Maybe if I'd Googled the bastard before our date I would've had more ammunition.

"I never expected you to be the type to make a snap judgment, Lola," he said, yanking me from my thoughts.

"I'm not!" I objected.

"You looked at me and saw that I have money, dress well, appreciate nice things, and am a single thirty-five-year-old man, and you automatically jumped to the conclusion that it means I have an issue with commitment. Am I wrong?"

"And you're telling me you're not?"

"That's exactly what I'm telling you. Yes, I'll give you that most men who fit the description I just laid out are more than likely in the market for nothing more than a quick fuck. Hell, my best friend's one of them. But you made an unfair assessment and haven't even given me the benefit of defending myself before acting as judge, jury, and executioner. I have to say, Lola, I'm disappointed. I expected more from you."

Oh my God. In two seconds flat, he'd managed to make me feel worse than every single one of the nuns in my old Catholic school put together. And that wasn't something you saw every day. Nuns were notorious for their guilt trips, only coming in second to Italian mothers. I was well versed with *both*.

"I...." Then I went on to say the two words I never expected to say to Grayson Lockhart. "I'm sorry."

Well sonofabitch.

CHAPTER TEN

DID I feel bad for manipulating the situation with Lola by laying on a Nana-sized guilt trip? Not one goddamned bit if it meant getting what I wanted. Sure, she was wrong to make assumptions about my character, but it wasn't like I was a choirboy growing up. I screwed around plenty, but I also committed when I met someone I felt was worth it.

The waiter came with the appetizer, placing it carefully in the center of the table, then offering us a nod before disappearing once again. I looked at the oysters topped with shiny black caviar and small shavings of black truffles and couldn't help but curl my lip in disgust.

After several seconds of staring in horror, I lifted my head, no longer able to stomach the sight of all the blacks and grays and slimy bits on the plate in front of me. How in the hell Lola found oysters appetizing was beyond me, let alone oysters topped with fish eggs and fungus.

I expected to see a happy smile on her face when my gaze locked on hers. What I hadn't expected was to see the same repulsion that I felt written all over her delicate features.

Oh I'm going to enjoy this.

My lip curl quickly morphed into a smile as I picked up my wine and took a sip. "What?" I asked. "Doesn't it look as good as you expected?"

"Of course!" she answered, smiling brightly to mask the cringe. "It looks... great."

"Well then, dig in. I can't wait to see the enjoyment on your face once you take your first bite."

She hesitated, looking back down at the food in question, trying her best to hide her repulsion before her eyes came to mine once again. "Uh... sure," she replied, sounding anything but sure. "Do you... would you like one or two?"

I held up my hand. "Oh no, those are all yours. I wouldn't dream of taking your food."

I could have sworn she was about to throw up. Her hand visibly trembled as she slowly lifted one of the oysters off the plate and brought it to her mouth. The closer it got the worse it shook. She looked so adorably ridiculous with her mouth hanging open, her hand suspended in the air as her face grew paler by the second, that it was impossible for me to hold back my chuckle.

"I can't!" She finally cried out seconds later, dropping the offending-looking mollusk onto the plate like it had bitten her. "I can't, all right! I'm sorry but that just looks revolting!" Her top lip curled up as she looked down at it and my chuckle turned into full-blown laughter.

Once I was finally able to stop, there was no missing the glare she shot me from across the table. "I'm sorry." I sucked in a much-needed breath. "I'm sorry, but you have to admit that one came back and bit you in the ass, sweetheart."

She sighed and dropped her hands into her lap. "It really did, didn't it?"

"Yep." Picking up my wineglass, I took a sip, keeping my eyes locked on hers over the rim of the glass. "But it was commendable, I'll give you that. For a second there, I really thought you were going to eat it."

"And I would have! If it didn't look like something a frat boy throws up after a kegger."

"You have a gift for painting a colorful visual." I laughed again, that time earning myself a smile from the other side of the table.

She shrugged casually and picked up her own glass. "What can I say, it's a talent."

"Oh I'm aware. I listen to the show."

Those beautiful chocolate eyes went wide as she set her wineglass back on the table. "You do? Really?" I loved that I just caught her off guard. On top of her beauty, she had a quick wit I'd never known another woman to have. That veneer she coated herself in sometimes seemed impenetrable, so it was nice to see she could be taken by surprise just like the rest of us.

"Of course. After our interesting little segment, I couldn't help but be curious about KTSW's most lucrative talk radio show. But I'll admit that I haven't figured out if I find the things I've learned about the inner workings of the female mind to be knowledgeable or terrifying."

Her grin couldn't be described as anything but wicked as she answered, "If you're a smart man, you'd find it to be both."

I returned her grin with one of my own, one I knew affected women the way I wanted it to. "Oh, I'm a *very* smart man."

Lola scrunched her face up and tilted her head to the side speculatively, pretending to study me before finally saying, "I'm not so sure about that. A smart man is usually able to take a hint. You seem to love bashing into a brick wall over and over again, expecting to see a different result."

"You're having dinner with me, aren't you?" I quickly countered.

"Not of my own free will," she rebutted without missing a beat.

I pulled in a deep breath as I watched her across the table. Humor flashed behind her eyes, and I could see her trying hard to fight a smile. "Just admit it. You're having fun right now."

Her chest rose and fell with each breath as she contemplated her answer, but I could see it on her face clear as day. She was enjoying herself.

Eventually she let out a huff. "Fine, I'll admit it. I'm having *a little* fun." She teasingly held her thumb and index finger a millimeter apart to make her point.

Thankfully, the server came to clear the uneaten appetizer away and refilled our wineglasses.

"So, tell me about yourself, Lola Abbatelli."

She smirked at me over her glass, one dark brow quirked up. "Not a very original start, now is it."

Christ, I loved that fiery attitude. If my dick didn't start behaving, I was either going to be stuck sitting all night or forced to go into the bathroom and take care of myself. I'd have preferred to bend Lola over the table and fuck her until she screamed, but self-preservation told me the timing was way off.

"Doesn't matter if it's unoriginal if it's true." I shrugged. "I'm genuinely interested in you. I think you know that."

She paused momentarily, and that was all I needed to confirm that she felt the exact same thing brewing between us that I did. No matter what came out of her mouth.

"And I think you're just begging for a sexual harassment lawsuit."

"How can I possibly sexually harass you when you want me just as much as I want you?"

Her mouth dropped open with a bewildered laugh. "That! That right there is why I accused you of being a playboy. You think you can just throw that stuff out there and expect me to drop my panties, just like that?"

Before I could respond, two servers interrupted our conversation just long enough to place our meals in front of us. I didn't bother looking down at my plate, maintaining eye contact until we were once again alone.

"I'm not a playboy, Lola—I'm determined. There's a difference. I'm a man who sees something he wants and is willing to break his back working to get it. I'm upfront and honest in all things. Don't confuse the two."

Her eyes narrowed. "So you're telling me that you're willing to break your back for a one-night stand?" She scoffed. "That's ridiculous, Grayson. Not to mention a complete waste of time."

"Who said anything about one night?" Her entire body froze with the exception of her chest, which seemed to rise and fall quicker than it had been just moments before. I was definitely getting in there. "And I'd rather risk breaking my back doing something *much* more pleasurable with you, but like I said, I work for what I want."

Lola let out a slow, measured breath as she studied me. "And you want me."

It wasn't a question, and I had no intention of lying. "I do. Very much. But you already knew that, didn't you?"

Her eyes finally broke from mine just long enough to repair any damage I might have managed to cause to that goddamned wall she kept around her like a fucking fortress.

"What was your longest relationship?"

My head jerked back slightly, and I'm sure my expression mirrored the surprise I experienced at her unexpected question. "What?"

"Relationship. What's the longest one you've had?"

"Four years," I answered. "We'd grown up together, our families close friends. We started dating after I graduated college, but she wanted to move the relationship along faster than I was ready for. Before that it was a year, and the one before that was two. Both of those were in college. And I was with my high school girlfriend for three years. Have I passed the interview process?" I finished, the frustration I felt seeping into my tone.

She sat back in her chair with a huff. "God, you really aren't a player, are you?"

"You know," I started in bewilderment, "I'm really trying to understand why you sound disappointed by that, but I just can't figure it out."

Instead of answering, she carried on. "My longest relationship was *maybe* a year. But if I were to really sit down and do the math, it would probably be closer to nine months."

"*Okay*," I said slowly, unsure where she was going.

"Why weren't you willing to take your relationship with her to the next level? I mean, four years is a long time, isn't it?"

I was afraid that if she didn't get to her point soon my head was likely to explode. "She wanted to get married and have kids. I wasn't ready for that. I was twenty-six and just starting to make a name for myself in my father's company. It took a while to earn the respect of the employees, convince them that I was there because I'd earned it, not because my dad handed it to me. I wanted to be stable in my career before I started a family. I didn't feel that I was there yet."

From the look on her face she seemed to accept my answer, but it was her next one that caused the lightbulb over my head to go off. "So, if you'd been more stable in your career, would you have married her?"

I knew exactly what she was doing. "I'm not answering that." I smiled triumphantly at having outwitted what had to be the wittiest woman I'd ever met.

"What? Why not?"

I finished my wine and poured more into my glass, not bothering to wait for our server to appear and do it for me. "Because I'm not playing into your attempt to bait me." She snorted and opened her mouth, prepared to deny it, but I didn't give her a chance. "No matter what my answer is, you'll twist it to use in a way that won't end favorably for me. If I say yes, you'll claim I'm still in love with her and pining away. If I say no, you'd probably accuse me of wasting her time when I knew all along I wasn't going to settle down." What flashed in her eyes told me I'd hit the nail right on the head, so I pushed on. "That was a past relationship that doesn't play into what's happening between you and me whatsoever. There's no reason to dredge up the past, especially when it's been over for years. But I will tell you this." I leaned in, making sure I had all her attention before lowering my voice and finishing. "You're going to have to work a *lot* harder if you're hoping to dissuade me."

Her face scrunched into a glower that did nothing to detract from her stellar looks. Picking up her fork and knife, she began tearing into her steak while I reveled in my defeat for a few more seconds.

"You're really annoying when you're being stubborn."

I chuckled as I picked up my own utensils to begin eating. "I'm probably the only person you've met who's even half as stubborn as you, aren't I?"

She made a little grunting noise deep in her throat and focused on her food.

"And you're really fucking gorgeous when you're pissed off," I added—you know, just for fun.

CHAPTER ELEVEN

LOLA

"SO TELL ME SOMETHING," Grayson prompted once our entries had been cleared away and the mouthwatering dessert was set before us. I hadn't been able to eat the entire thing, but what I'd managed to eat was decadent. The food and wine really were divine, and the company—to my utter dismay—was equally as good. I'd lost count of how many times I'd laughed throughout our meal. I couldn't remember the last time I'd had so much *fun* with a member of the opposite sex that didn't include naked mattress dancing.

"What's that?" I asked, picking up my wine and finishing the last of it. I was on my third glass and already feeling happily warm from the inside out.

"How did you get into the business of giving relationship advice?"

"What do you mean?" I asked around a mouthful of crème brûlée with no shame whatsoever. The dessert was pure *heaven*. I wanted to marry it and have little baby raspberry crème brûlées. Before I swallowed the last of what was in my mouth, I was already shoveling in more. "You know," I said after I managed to swallow. "You might want to get your own, because

I'm totally not sharing this." I pulled the plate closer to me and wrapped a protective arm around it so Grayson couldn't steal any of my precious.

His low, raspy chuckle was *almost* as good as my dessert. *Almost.* "I take it you like it," he said, his voice filled with amusement.

"*Soooo* good," I groaned, my mouth full once again. It was tart and sweet and silky with a hint of chocolate from the truffles. It was officially one of my favorite things on the planet.

"I'm glad you're enjoying it." He smiled at me. "But you still haven't answered my question."

It took my sugar-addled brain a second to remember what he'd asked just a minute before. "Oh yeah. Sorry." I swallowed the last bite and delicately wiped my mouth with the cloth napkin, barely able to hold myself back from licking the plate clean. "Well, it's not a very interesting story, really. Daphne, Sophia, and I all went to college together. Daph was the only broadcasting major out of the three of us and got a job hosting a late-night show for our campus station. We used to go with and keep her company since she was there mostly by herself, and one night we were screwing around when a girl called in crying about how her boyfriend cheated on her with her best friend."

"If Daphne was the only one hosting, how did you and Sophia get roped in?"

A sneaky smile stretched across my lips as I recalled that particular night. "Let's just say tequila helped. What I didn't mention was that the three of us headed to the station *after* an Alpha Phi luau."

"Ah." He sat back in his seat and regarded me, his stupid sexy eyes doing that attractive glimmer thing again. "I see."

"Yep." A wine-induced giggle worked its way from my throat. "To be honest, we didn't even remember what happened until the following day when we all got called in. Daphne was scared she was going to lose her job, but they ended up making it a three-person show instead. It just kind of snowballed from there. More girls started calling in, asking advice, and we just gave them our opinions. It was more a fluke than anything else. The three of us have never really had much luck in the relationship department, so when we weren't offering advice, we were telling our own dating horror stories. People seemed to love it and"—I held my arms out at my sides—"here we are ten years later."

Silence ensued after I finished my story, and the inquisitive way he studied me from across the table made my skin start to tingle. It was like he was trying to see inside me and figure out all my secrets. I began to fidget in my seat, disconcerted by the intensity of his stare. When he finally spoke, his words were just as confusing as his expression.

"You said *have*."

I cocked my head to the side, not understanding. "Excuse me?"

"You said the three of you *have* never really had much luck with relationships, not *had*. You spoke in present tense. Does that mean you still find yourself unlucky?"

I forced myself to swallow the sip of wine I'd just taken, the liquid going down painfully in my suddenly tight throat. On top of attractive, rich, and funny, it would appear that Grayson Lockhart was intuitive as well. "I don't do relationships," I answered, once I was able to work the uncomfortable knot from my throat. I tried my best to appear unaffected by the insightfulness of the question, but the truth was I'd suddenly gone from comfortably relaxed to on edge in a split second.

"You don't do relationships?"

"That's right."

His gaze grew curious and I could've sworn his lips twitched with a suppressed smile. "May I ask why?"

I shrugged, staring longingly at the empty dessert plate before answering. "I just don't believe in them."

"You don't believe in them," he repeated.

"Yep." I popped the P, growing frustrated at his repetition of my answers. "And can you please stop repeating everything I say like I'm some wackadoo?"

He lost the grin he was fighting and full-on smiled, making my belly swoop pleasurably. "I'm sorry. I just don't understand how you don't *believe* in relationships. I mean, you offer relationship advice as a profession."

I spun my wineglass by the stem as I thought on how to answer. "Well, all adults know Santa and the Easter Bunny aren't real, right? But they still pretend for their kids. It's kind of like that."

"Wait." Grayson's eyes grew huge with mock disbelief. "Santa and the Easter Bunny aren't real? Sonofabitch!"

"Shut up," I giggled. "It's a belief that's been engrained in me from a young age, starting with my dysfunctional parents."

"So you learned by example, then."

"No, not necessarily. You know the phrase 'Once bitten, twice shy'? Well, I'm pretty sure that phrase was coined for me. It wasn't just my parents who turned me off relationships— believe me, I had my fair share of disasters on my own. And if I wasn't living it, I was watching my friends be cheated on or taken advantage of. As time passed, I just decided it wasn't worth it. I'm happy with how my life is. I don't need a man in it to feel complete."

It was the very same argument I'd given a million times throughout my adult life. You couldn't remain single in my particular profession without some explanation, after all. The more I spoke that scripted argument over time, the more I actually started to believe it until it just became a way of thinking. But for some reason, sitting across from Grayson Lockhart, speaking those familiar words just felt... underwhelming. I felt like a fraud, a feeling that was completely foreign to me.

"I have no doubt that you can be complete without a man in your life, Lola. But don't you ever get lonely?"

I picked up my wineglass and took a long fortifying sip. "Nope." And normally that was the truth. Usually I ended my days with a comfortable sense of contentment. I had a great job, great friends, a fabulous apartment. My life was amazing simply because I'd worked my ass off to make it so. But for some reason, Grayson's sudden appearance had turned everything in my cozy little world on its head. Thanks to his question, that contentment I felt on a regular basis was replaced with something not at all pleasurable. *Stupid men, always messing with stuff.*

"Well, what about the people you know who have been in healthy, loving relationships for years? Take my parents, for example. They've been happily married for almost forty years."

"There's an exception to every rule," I answered simply. "Your parents are the exception. I learned a long time ago that only a lucky few get to call themselves that. Most people are just the rule."

His penetrating gaze sent a shiver down my spine. I had the acute sense that he could read every lie I was telling, clear as day. Fortunately, he seemed to realize my growing unease at the current topic and took pity on me, changing the subject to such things as my friendships with Sophia and Daphne, and how I liked working with my best friends every day.

The waiter finally brought the check, and I watched as Grayson pulled a credit card from his wallet and slipped it into the small black billfold. It was then that I noticed he had really nice hands. They were large with long fingers that looked like they could hold tight to my hips while—

Get your shit together, Lola!

My mind had quickly dived straight into the gutter. I gave

my head a small shake, trying to clear it of all the ridiculous thoughts that were suddenly bombarding me.

I wonder if what they say about the size of a man's hands is true?

Damn it, Lola!

I totally blamed Grayson for being so... so... damn *yummy!*

"Lola?"

My gaze jumped from his hands back to his eyes, my cheeks suddenly warm with embarrassment that he could possibly see the desire written all over my face.

"You okay?"

"Y-yeah. Yeah, I'm good. Sorry. Too much wine, I guess." I pasted on a smile and balled my hands into fists in my lap to keep from fanning my face. *Stupid sexy jerk with all his sexiness.*

Grayson stood and extended one of those strong, manly hands at me as he said in a low rumble, "Let's get you home, then."

My lady parts might have actually quivered. *Quivered!* He had the most seductive voice when he talked all quietlike. He sounded so good I'd have gladly listened to him read the phone book, or the back of a shampoo bottle, or the label that came on the back of the cookie dough packages warning not to eat it raw.

Swallowing against the sudden dryness in my throat, I placed my hand in his and let him help me from my chair. Just as I knew it would, his large hand completely engulfed mine.

You can't stand this guy, I reminded myself. *He's the devil. He's a manipulator. He schemed to trap you into fake-dating him. You. Do. Not. Like. Him.*

The silence that enveloped us as he led me through the restaurant and out onto the sidewalk had me feeling like a jittery mess. Not because it was awkward but because it *wasn't*. The knowledge that I actually *enjoyed* being around Grayson sat like a lead weight in my belly. I was discombobulated by the warring feelings taking place inside me. I liked him, but I didn't want to like him. He wasn't a guy I could use and then disregard like a pair of worn-out shoes. He was nothing like the men I was usually drawn to. He was too powerful, too masculine, too... all-consuming.

He was dangerous to my mental well-being.

Not to mention the fact that he was *my boss*.

"I enjoyed tonight," he murmured, pulling me from my unpleasant thoughts.

"Yeah, me too." I allowed myself to look up at him and smile as he opened the back door of the waiting town car. I moved to step in but his grip on my hand tightened, halting me between his large body and the car door.

"What's wrong?" I asked, glancing up to find him looking at something over my shoulder.

"Don't look," he warned as I went to turn my head. "There's a photographer about twenty feet away."

My back shot straight at his quiet words. "Are you serious?" I whispered, drawing his eyes back to mine. Something in their green depths flashed, an almost wickedness that heated me from the inside and set me on edge all at the same time.

A Cheshire grin stretched across his lips as he leaned in closer, releasing my hand in order to wrap his arm around my waist. "Looks like you're going to need to put on a good show," he said in a low rumble. "Hope you're a good actress."

Before I could question Grayson's puzzling statement, his mouth crashed down on mine in an unexpected yet captivating kiss that stole all the air from my lungs. My lips parted on a surprised gasp, giving him the access he needed to slip his tongue inside. He tasted of wine, decadent chocolate, and tart raspberries from our dessert. The flavors exploded against my tongue and I moaned appreciatively.

With my body no longer under my control, my arms lifted to twine around his neck as my mouth dueled with his. It was, by far, the most delicious, enthralling kiss I'd ever experienced in my life. For the first time in more than ten years, I found myself melting into a man and allowing him complete control.

By the time he pulled back, I was so kiss-drunk that I probably would've given him anything he wanted. I stood in a stunned haze, my eyelids fluttering open as my tongue darted out and ran along my plump, sinfully bruised bottom lip.

"That was...." I breathed as he smiled down at me like the cat that got the canary. Then he spoke, effectively shattering the perfect moment into a million tiny pieces.

"That'll surely make for an interesting piece in tomorrow's edition."

Sonofabitch. I'd been played and hadn't even put up a fight. His words pissed me off at the same time as they strengthened my resolve. There was no way I was going to allow myself to get stupid over some guy. Not again. Not ever. He was a pain in my ass, nothing more. And once my job was safe and Grayson's reputation was cleared, I was determined to put this entire ridiculous debacle in my rearview mirror.

Or at least that's what I told myself.

Unfortunately, my traitorous body didn't seem to be on board.

CHAPTER TWELVE

LOLA

THANKS to the NC-17-rated dreams I had after mine and Grayson's sham of a date, I was a panting, sweaty, horny mess when my alarm sounded and jolted me awake. Three things that led to me being in an epically shitty mood.

Sexual frustration and I did *not* get along. Usually, whenever I was in the mood, I'd scroll through my contacts in search of one of the men I kept on my roster for when I needed to be wham-bam-thank-you-ma'amed, but for some ridiculous reason, none of those names held any appeal when I'd looked through them earlier that morning.

There was only one number I wanted to dial and I refused to allow myself to cave, no matter how insanely good-looking he was... or how amazing he smelled every time he came close to me, or how good he was at kissing.

Damn it! Now I'm thinking about kissing and sniffing him!

If this went on for much longer, I was afraid my poor neglected va-jay-jay was going to turn on me. And who knew what kind of trouble that hussy would cause if set loose.

By the time I made it to my office building, Starbucks in hand, I'd gone from aggravated to straight-up pissed right the hell off. And it was all *his* fault! Grayson Lockhart was a dick! A sexy, chiseled, walking wet dream *dick*!

I bet he has a really good-looking dick.

Stop it, *Lola!*

"Hoo-we! Looks like someone woke up on the wrong side of the bed this morning," Bob teased as I made my way past the security desk in the lobby. I wasn't even in the mood for our typical morning banter.

"Push your luck and you're going to have my size seven-and-a-half planted somewhere even Loretta won't be willing to go," I shot back, causing him to throw his head back and hoot with laughter.

"Only thing I've ever known to put that kinda sour expression on a woman's face was a man. You finally meet your match, sweetheart?"

Bob clearly wants to die today. Shooting him a look that I hoped melted his skin, I clamped my lips between my teeth and proceeded toward my elevator bank, ignoring the raucous laughter that followed me.

I hit the Up button and let out a relieved sigh when one of the elevators dinged and the door instantly opened for me. I was hoping for a short ride to my floor and was almost home free, watching the doors close, when a hand suddenly appeared between them, halting their progress. And not just any hand —*his* hand. The hand I'd spent an unhealthy amount of time thinking of the night before. Had I been close enough, I probably would've jabbed the Door Close button a million times.

What did he do, run to catch up with me? The stalker.

"Well." The jackass grinned smugly. "My morning just keeps getting better and better."

"God hates me," I muttered between clenched teeth, looking up at the ceiling as Grayson moved close, forced to step behind me as the onslaught of people *he* allowed to get on with us took up the confined space.

My back remained ramrod straight, my heart pounding against my breastbone as his warm breath tickled the small strip of exposed skin where my shoulder met my neck. He was close. *So close.* I imagined I could feel the heat radiating off his body, my skin prickling with awareness.

"You look beautiful," he whispered against my ear, sending a shiver down my spine.

I shot him a cutting look over my shoulder in warning and mouthed, "Stop it."

He grinned cheekily, making me hate him even more because I really, *really* loved that smile.

I turned back around, doing my best to ignore his presence, hoping our little exchange didn't garner any unwanted attention. To my astonishment, he moved even closer, so much so that I could feel his chest vibrate with a silent chuckle.

I shoved my elbow back, jabbing him in the solar plexus, and smiled at the sound of his muffled grunt of pain.

"That wasn't very nice," he whispered once again, only that time he placed the hand closest to the wall on my hip. I gasped as his fingers tensed in a gentle squeeze. Heat suffused my entire body at the simple yet intimate touch.

The elevator stopped and the doors opened to allow some of the people off at their floor.

"When someone compliments you, the normal response is to say 'thank you.'"

I glanced back as the doors began to close once again and hissed, "There are no cameras around. What the hell are you doing?"

That cheeky smile returned and I felt it *low* in my belly. "I'm paying you a compliment. Say 'Thank you, Gray.'"

The glare on my face was a contradiction to the warm, happy whoosh in my stomach.

"Thank you, Gray," I ground out for no other reason than to put an end to our interlude before someone caught on... or at least that's what I told myself.

"You're welcome," he answered cheerfully before standing tall and looking straight ahead.

The elevator stopped three more times, allowing people off at one floor after another until there was no one left but Grayson and me. Despite all the available space, he didn't move away, and when I attempted to step to the side in order to create room between us, his fingers, still firmly on my hip, tightened their grip and he grabbed my other hip with his available hand, effectively holding me in place.

His nose brushed the delicate skin behind my ear, and I had to close my eyes against the onslaught of warring emotions and hormones raging through me. "Wh-what are you doing?" I stuttered, swallowing thickly to ease my suddenly dry throat.

"You smell amazing." His words weren't soft whispers; instead they came out in a sort of growl. "What perfume are you wearing?"

Goose bumps broke out across my skin. My head screamed, *Abort! Abort!,* while my body wanted nothing more than to turn around, tackle Grayson to the floor of the elevator, and have its wicked way with him.

"I-I—" I cleared my throat, an unfamiliar sense of being flustered suddenly taking hold of me. It was all the more reason not to like this man. I wasn't the type of woman to fluster easily. I was a strong, independent, career-minded woman. Men had no power over me unless *I* allowed it... or so had been the case before the exasperating Grayson Lockhart waltzed into my life and turned it on its head. "I'm not wearing any... perfume, that is."

The sound that rumbled from his chest was a cross between a hum and a moan... and I *loved* that sound. *Damn it all to Hell!* "Christ, that's all you, then?"

"I... guess so?" I ended on a high-pitched inflection, turning what should've been a statement into a question. I just didn't know how to handle this enigmatic man. I felt out of my depth, out of my league... hell, out of the damn ballpark. It was *not* something I was used to.

"Well, I approve," he grunted.

Some of my bearings thankfully returned in that moment and I was able to reply bitingly. "Oh, I'm so pleased you approve. Now I can die a happy woman. Grayson Lockhart likes how I smell. My goal in life has been fulfilled."

His fingertips skimmed up and down, coming to a stop on my waist, and I swear to God, I could feel his touch through my dress as if I were wearing nothing at all. "You know, your smart mouth might just be the very thing I like about you most."

Spinning around to face him for the first time since we stepped on the elevator, I leveled him with my most intense glare, all the while my body acutely aware of the fact that the move had caused me to lose the touch of his hands. It was *not* happy with me.

"You know this goes beyond sexual harassment, right? This entire conversation doesn't even border on indecent—it sailed right over that line and has now entered lawsuit territory." Not that I'd ever consider filing a complaint, not when I secretly loved his attention as much as I did. I wasn't delusional; even though part of me couldn't stand him, I could admit to myself that there was another part of me that was wild for him—but there was no way in hell I'd ever admit that out loud. My dichotomous emotions were going to drive me to insanity.

"I might be concerned if I wasn't certain you enjoyed it just as much as I did," he replied, leaving me speechless as the doors once again slid open. "I believe this is your stop, Ms. Abbatelli."

My mouth dropped open at the outrageousness of his statement. I was momentarily stunned, only coming to my senses when Grayson moved to hold the closing doors open. It was in that moment I realized Grayson hadn't bothered to hit the button for his floor. He'd planned this whole thing. He wanted the chance to discombobulate me. He seemed to get off on my reactions. *The stupid, sexy jerk.* He'd played me like a violin. *Oh, he's good.*

With a harrumph, I spun on my heels and flounced out of the elevator insolently, telling myself that the sensual laughter that followed after me had no effect. I was a big fat liar.

"Have a wonderful day, Lola. I know I will," he called to me.

I chanced one last scowl over my shoulder at him before flipping my hair and turning back around... and running smack into a glass wall.

CHAPTER THIRTEEN

LOLA

THE THROBBING in my nose was only outshone by the throbbing between my legs, thanks to Grayson, the asshole.

Daphne and Sophia were already hovering around my desk when I stomped to it and slammed my beloved red Kate Spade bag down on the top. I was dangerously close to full-on tantrum mode. Despite my physical attraction, Gray seemed to bring out the worst in me.

"Morning, sunshine." Sophia gave me a saucy grin. Daphne did a half-assed job of trying to cover her giggle with a cough. I stared daggers at the both of them before dropping down into my chair and rubbing at the sore bridge of my abused nose.

"Oh no," Daphne started, her tone full of sympathy. "Did you run into the glass again?"

I seriously hated my life at that moment. That was twice now I'd tried to make some dramatic exit from Grayson only to humiliate and injure myself at the same time. "This entire place is a death trap," I grumbled. "I'm lucky I haven't concussed myself yet."

"You're like those birds from the Windex commercials," Sophia added unhelpfully.

I frowned at my so-called friend. "Thanks."

She smiled cheerfully and dropped a newspaper on my desk. "If it's any consolation, you looked hot last night."

"What?" I asked, snatching up the copy of the *Seattle Times* and thumbing through.

"Try the Entertainment section," Daphne offered.

The thin pages rustled loudly as I whipped through them. When I finally landed on the photo that had caught my girlfriends' attention, I froze. Okay, yeah. Sophia might have been right. I was rocking that dress, but that wasn't what I was focused on. No, what held my rapt attention was the fact that the photo was of Grayson and me wrapped in a tight clinch, making out like two horny teenagers next to his car on a public sidewalk.

"Damn it!" I hissed.

"That's quite a show you put on for the cameras," Daph teased, clearly enjoying my discomfort.

"Jesus, how the hell did this make it into the papers so fast?"

"Well the headline says it all, don't you think?"

I looked from the photo to the black, bold letters printed above it:

THINGS HEAT UP BETWEEN LOCAL CELEBRITY LOLA ABBATELLI AND ONE OF AMERICA'S MOST ELIGIBLE BACHELORS.

"Gossip sites are already starting to speculate how long this has been going on," Sophia told me. "There are even a few reports saying you two have been hooking up for a while and are secretly planning to run off to Vegas and elope soon."

My head shot up at that announcement, and I noticed my friend looked way too amused by the news.

"This isn't funny," I demanded, but truth be told, if the shoe was on the other foot, I'd probably be having just as much fun at Sophia's expense as she was at mine.

"*Au contraire*, this is *hilarious*. The rumor mill is already running rampant. Seems the folks in PR and our lovely Sam are beside themselves with glee. They're absolutely thrilled at the thought of the publicity this relationship could bring to our show."

My eyebrows dipped together, my head starting to ache as my brain worked feverishly to keep up with just how epically my life was crumbling before me. "It's not a relationship," I insisted.

"Sure looks like one to me," Daphne chimed in. "I mean, look at that kiss." She yanked the paper from my grasp and waved the photo in front of me. "No one is *that* good an actress. You look like you're trying to eat his face and he looks like he's two seconds from ripping that dress off and taking you against that car. You can't fake heat like that, babe."

"Yes, you can," I lied. "You can totally fake it, because that's exactly what I was doing." My brain shouted *Bullshit!* as I said the words. I mentally flipped it the middle finger. From the looks on my friends' faces, they didn't believe that anymore than I did.

Clenching my eyes closed, I lifted my hands and began rubbing at my temples to try and stave off my oncoming headache. I needed a do-over of the past few days. I needed this all to be a nightmare.

I was praying for some sort of reprieve when my cell phone began ringing from inside my purse. I pulled it out and released a pained groan at the sight of the name on the screen. I must have really done something big to piss Karma off, because not only weren't my prayers answered, but things only seemed to be getting worse.

"Hi, Ma," I answered.

Those two words were cut off by my mother's shrill, hysterical scream coming through the line. "*Cara!*" she shouted. "Oh, my dear, sweet girl! You've made me so happy!" She started spouting off endearments, bouncing between Italian and English in her excitement. "It's all over the interweb that you've landed yourself a handsome young man!"

I wasn't sure where to start first, so I decided to grab hold of the easiest thing. "It's the Internet, Ma, not the interweb."

Her snort echoed through the receiver. "Whatever. I don't care about that. All that matters is that my little girl's finally got herself a man! Oh, *cara*, I'm so happy." Ah hell, her voice was watery and wavered like she was just moments away from crying happy tears. "I'm not happy you were so public in your affection, but I can't be too mad, not when it means I'll finally get my dream of little grandbabies! But you really should consider being more private in your liaisons, darling. You'll get a reputation."

"Whoa! Whoa!" I cried out. "Slow your roll. No one said anything about babies. Have you lost your mind? Jeez, Ma, it was one date!"

"And such a good-looking boy," she mused. Only my mother would call a grown man in his midthirties a boy. "And from the article it looks like he's *very* well off."

"Mom!" I snapped, desperate to pull her from her tangent. "Just stop, okay? It isn't what you think. Grayson and I aren't—"

"And what a masculine name, don't you think? *Grayson.*" She said it almost reverently. "So strong and commanding, yes?"

That was such a spot-on description of not just Grayson's

name, but his presence as well—not that I'd ever admit that to my mother; she was already foaming at the mouth because of a simple picture. Trying to talk her down right then would've been pointless. I didn't have the inclination or the time to talk her down. I needed to get to the studio.

"Look, Ma, I have to go, okay? We're going on the air soon. I'll call you later." *Like in a year or two.*

"Okay, sweetheart. I'll talk to you soon. Maybe I'll come for a visit," she said, sounding like she was speaking more to herself than to me. That declaration sent chills over my skin. "It'll give me a chance to see you, *and* meet your new young man."

"Sweet, merciful hell," I grunted through the line.

"Language, Lola Arianna Abbatelli!" she scolded.

"Sorry," I sighed. "We'll talk about this later, okay?"

"All right, honey. Talk soon. I love you."

"Love you too, Ma."

I hung up and dropped my head to my desk, banging my forehead against the cool, smooth surface three times before sitting up straight.

"So..." Sophia dragged out, "nice chat with your mom?"

"She wants to visit," I told them.

They both stared at me with matching expressions of horrified astonishment. They were my best friends; they knew that, despite how much I loved my mother, being in her company for more than a short span of time was a recipe for disaster. One of us was bound to kill the other if we were cooped up in the same room for too long. There was a reason we lived on different coasts. Our relationship did much better with a continent dividing us. When I was growing up, we butted heads like crazy, the both of us being strong-minded, stubborn women. It wasn't until I moved away to college that our relationship finally began to flourish.

"You'll kill each other," Daphne stated the obvious.

I let out a humorless chuckle and added, "She says she wants to 'meet my new young man,'" I told them, using finger quotes to emphasize my point. "When did my life get so effed up?"

Sophia smiled evilly. "When you met your match and caught the guy's eye at the same time. Grayson Lockhart is totally your equal when it comes to getting what he wants."

I scowled again. If this kept up, I was going to have wrinkles long before I was ready. "I didn't catch his eye," I objected petulantly. "I just... pissed him off, and now he's making me pay for it."

Daphne picked up the paper once more and shook it playfully. "Looks like you caught more than just his eye," she singsonged.

I snatched the paper from her hand and crumpled it up, tossing it into the recycling bin.

"You're right. I also caught his disdain. We can't stand each other."

My friends gave each other a knowing look. "Just keep telling yourself that, Lo," Sophia said.

I stood from my chair and propped my hands on my hips, replying in a snotty tone, "I will, thank you very much. Now if you two don't mind, we have a show to do. Can we please stop talking about my fake love life and focus on our jobs?"

Again, they shared a look that made me want to smack them both. But before I could, they both stood up and started out of my little cubicle toward the studio. I breathed a much-needed sigh of relief as I followed after them. I thought the topic was dropped, that I was finally granted my reprieve, but I should've known better.

"Hey, Lo?" Sophia asked, watching me over her shoulder.

"Yeah?"

"Can I be your maid of honor when you and Grayson get married?"

While she and Daphne giggled like little schoolgirls, I was contemplating how I could dispose of my two friends' bodies after I murdered them.

CHAPTER FOURTEEN

GRAYSON

IT HAD BEEN NEARLY a week since my last interaction with Lola. After leaving her so out of sorts that she'd walked into a glass wall, I figured it was best to give her a small break. But that break was coming to an end today. It seemed I couldn't get that woman off my mind no matter where I was or what I needed to get done. I couldn't remember the last time I wanted a woman so much I was driven to distraction. Hell, my longest relationship ended because I put my job first, but just a few days with Lola and I couldn't focus on shit.

My office door swung open, yanking me from my thoughts of Lola. Caleb came waltzing in with the same casual, happy-go-lucky attitude he wore like a mask. I knew him well enough to know it was all an act, that he played up the playboy title he'd been given, thinking nothing more would ever be expected of him. Caleb was my closest friend and one of the most loyal people I'd ever known, but growing up being beaten down and cowed by the people who were supposed to love you unconditionally could seriously damage a person's outlook on life.

"You're in a good mood this morning," I stated, noticing the faint smile that lingered on his lips.

That smile only grew at my observation. "What can I say? Hours of world-class sex will do that to a man. You should really try it sometime."

Oh, I fully intended to... as soon as I could get Lola on board, which was proving to be more of a pain in the ass than I'd considered.

"Maybe if you'd finally tap that hot piece from the gossip rags all week, it would improve your disposition."

I threw him a killing look at referring to Lola as a "hot piece." Caleb might've been my best friend, but that didn't mean I wouldn't beat the shit out of him if he continued to disrespect her. And by the way his mouth snapped shut, I knew he interpreted my expression correctly.

His hands went up in surrender as he moved toward one of the chairs on the other side of my desk. "Sorry, sorry. I won't talk about your girl like that," he chided as he fell into the seat and placed his ankle on the opposite knee. With a teasing smile, he added, "Didn't know it was so serious."

"It's not serious," I replied flatly, the admission souring my mood somewhat. "From the way she acts whenever I'm around, you'd think I had the fucking plague."

A sharp bark of laughter erupted from Caleb. "Oh man! This is great." He laughed hysterically.

A scowl darkened my features as I watched him laugh his ass off at my expense. "Glad I could amuse you, man."

"I'm sorry," he gasped, his laughter finally starting to die down into an annoying chuckle. "But you have to admit that the irony is kind of funny, brother."

"How do you mean?"

"Well, think about it. Women all around the country would drop their panties if you asked—"

"You're exaggerating," I interrupted.

"Hell, man, you actually had a chick stalk you because she

was convinced you were *the one*. Have you ever had to work to get a woman's attention before?"

Crossing my arms over my chest, I leaned back in my chair and regarded him. "I'm assuming you have a point you'll eventually get to?" I said instead of admitting he was right. I might not fuck every woman who threw herself at me like he did, but that didn't mean I hurt for female company when the mood arose.

"The point, man, is that you've finally met your match." The asshole really didn't have to sound pleased about it. "And she's one damn good actress too, if those pictures are anything to go by."

That wasn't an act. I didn't bother to correct Caleb, or try to explain it, but I knew. I could feel it every time I got close to her, the way her entire body melted into mine when I kissed her, and how she greedily kissed me back. It wasn't an act—no fucking way. She wanted me, but there was something holding her back.

"Looks like you've got your work cut out for you with this one." Caleb grinned. "Hope you've got a game plan. You're going to need it."

"Oh, I'm sure I'll think of something," I responded with a determined smile. I wasn't afraid of hard work, and when I wanted something, I was determined to get it... no matter what it took.

"Maybe you should enlist Mama Lockhart's help. We both know that woman'd give her little boy anything he wanted." He said it jokingly, but his words made me stop. There was actually some merit to that suggestion. My father was never one to spoil his child, but my mom most definitely was. Lola might be stubborn as shit, but she was no match for my mother. And the plus side was that my mother was unaware of the scheme I'd worked up after that disastrous phone call that had been aired so publicly. My father had thought it best to leave her in the dark, so she'd been operating under the misconception that what was being splattered in the papers was real. It was *perfect*.

"Dude. I was just kidding, Gray. I see those wheels of yours spinning. You really want to sic your mom on her? She'd eat the poor girl for lunch."

I propped my elbows on the arm of my chair, and stroked my chin as I thought. "Hey, you're the one who said I needed a game plan."

Caleb studied me silently for several seconds. "You're really gone for this chick." It wasn't a question so I didn't bother with an answer. "I figured that was the case when you didn't get all pissy at your face being splashed around the gossip columns, but I didn't think you were this far gone."

"What can I say? You know how much I love a challenge."

He suddenly grinned, his face showing he was down for whatever scheme I was working up. "That I do. And I have to tell you, Gray, that's one fuck-hot challenge. Be honest. Are those real?" He held his hands out in front of his chest like he was gripping a couple melons.

"Fuck off," I said by way of an answer, then looked down at the watch on my wrist.

"Come on, man," he whined as I stood from my seat and started around my desk. "You can't leave me hanging like that. Best friends are supposed to share this kind of shit. Hey, where are you going?"

I didn't look back as I headed toward the door. Lola's show had already started, and I could no longer ignore the niggling desire to see her any longer. "To get a front row seat of the show."

"I'll join you. I've been meaning to head down and see the woman who's got you twisted in knots in person," Caleb muttered, shooting from the chair and following after me.

The elevator took us up and the instant we stepped off, I

knew everyone on the floor not only knew who I was but that they'd all seen the articles in the papers. The curiosity and speculation of what was going on between Lola and me was written on all their faces.

"M-Mr. Lockhart. Oh... h-hi. Hello," the receptionist stammered as Caleb and I entered KTSW's lobby. Her eyes grew wide at the sight of us. "C-can I help you?"

"Well, hello." Caleb gave the young blonde receptionist what he called his "panty-drenching" smile and leaned against the credenza. "And what's your name, beautiful?"

I smacked him upside the back of his head and grabbed him by the elbow, jerking him from the poor, unsuspecting woman.

"Ow! The fuck was that for?" he pouted as he rubbed his head.

I looked back to see the receptionist's eyes bug out and her jaw drop. "I know the way. Thank you." I didn't break stride as I answered, pulling my man-whore of a best friend behind me. "Don't shit where you eat, asshole," I gritted as we headed for the sound booth.

"Why not? That's what you're doing. Or at least trying to."

"That may be, but I know you. You'll fuck her, drop her, then pretend like she doesn't exist when you see her in the halls. That's a lawsuit waiting to happen that the company doesn't need."

"Jesus, Gray. You make it sound like I'm a heartless prick."

I shot him a side-eyed look. "Tell me that's not exactly what you planned to do if she gave you a shot."

He opened his mouth like he was prepared to argue but then stopped, realizing I was right. "Whatever," he grumbled as I brought us to a stop in front of the door to the sound booth.

"Now can you behave or do I need to send you back down to your room?"

He flipped me off and twisted the knob, pushing the door

open and stepping in. I followed behind him and closed us into the room with a red-faced, startled Jerry, the producer, and the other young guy I'd seen last time I was in there.

"Mr. Lockhart... what are you... I mean, how, um, how are you?"

"Gentlemen." I tipped my chin at them and made introductions between the two of them and Caleb. "We just wanted to come check out the show for a bit."

"Oh... uh...." Jerry's face grew even redder as the kid, Andrew, began to fiddle with the soundboard. "Okay... sure. Just pull up a seat, I guess."

Caleb and I made ourselves comfortable in the chairs near the back wall, mindful to stay out of the way while Lola and her friends were on the air. I wasn't sure what I expected, but listening to the three of them banter back and forth and interact with their callers while we watched from the other side of the glass was pure entertainment. Those three women had an enthusiasm that was damn near palpable. It was no wonder *Girl Talk* brought in such high ratings. As I listened, my mind whirled with ideas of how to promote not just the station and the show, but the three hosts as well. We needed to get them out in front of the public, really put their faces to the voices people listened to on a daily basis.

"Dude," Caleb whispered, drawing me from my musings. "I had no idea these chicks were so damn hot. Have you checked out the blonde? Christ, she's a perfect ten."

Andrew turned to look at us over his shoulder, giving Caleb a commiserating look. It would appear that it wasn't just the listeners who were charmed.

"Don't even think about it," I warned quietly.

Lola's voice cut through our conversation as she spoke into the mic. "If you're just tuning in, we've opened up the lines and are taking calls from you guys. This is your time to vent. If you've got some issues in your relationship, this is a chance for you to call for some advice. We've got Rose on the line right now. Hey, Rose, how can we help you out?"

"H-hi, guys," a hesitant voice sounded through our small room.

"So what's happening in your relationship that made you call in today?" Sophia asked.

"Well... I've been with my boyfriend for about six months now, and lately I've been thinking about breaking up with him."

"Seriously?" Caleb leaned in and whispered. "You dragged me down here to listen to some ya-ya traveling pants shit?"

"I didn't drag you in here, dick. Now shut up and listen," I hissed back.

"And why have you thought about breaking up with him?" Lola prodded. I looked back toward the booth to see all three ladies with matching expressions of concentration.

"The thing is... God, this is so embarrassing."

"Nothing to be embarrassed about," Lola said in a soothing voice. "We're all friends here. Just let it out."

Caleb let loose a derisive snort, earning himself my elbow to his ribs.

"Okay," Rose sighed. "Well you see, my boyfriend... he's...."

"Is the sex bad?" Daphne asked when the caller continued to waver.

From the corner of my eye, I saw Caleb perk up at the mention of sex. "Say what?"

"No, no. The sex is good. It's... the stuff leading *up* to the sex that's bad."

"There's stuff *before* sex?" Caleb asked in a quiet, curious voice.

Sweet mother of God. I need new friends.

"You mean foreplay?" Lola asked.

"Ohhh." *Now* Caleb was following. The dumbass.

"Yes. Foreplay. You see... my boyfriend's not very good at... going downtown."

"The hell?" Caleb choked.

Jerry's face burned even redder as he cleared his throat uncomfortably.

Andrew blushed in a way only a young, twenty-year-old, semi-experienced kid could.

Me... well, I just sat there with rapt attention, curious to see what these three ladies would offer up as advice.

"Ah... we're following," Daphne spoke up as Lola rolled her eyes. And for some reason Sophia threw her arms out, as though the topic was frustrating.

"Okay, look," Lola cut in. "You're not the first woman to call in with this particular complaint, Rose. I've got to ask... have you bothered to try and *teach* your boyfriend what you want him to do down there?"

"Well... no... not really. I mean, he's twenty-five years old. Shouldn't he know what he's doing by now?"

Daphne smacked her forehead as Lola began to talk once again. "See, this is the problem with the younger generation." Now *that* definitely hadn't been what I was expecting to hear. As she continued to talk, I was reminded that this woman was just full of surprises. "You expect to get whatever you want without having to actually work for it. Here's the hard truth, Rose. Men aren't born with the innate ability to give amazing oral. Just like everything, it's an acquired skill, something taught over time. You can't possibly expect him to just dive in and know what he's doing if you and all the girls before you never bothered to guide him in the right direction."

"Bloody hell," Caleb breathed, but I was too enraptured by Lola's passionate monologue to pay attention to anything else.

"You need to pull up your big girl panties and take the bull by the horns... literally. Grab hold of his hair next time he goes downtown and show him what you want. Use your words. When he hits a spot you like, moan, scream, '*Yes, right there!*' Do *something* to let him know what works and what doesn't. Don't be afraid to be vocal. You're in your midtwenties, sweetheart. If you're unhappy with the foreplay in your relationship, there's really no one to blame but yourself."

"But... wouldn't he find that offensive?"

"We aren't telling you to give him a bullet point list of instructions," Sophia chimed in, drawing a chuckle from me. "There's no need to bruise his ego or insult him. You can do it without him even realizing what's going on. Make it sexy. Compliment him when he does something right. Reward him for a job well done by returning the favor. Trust me, he'll get off on it and keep doing what you like if he sees it's getting results."

"We've said it on this show a hundred times, and we'll say it again," Lola added. "You're just as responsible for your own pleasure as he is... maybe even more so. You can't just sit back and expect to see the results you want. You have to demand them, work for them. You want the best sex of your life? Then teach your man to give it to you."

"I think I'm in love," Caleb whispered reverently. I glanced over at him to find him gazing through the Plexiglas in complete awe.

"You really think that will work?" the caller asked, her tone a mixture of trepidation and hope.

"Oh, most definitely, honey." Lola smiled into the mic. "Now, you be sure to call us and let us know how it goes."

"Okay, I will," Rose replied enthusiastically. "Thanks, you guys. This was exactly what I needed to hear."

"No problem. We're happy to help out. And we look forward to hearing from you again, Rose."

The call dropped and I listened with an amused smile on my face as the show came to a close. Jerry flipped the switch that allowed them to hear what was happening on our side of the booth. "All right, ladies, that's a wrap. Good show."

I stood, prepared to make my presence known, when Caleb spoke, pulling my attention back to him. "Now I see why you're so hung up on this chick, man. She's hot *and* fucking brilliant."

He wasn't telling me something I didn't already know. Lola Abbatelli was the total package.

CHAPTER FIFTEEN

LOLA

I GAVE a small start after I removed my headset and turned toward the control booth, only to come face-to-face with the man who'd been plaguing my thoughts for the previous two weeks. To say the images that had been running through my head for the past several days were not safe for work would've been a massive understatement.

The second his green eyes met mine, a wicked smile spread across his face, sending a bolt of electricity straight between my thighs. I was in *big* trouble.

"Looks like someone's got an admirer," Sophia teased, tearing my rapt attention from Grayson.

I skewered her with a glare and muttered, "Shut it, jerk," just as the door between the sound booth and the studio opened.

Grayson sauntered in like he owned the place—because he kind of did—followed closely by a man of equal height and similar stature. The stranger's hair was a few shades lighter than Grayson's but his smiling eyes had hints of brown in the grassy green. While Grayson's friend was definitely handsome, he didn't possess the same all-consuming charisma. His presence wasn't as potent... at least not where I was concerned.

Turning my gaze from the unknown man, I narrowed my eyes at Grayson and demanded, "What, are you stalking me now?"

My attitude—the very same attitude that had men running scared all my life—didn't seem to faze him in the slightest. His smile expanded as he came closer, stopping only a few feet away —far enough to maintain an air of professionalism, but still close enough for me to get a whiff of his woodsy cologne. He looked good... *damn* good. The pale green button-down shirt he wore highlighted the color in his eyes. Two buttons at his collar were undone, giving me a tantalizing peek at the tan skin of his neck. His sleeves were rolled up to his elbow, his thick, corded forearms on prominent display. I hadn't really noticed the appeal of a man's forearms before, but something about Grayson's drove me crazy. He had sexy forearms. He had sexy *everything*.

"Just wanted to catch the show in person. Once again, you ladies didn't disappoint."

My cheeks caught fire at the realization that he and his friend had a front row seat as I offered advice on the art of cunnilingus to a caller. Instead of letting my insecurities show, I straightened my shoulders and lifted my chin, propping my hands on my hips in an effort to appear unaffected. "Well, glad we could keep you entertained," I replied snootily.

"Hi. Caleb McMannus. Huge fan of the show. *Huge*." The stranger who'd been standing silently next to the bane of my existence stuck his hand out for me to shake. I returned his gesture and introduced Sophia, Daphne, and myself, in that order. As soon as I spoke her name, he turned his attention on Daphne. The way his eyes flared with desire as he looked at her was impossible to miss.

Poor guy didn't stand a chance.

"Hi, I'm Caleb," he repeated, as though dazed by just the sight of her. "I'm an Aquarius, thirty-five years old, the CFO of Bandwidth, and I learned the proper way to go down on a woman when I was sixteen."

Daphne's eyes bugged out.

Sophia snorted.

I choked on my tongue.

And Grayson rattled off a litany of cuss words. "Excuse my friend," he offered up as an apology. "He was dropped on his head as an infant... a lot."

Daphne visibly bit the inside of her cheek to keep from bursting into laughter. If the guy who'd just made a complete ass out of himself wasn't the CFO of the company that owned *our* company, we never would've let him live down the word vomit he'd just subjected us all too.

"Uh... good to know, I guess," she offered somewhat amicably before looking at me with an expression that screamed "Help a sista out."

"Well, it's been a pleasure and all, but we were just heading out to lunch, so...." I threw my thumb over my shoulder as I slowly started backing away.

"Ah, ah, ah," Grayson chided. "Not so fast. You and I have lunch plans."

"We most certainly do not!" I shouted, knowing damn good and well that being alone with him would ultimately lead to my downfall. I'd had a weeklong break from the man and my lady bits *still* got tingly every time I thought about him. I needed to stay as far away from him as possible. Only he was making it impossible. The son of a bitch.

Stuffing his hands in his pockets, Grayson appeared completely at ease as he declared, "Ah, but we do. Or have you forgotten our little ruse already? You owe me. I'm here to collect."

That motherfu—

"Well, we should be going!" Daphne chirped. "We'll see you later, Lo." Then the traitorous wench hooked elbows with Sophia and the two of them bolted for the door. I was going to kill them, murder them dead. I'd been dying for Dough House's dumplings for *ages*, and they'd just abandoned me. The backstabbing bitches.

"I'll walk you out!" Caleb shouted after them. Seconds later the door to the studio clicked shut, leaving Grayson and me alone—painfully, *obviously* alone.

"My friends are dead to me," I muttered to myself before pulling in a fortifying breath and turning back to the man who made my blood pressure spike. "Well, if you're going to feed me, let's do this thing. I'm starving, and I have a tendency to be very dangerous when I'm hangry."

"Hangry?" he asked on a laugh.

"Hungry and angry. Not a good combination." I yanked the door open and started for my desk to get my purse. The sound of Grayson's footsteps echoed the click of my heels the whole way to the elevator bank. I was acutely aware of all the attention we'd drawn; if I wasn't afraid of getting fired—or walking into another glass wall because I wasn't paying attention—I would've flipped each and every one of them the bird.

"So where are we going?" I asked as the heavy steel doors closed and we began our decent.

"I made a reservation at Altura. I hope that works for you."

I stared in silent amazement for several seconds. My mouth was more than likely hanging open, and I wouldn't have been surprised if there was a bit of drool. Altura was one of the best Italian restaurants in Seattle. It was the mother ship for all the Italians in the city. Of *course* that worked for me.

His laughter reverberated off the walls of the near-empty

elevator. "I'm taking it by the crazy look on your face that Altura works for you."

"It'll do," I answered haughtily, not wanting to give away the fact that my mouth was practically watering. "You should have led with that. I wouldn't have put up a fight about going to lunch with you if I'd known where we were going."

Grayson stepped closer, leaving barely enough room between us for air to slide through. "Yeah, but I'm quickly coming to realize that I like it when you put up a fight. You're attractive always, but there's just something addictive about you when you're fighting mad."

I tried my best to appear disgusted while my neck burned like fire and tiny bolts of lightning shot straight to my core. "A psychiatrist would have a field day with you, you know that? Maybe you should consider making an appointment. I think you need help."

I needed help. I needed a lot of help when it came to Grayson Lockhart.

Maybe I should consider taking my own advice.

His hand rested against the small of my back, sending an electric current of awareness through my body. Common sense told me to shake off his touch. But I told common sense to screw the hell off. I wanted to feel that warmth against my back. I wanted it more than was healthy.

We remained in silence as we stepped off the elevator into the lobby. People all around us seemed to stop and stare, not that I could blame them; Grayson was fine enough to stop traffic. But the attention was more than just a little disconcerting, especially when the hand on my back slid around my waist and his large palm settled firmly on my hip, pulling me against his side.

I could see people from the corner of my eye leaning into each other and whispering as we passed. One of America's most eligible bachelors appeared to be smitten. Us canoodling in the lobby of Hart Tower for all to see was apparently pretty head-line-worthy.

"How much longer do we have to keep up this charade?" I asked in a hushed tone. Walking side by side, one of his arms holding me close while both of mine hung at my sides, was too awkward. I had no other choice but to return the gesture and wrap an arm around him to make it less uncomfortable. I tried my hardest not to fixate on the solid, rippled muscles beneath his shirt. *Stupid gorgeous muscled man.* "Your image doesn't look the slightest bit stained to me. So how long am I going to be forced to keep this up?"

His arm tensed, forcing me even closer. "You make it sound like being in my company is miserable." I looked up to find him grinning down at me, humor glinting in his mesmerizing eyes. "Careful, Lola. You might just bruise my delicate ego."

I snorted as we pushed through the wide glass doors and headed out onto the busy sidewalk. "Something tells me there's nothing delicate about you." *For crying out loud, Lola! Are you flirting?* I was quickly losing my mind. Sad thing was, it kind of excited me.

"You know what I think? I think you're starting to like me."

I didn't say anything because there was nothing to say. I'd always been a horrible liar, so telling him he was wrong would've been pointless. He'd have seen right through my lie. The truth was I *did* like him. And that terrified the shit out of me.

"What?" he chided as he opened the back door of a sleek black town car and helped guide me in. "Nothing to say? No witty comebacks or cutting barbs? I'm a little disappointed in you."

That made two of us.

I worked to keep the conversation light and innocuous the

whole way to the restaurant. It was safer that way, at least for me. As soon as we entered the restaurant, he pulled me flush against his side once again, and once again it didn't go unnoticed.

"How do you stand it?" I asked once we were seated at our table and the busboy disappeared after quickly filling our water glasses.

"Stand what?" he asked, his forehead furrowed with curiosity as he gazed across the table at me.

"Being watched. I've been out with you twice now and even I'm getting uncomfortable by the amount of attention you garner. How can you stand it?"

Before he could answer, the waiter stopped by. We gave him our order—I didn't even have to look at the menu to know what I wanted—and he left us alone once more.

Grayson took a slow drink of water, appearing to give my question serious thought. "Honestly, I've just been forced to get used to it. The attention on me started to get really bad after I graduated college. It got to the point that I actually got into a fight with one of the photographers who'd been following me around. I was in a relationship at the time and we were coming back from a date. The fucker was lurking around outside my house, waiting for us to get back, and when we finally showed up he started in on Fiona, saying some nasty shit to try and get a rise out of me."

"Fiona?" I found myself asking as a heavy ball of tension settled in my stomach. It was completely ridiculous, but hearing the name of one of his exes made her seem more real. And I really didn't like that.

"My girlfriend at the time," he confirmed, making that ball twist even more.

"Is that the one you dated for several years?" I knew it was irrational, but I couldn't help the sudden spike of jealousy.

"Yeah. Anyway, he was spouting some pretty foul stuff, and I kind of lost it. I ended up smashing his camera and breaking his nose in the process." My eyes nearly bugged out of my head as I imagined Grayson kicking some piece-of-shit photographer's ass. I had to admit, the mental picture was hot as hell.

"Good. Sounds like the asshole deserved it. I hope it was painful."

"Well...." He chuckled quietly. "I think in the end it hurt me more than him. I was arrested for assault and battery. The charges didn't stick, but he filed a civil suit that cost me more than it was worth. After Fiona and I broke up, I realized that dating anyone was going to be impossible if I didn't grow thicker skin. As the years passed, they stopped being so relentless when I quit giving them shit to write about. Unfortunately, it's jaded me a bit. I've had to be a lot more careful about who I bring into my life. It's insane how many women out there get off on a few pictures in a magazine. But I will say this." His smile grew wicked, sinful, and it made me quiver a little bit. "Hearing the sound of that bone breaking was satisfying as fuck."

I couldn't have held my smile back if I wanted to, but I found that the longer I stayed in his company the more I *wanted* to smile. He made me feel things I hadn't felt in a very long time, excitement being the most prominent of them all.

"God, you really have a beautiful smile." The awe in his tone made me pause with the water glass halfway to my mouth.

I never felt as out of sorts as I did when I was with him. Because of that I found myself asking a question I hadn't expected.

"What do you want from me, Grayson?"

CHAPTER SIXTEEN

LOLA

HE DIDN'T EVEN HESITATE in answering. "I think I've made it quite clear what I want from you, Lola."

Those electrified, reinforced walls I'd built to protect my heart from being trampled on ever again started to shake and buckle under the weight of his penetrating gaze. I had to stand strong or I'd risk being hurt. It was pathetic to think that I made a living giving other women relationship advice yet was too much of a coward to go after something of my own, but that was just my reality. Fool me once, shame on you and all that... but to have been fooled as many times as I'd been was my own damn fault. I wouldn't go there again.

"If this is about getting in my panties, I have to tell you, there are easier ways." The words came out biting, angry. The uncertainty of everything I was feeling caused me to lash out.

"You really think that's what I'm after?" he asked in a low, ominous voice as he leaned over the table.

"Isn't it? Isn't that all men are really looking for, a woman who'll put up a challenge just long enough to be fun? But once it's over—" I shrugged. "—what then? You don't really expect me to believe you're interested in me for more than a couple of fun rolls in the hay, do you?"

"Jesus Christ." He let out a perplexed laugh but his features held no animosity, no frustration at my stubborn refusal to believe it was anything more. "What happened to make you so goddamned cynical?"

"Life." I shrugged again, picking up my water and taking a huge gulp to alleviate the dryness in my throat. "Life happened."

I shouldn't have said it. I *really* shouldn't have. Because I'd just given him the ammunition he needed to continue pushing.

The waiter quietly dropped off our orders as Grayson and I studied each other like specimens under a microscope. Once we were left to our meal, he insisted on knowing all the dirty details. "Tell me. Who caused you to be so pessimistic?"

"It wasn't just one person, Gray," I answered honestly. "Believe it or not, I used to believe in happy ever afters and all that naïve bullshit. Even when my father cheated on my mom over and over again and I'd lie in bed at night listening to her cry. I should've learned my lesson then, but I guess I'm too hard-headed." I twirled strands of angel hair pasta with my fork and let out a self-deprecating laugh as I continued. "It took me a while, but after dating cheaters, liars, and one closeted homosexual, I finally started to see men for what they really are."

"And what's that?" he asked as I took a bite of my food. The question wasn't ridiculing or sarcastic in the slightest. He really seemed genuinely curious about what I had to say.

I swallowed and wiped my lips with the impeccably clean cloth napkin. "That monogamy and commitment are a joke. And before you accuse me of being disenchanted because of a few bad experiences, let me just tell you, it wasn't only my own bad experiences that made me this way. It was watching the people I love go through it too. Daphne was crushed when her fiancé broke off their engagement a month before the wedding. I sat with her for days while she cried her eyes out, trying to figure out what went wrong, only to find out the son of a bitch had been screwing her own mother for *a year*. Sophia was head over heels in love with my brother, thought the sun rose and set with him. She was convinced he was the one until she walked in on him banging the receptionist where he worked in *their bed*."

He sat and stared at me for so long I began to feel like I was being examined. "So, because of what you, your mother, and your friends went through, you've convinced yourself that we're all cut from the same cloth. Is that it?"

I took another bite while I considered his question. "No, I don't honestly believe that *all* men are cheaters and users. I just think that the percentage of them that are out there is too high to warrant taking a risk. It's not worth it, not when there are no guarantees."

"Well, that's going to be a problem."

My heart dropped into my stomach as dread set in. Despite everything I'd just said, everything I truly believed, I was still overcome with fear that my negativity might just prove to be too much for Grayson to deal with.

"Oh? How's that?" I asked, surprised I could emit a carefree tone. I was shocked that my voice hadn't broken. Outside, I was the picture of calm, but my insides raged like a sea during a thunderstorm.

He set his fork down and clasped his hands on the table in front of him. The unaffected coolness he'd been radiating just seconds before gave way to the fierce determination that took its place. "The problem is I'm a very determined man. I see what I want and I bust my ass to get it. I don't give up—*ever*. Not until I have what I want. And despite what you may think, what I want from you is more than just a quick, meaningless fuck."

I wanted to believe him. Desperately. But experience had

proven that words couldn't be trusted. I rolled my eyes toward the ceiling, and when I focused on Grayson once again, he still regarded me with such conviction that the breath froze in my lungs.

"Don't mistake me, Lola. I want to fuck you. I'm dying for it. But I also want to *know* you. I want to know what makes you tick. I want to know what your childhood was like, how you were as a teenager. I want to discover all the ways I can make you laugh and smile. I want to know what I have to do to make you take a chance on me."

My chest ached with the need to draw in air, but I couldn't seem to get my body to behave.

"I might want what's in your panties, but I also want what's in your head. You fascinate me. Everything about you is enchanting to me. And that's where the problem lies, because you're too stubborn to believe me, but I'm too stubborn to give up."

By the time he finished, my mouth was hanging open in shock. I snapped it closed as I struggled to put my tumultuous feelings into words, but all I could manage was a disconcerting sputter. "I... you... what the... *what?*"

He sat back with a pleased smirk wreathing his face. "I'll give that a chance to sink in. But there's something else you need to know." I could only imagine what that would be after the bomb he'd just dropped. "This *charade*, as you like to call it, is far from over. I'm going to milk this for everything it's worth. I'm gonna take advantage of our situation so I can touch you and tease you and beat at those goddamned walls of yours until you have no other choice but to let me in. This is the only warning you're going to get, so you better brace yourself. I'll use my position as your boss, the media, I'm even willing to use your own friends if that's what it takes. Once I'm done with you, I'll have burrowed so far under your skin there won't be a goddamned thing on this planet that could get me out. Is that clear enough for you, or do I need to explain what I want in greater detail?"

My mouth opened and closed a few times like a fish out of water. I was at a complete loss for words—something that had never happened *in my life.* Given no other choice, since my vocal cords seemed to be failing me, I nodded. I didn't think I could possibly handle him going into even *greater* detail; if he did that I would probably spontaneously combust. As it was, I was struggling not to launch myself across the table and give my body everything it was craving, right there in the middle of a crowded restaurant.

Grayson picked up his fork and began cutting into his veal. "Good. I'm glad we got that taken care of. Now eat up. You're going to need all your strength if you have any hope of fighting me off."

Those walls around my heart groaned and quaked under Grayson's pressure. There was no doubt about it—if this continued on much longer, they were going to come crashing to the ground.

I WAS no less flustered by the time we arrived back at Hart Tower after lunch. My mind was racing a million miles a second, never settling on one thing long enough for me to process the brutal truths Grayson had laid down. I couldn't seem to process a single thought.

It went something like this:

Want him.

He smells good.

I'm in big trouble.

I bet he tastes yummy.

...squirrel!

My body was on autopilot, letting Grayson lead me through the lobby to the elevator banks.

He hit the call button for the elevator and we waited in silence, standing side by side. "Hey. You okay?" he asked, pulling me from the jumbled mess inside my head.

"Uh... yeah. No." I gave my head a brisk shake, hoping to piece my brain back together. "I mean I am. I'm just... a little overwhelmed."

He took me by the shoulders and turned me so we were both face-to-face, leaving his hands on me as he hunched down to meet my gaze. "Because of me?"

I arched an eyebrow and fought the smile tugging at my lips as I replied, "Well, you *are* the only one driving me crazy at the moment."

I hadn't realized the double meaning of my answer until Grayson leaned in and whispered suggestively, "The feeling is definitely mutual."

"I didn't... I meant.... *Argh!* See? This is what I'm talking about right here! I can't *think* when I'm around you."

"Good," he said in a hushed tone, stepping close, trailing one hand up my neck to my temple. He tucked my hair behind my ear, making my body—the hussy—shiver wantonly. His breath flittered over the shell of my ear as he whispered, "You think too much anyway."

Then he kissed me... for the second time. And I melted into a needy puddle of goo... for the second time.

I was so lost in his kiss, so enveloped by all that was *him*, that I'd completely forgotten where we were. All I could think was *want, crave, need, more* as his tongue invaded my mouth and began warring with my own for dominance. My body responded, my hands diving into his silky hair and holding on tightly, as if scared he was going to pull away. In that moment, he was absolutely everything. Nothing else existed.

That was until the sound of someone's throat clearing cut into our private little moment and shattered it to pieces.

My head jerked to the side to find Sophia and Daphne watching us with similar expressions of "Giiiirl, get you some" on their faces.

"Sorry to interrupt the public snog-fest, but you're blocking the button."

At Sophia's words, I realized I hadn't even noticed that the elevator had come and gone while Grayson and I were playing tonsil hockey in the middle of the lobby.

"Shit," I hissed. I tried to take a step back, gain some much-needed space, but at some point during the kiss Grayson's hands had slid to my hips. At my movement, he tightened his hold on me, refusing my escape.

"Sorry, ladies," he said, not sounding sorry in the least. "Let me."

One hand released me just long enough to hit the call button again before coming back and wrapping around my waist. In the back of my mind, I heard the elevator ding and the doors slide open. But I was too focused on the man staring down at me to give it much thought.

"Thanks for lunch," he said, drawing my focus to his inviting mouth. "I'll see you tonight."

He abruptly let me go and stepped into the elevator. I missed his touch instantly, but losing it gave me the clarity to realize what he'd just said.

"Wait... tonight?"

"Yeah. Dinner at my place."

"At *your* place?" I squeaked. "But—"

The doors began to slide closed before I could finish my argument. The last thing I saw was Grayson's smirk, and the last thing I heard was his rich voice telling me, "I'll send my driver to get you at seven. And don't make me track you down, Lola."

Then he was gone.

Daphne's low whistle hit my ears. I turned and shot a glare at my two friends. "Someone's getting lucky," she singsonged.

Sophia laughed and hit the button for the elevator again.

I shot daggers at them as I declared, "I hate you both."

CHAPTER SEVENTEEN

LOLA

I'D BEEN hot and bothered ever since that kiss by the elevators just hours before. As I got ready for dinner at Grayson's house, I tried to smother the desire burning hot in my veins. My entire body felt like a livewire, like just one touch and I'd combust. I could barely go a minute without replaying that kiss in my mind. And each time the images replayed, that tingle between my thighs grew stronger.

My cell phone trilled from the vanity as I leaned closer to the mirror to swipe a second coat of mascara on my lashes.

Screwing the wand back into the tube, I looked down at the screen, surprised to see my father's name flashing back at me insistently.

I slid my finger across the face of the phone and answered, putting the call on speaker so I could finish applying my makeup. It was already close to seven. "Dad. What can I do for you?"

"Ah, my beautiful girl! So good to hear your voice. I've missed you, *bella*."

I'd been in the middle of applying lipstick when his exuberance made every muscle in my body lock up. My father and I hadn't had a good relationship since I was old enough to understand just what a despicable human being he truly was. Dominic had been better at looking past our father's faults than I ever had. At best, he and I barely tolerated each other. I learned early on, and through countless heartbreaking disappointments, that Roberto Abbatelli wasn't the type of man you put your faith in. He rarely ever called, but when he did, it was because he wanted something from me. Usually it had to do with some photo op for a piece being written on him so he could look like the doting family man.

To have him call out of the blue was unexpected, but to hear him speak so lovingly set my teeth on edge.

"What do you want, Dad?" I asked dryly. Cutting to the chase was better than dragging out whatever shit-show my father was trying to pull me into.

"Now, baby girl, is that any way to speak to your dear old dad?"

I rolled my eyes at my reflection in the mirror. "It is when the 'dear old dad' in question would sell his own kid to the devil to make himself look good."

In typical Roberto Abbatelli fashion, he attempted to lay on the charm. "Aw, baby girl. You break my heart."

"You'd have to have a heart in order for it to break. Pretty sure all you've got in your chest is a block of ice. Now tell me what you want or I'm hanging up. I have something to do."

"Would that something have anything to do with your new boyfriend?"

And there it was. That son of a bitch.

"You've got to be kidding me!" I let out a loud bark of astonished laughter.

My father's entire demeanor changed as he asked, "Do you even know who you're dating, Lola? Just how important of a man Grayson Lockhart is? How important his *father* is?" Gone were all pretenses of the doting father. He sounded frustrated and cold, like he sounded during his board meetings.

"I'm well aware, Dad," I deadpanned. "What I don't understand is how it's any of your business."

"Have I taught you nothing about business? It's all about who you know. Having a connection to the Lockharts would be career gold. Can you imagine how it would make the company look if we handled the investments of the Lockharts? If things are serious between you two—"

I cut him off, hot seething anger coursing through my blood. "What I do with my life and who I associate with doesn't have a goddamned thing to do with you," I snapped. "As far as I'm concerned, you're nothing to me but a sperm donor. You think you can use to me to get to Grayson and his family, get in their good graces? You're out of your mind, old man. You used Mom up until there was nothing left, and I'll be damned if I let you do the same to me. Don't call me again."

I disconnected the call and slammed my hands down on the vanity. My head dropped and my shoulders drooped like the weight of the world was resting on them. Nothing could put me in a foul mood like a conversation with my own father.

I took several deep breaths to try and calm my raging heart. By the time I managed to get a hold of myself, the phone rang again, startling a short, high-pitched scream from my lungs.

"Jesus!" I hissed. "Get a hold of yourself, Lola."

I grabbed the phone and answered the call with an agitated "Yeah?"

"Ms. Abbatelli," Maury's voice returned through the receiver. "There's a car here to pick you up, ma'am."

I let out a sigh and tried to rein in my temper. "Okay, Maury. Thanks. I'll be right down."

"Yes, ma'am."

I hung up and gave myself one last cursory look in the

mirror. My paisley-patterned Boho dress nipped in at the waist and flowed down to just above my knees. It was casual yet cute, making it appear that I wasn't trying too hard. I thought it looked fun and flirty. Not that I *wanted* to be fun and flirty... *whatever*. I paired the dress with a pair of silver strappy cork wedges that gave me the much-needed height I required and went for a light, natural look with my makeup. I grabbed the pale pink lipstick I'd just applied and tossed it into my silver clutch before heading out the door.

I recognized the driver as the same man who'd taken Grayson and me on both our so-called dates. I felt a little embarrassed that I'd already met the man twice and still didn't know his name. "Hi, I'm Lola," I introduced myself as we pulled away from the curb and started the trip to Grayson's.

"Yes, ma'am. Mr. Lockhart told me your name." That was all he said. *Uh... okay?*

I tried to continue—well, *start*—a conversation without distracting him from the road. "And your name is...?"

"Thomas, ma'am." I waited for him to say more, but nothing else came.

"Anyone ever tell you that you talk too much, Thomas? It's kind of annoying."

I was able to see the corner of his mouth kick up in a smirk just before he responded, "All the time, ma'am. It's a real problem."

"Oh!" I clapped. "You've got jokes! I get it. You're the silent stunner. You like to sneak attack. I can appreciate that, Thomas. Kudos to you." I sat back in my seat, triumphant that I'd forced the quiet Thomas from his shell, somewhat. The town car filled with silence for several seconds before I finally worked up the nerve to ask, "So, Tommy. Can I call you Tommy? Tommy, how long have you worked for Grayson?"

"Going on seven years, ma'am."

In the short time I'd known Thomas, I discovered that I was going to have to pull answers out of him. That was fine, I could live with that. What I couldn't live with was being called "ma'am" over and over again like I was a senior citizen and this was some bizarre *Driving Miss Daisy* moment. Although... I studied Thomas the best I could in the darkness of the car. He *could* pass for a younger Morgan Freeman if I squinted and tilted my head a little to the right.

"Tommy, call me 'ma'am' one more time and I can't be held responsible for my actions."

Surprisingly enough, the deep baritone of his chuckle filtered toward the back seat. "I'll refrain from calling you 'ma'am' if you'll stop calling me 'Tommy.' How about that?"

"Deal. Now quick, before we get there, give me all the dirt you have on Grayson. The man's too damn perfect. I need *something* to hold against the stupid jerk." I hadn't planned on saying that last sentence out loud, but the words escaped before I had a chance to stop them.

Thomas laughed at that. "I'm sorry to disappoint, ma—uh, Miss Lola. But there's really no dirt to give. He's a decent guy and a good boss."

"Well...." *Think, Lola. Think!* There had to be *something*. Those stupid, cheaply built walls around my heart were crumbling; I needed something to refortify them against that man. "How often have you done something like this? Pick up and deliver his dates to his house, I mean. I bet's it's a lot, huh?"

"Actually, you're the first."

"Really?" My question came out as a shocked squeak. I hadn't been expecting that.

"Mr. Lockhart doesn't date all that often, but when he does, he rarely ever brings them back to his house. He's had a few bad experiences."

My mind quickly went to the scene with the psychotic

Brooke and was immediately swamped with regret at the part I'd played in that whole mess.

"I can imagine," I said softly, sitting back against the soft, buttery leather of the seat. Thomas proved to be no help at all. The jerk. How was I supposed to protect myself against this man if I had nothing to hold over him?

"We're here, Miss Lola."

I turned my head, looked out the window, and gasped. I wasn't sure what I'd been expecting, but the beautiful Tudor surrounded by tall, impressive trees most certainly wasn't it. I allowed Thomas to help me from the car, then gave him a friendly smile and a polite goodbye before starting up the walk to the front door. The yard, large as it was, was impeccably land-scaped. In the waning sunlight, I could see the flashes of color all around from the different flowers and plants. I bet it looked stunning in the daytime.

The walkway was laid with attractive cobblestones and surrounded on both sides by solar-powered garden lights. The only way I could describe the initial look of Grayson's house was... *homey*. It looked like the kind of home for a large family, not a single man. That was probably what surprised me the most; I could actually visualize Grayson raising a family there.

That thought was both terrifying and exciting all at once.

"You aren't going to have sex with him," I whispered to myself. "You are *not* having sex with Grayson Lockhart. You're not, you're not, you're not. No sex for Lola."

The short pep talk did very little to calm the rapid beating of my heart. Before I had a chance to knock, the front door was thrown open and all the air stole from my lungs.

I'd never seen Grayson in anything other than a suit, and I knew from experience that he wore those suits insanely well. But that was nothing compared to what he looked like in a worn pair of jeans and a plain T-shirt. The shift from Grayson the professional to Gray the relaxed was uncanny. And he was bare-footed. *Gah!* How was it possible for a man as good-looking as him to have sexy feet as well? It wasn't fair!

"Shit," I said on a slow, defeated breath. Because seeing him dressed casually in the comfort of his own home helped to make one thing perfectly clear.

I was totally having sex with him.

Damn it.

CHAPTER EIGHTEEN

GRAYSON

CHRIST, she was beautiful. At the same time her eyes went wide and began doing a sweep of my body, my own did the same. She looked stunning, as always, in a dress that accentuated her tiny waist and showed just a hint of those tits I'd been dying to touch.

"Shit," she hissed on a ragged breath, pulling me from my perusal of her delectable body as worry kicked in.

"Are you all right?"

My voice, dripping with concern, must have cut through her reverie. Lola gave her head a tiny shake, and I had to bite my lip to keep from laughing as she forced her gaze from my feet to my eyes. Her blatant ogling of my body couldn't have been more obvious. "Huh?"

"You said 'shit.' Is everything okay?"

Her neck and cheeks tinted pink and her eyes looked glazed with want as she stumbled over her words. "Oh... uh. Yeah. I, um, just stubbed my toe."

My eyes narrowed in a way that said "You're full of shit," but I didn't voice my disbelief in her claim. Instead, I stepped to the side to let her in.

"I hope you're hungry. I made—" And that was all I got out before Lola launched herself at me, wrapping her arms around my neck as her lips crashed against mine.

It took a second to realize exactly what was happening, for my brain and my body to get on the same page. But the moment her tongue prodded at my lips, instinct took over.

I wrapped one hand in her hair, using it to tip her head to the perfect angle, giving me better access to those full, pouty lips. My other arm slipped around her waist, yanking her body against mine as I feasted on her mouth like a starving man given his first meal in months.

"Oh God," she panted as I trailed kisses down her jaw and neck, licking and sucking until I reached the swell of her breasts. "This is wrong." But even as she said it, she held my head to her chest like she was afraid I'd stop. "We shouldn't be doing this."

"Stop thinking," I growled, moving back up to her mouth as I kicked the front door shut. I had her exactly where I wanted her. No fucking way was I letting her go this time.

Her body and actions contradicted the words she spoke. I knew she wanted me, had known for a while. And just like I'd hoped and prayed, she'd finally caved to her desire.

I bit down on her bottom lip and used my tongue to soothe some of the sting away as I grabbed her ass with both hands and pulled her against me, needing her to feel just how much I wanted her. She felt amazing; everything about her was like a dream. Having her pressed against me, my aching cock so close to what it wanted, was a lesson in willpower.

I lifted her and began heading in the direction of the bedroom. Her short legs twined around my waist as she held on, our mouths never disengaging. I needed her like I needed air or water. It wasn't just a craving. Sinking inside of her was necessary. I had to have her *now, now, now*.

Her hands tore at my T-shirt as I rushed down the hall. As

soon as we hit the room, I set her on her feet and reached for the hem of her dress, whipping it over her head as fast as I could, only to freeze at the sight of what was beneath. Nothing could have possibly prepared me for what I'd find under that goddamned dress. It was even better than what I'd imagined.

"Fucking *Christ*," I hissed, dropping to my knees in front of her and planting open-mouth kisses across her belly from hip to hip. She was a goddess. The white lace of her bra and panties against her olive skin made my mouth water. Lola had curves in all the right places; a woman's body that would make any man drool. And I'd be damned if I would ever let another man see what I was currently seeing, not after what I was about to do to her. I'd handcuff her to the fucking bed if that's what it took to keep her.

"Grayson," she said on a ragged breath, her fingers pulling insistently at my hair. "Come back."

No fucking way, not until I tasted her. I yanked her minuscule panties down her smooth, silky legs, nearly ripping them in my haste. She stepped out of them and kicked them away the instant they pooled on the floor, leaving her in nothing but that sexy bra and those fuck-me shoes. I was at risk of coming in my pants at just the sight of her, at the smell of her arousal. *I* did that to her—me.

I couldn't wait another second, burying my face between her thighs, right into that tiny thatch of curls.

"This is a mistake," she panted, jerking my head even closer. "We should stop."

My tongue darted out. That first taste was like pure heaven exploding on my tongue. She cried out as I flicked her clit, her words changing from protests to loud cries of "Oh God. Don't stop. Please don't stop."

I had no intention of stopping... not fucking *ever*. I'd happily die between her legs. I licked and sucked and flicked until her legs began to quake and her knees buckled. Guiding her back onto the bed, I used my hands on her hips to hold her in place as she collapsed backwards, undulating against my face as I stiffened my tongue and began to fuck her with it, diving in and out of her wet heat, needing to drive her as crazy as she drove me. I glanced up, transfixed by the sight of her heaving chest, her beautiful face twisted in ecstasy as she fisted the comforter in her hands. I'd never seen anything so glorious, never tasted anything sweeter.

Her breathing grew more erratic the closer she got, and I never let up, pushing her closer and closer until she burst, coming against my mouth with a long, loud moan. It was the most erotic thing I'd ever heard. If I wasn't buried inside of her in the next ten seconds I was going to explode.

As soon as the last tremors of her release drained from her, I stood to my feet, tearing at my clothes. Lola rose to her knees, her bra and shoes joining the quickly growing pile of discarded clothing littering my bedroom floor. She grabbed my waistband and began tugging at the button and zipper of my jeans.

"My turn," she purred, her voice deep and sultry with lust. Her eyes were still glazed over as she moved her hands, raking her nails up and down my chest and abs like she couldn't decide where she wanted to touch the most.

I saw the shift in her almost immediately. She'd gone from submissive to vixen in the blink of an eye, fighting me for control as we both struggled to get me naked. The moment the last stitch of fabric hit the ground and my cock was free, her tiny hand grabbed hold, pumping up and down as she licked her lips. It twitched under her ministrations as she moved closer, licking the head like a lollipop.

"*Shit*," I barked at the feel of her slick tongue against my shaft. It was pure bliss. But it wasn't what I wanted.

"Stop," I commanded, wrapping her hair around my fist to

hold her in place. "Lola, stop," I repeated as she fought against my hold. I yanked her hair, just hard enough to get her attention. She looked up at me with those unfocused eyes. The sight of her on my bed, on her hands and knees, was almost too much to bear. "I'm not coming in your mouth the first time."

"But I want it," she practically whined, trying to move in for another taste.

Talking wasn't going to do a damn bit of good; if I wanted to control this situation, I was going to have to force it. With my hands on her waist, I lifted her and tossed her farther up the bed, onto her back, crawling in after her. I lifted to my knees and bent to retrieve a condom from the bedside drawer. I straightened, prepared to rip it open, only to have the little devil beneath me snatch it from my hands and buck her hips, sending me to my back.

Lola ripped the condom open with her teeth and slowly slid it down my rigid length, a look of determination on her face as she straddled me and guided the tip to her entrance.

"This changes nothing," she sighed as she lowered herself. Both of our heads fell back in euphoria as she sank down, taking me until every last inch was sheathed in her tight, hot pussy. "Th-this is just s-sex," she stuttered as she began to rock her hips. "Nothing more."

Like fucking hell.

But I didn't say that out loud; instead, I declared, "Whatever you say."

It didn't take a genius to realize that this woman was used to being in control. But unlike the other dickheads she'd been with, I wasn't one to relinquish anything. I'd let her dominate our lovemaking over my cold dead body.

She began moving faster and faster, her head thrown back, eyes squeezed close as she attempted to use my body to get herself off. I could see it written on every inch of her face, she was doing her best to disconnect herself from me. I wasn't having it.

Not like this. Not with her.

Before she could process what was happening, I had her on her back, her long hair flung across my pillows. Her eyes shot open in shock as I gripped the headboard with one hand for leverage, the other holding her chin so she was forced to look at me.

"Wha... what are you—*oh fuck*, Grayson!"

I pounded into her, never breaking eye contact as I drove in and out of her body.

Her lashes fluttered and her eyelids began to drop. "Look at me," I demanded on a hoarse growl, burying myself to the hilt and circling my hips so my pelvis rubbed against her clit. "You keep your eyes open when I fuck you."

I stared, enraptured, while fear and lust warred in her amber gaze. "*Gray....*" My name on her lips was the best kind of torture, even if that one word sounded like a plea.

I continued to move, thrusting over and over as she tightened around me, her body letting me know how close she was.

"Amazing," I said in a hushed voice as I lowered my head and fed from her lips. "You're amazing, Lola."

Her hips began to snap, meeting mine every time I powered into her. Her hands slid around my neck, her long fingers tangling in my hair while her legs locked around my thighs. "I'm close. God, so close," she cried as we continued to move against each other. I wasn't far behind her. I desperately needed her to get there; I wasn't sure how much longer I could hold back.

"Come on, Lola," I coaxed as my movements turned faster, harder. I was getting lost in everything that was her. And I didn't care. "Give it to me, baby. Let me feel you."

"Gray... I...." Her eyes went wide as her pussy clamped down around me as if it was trying to hold me inside of her. "I-

I'm coming! Oh *God!*" Every muscle in her body locked as she screamed my name so loud her voice went scratchy.

"That's it. Fuck, baby, just like that," I ground between clenched teeth, ramming into her once, twice, three times before I fell off that ledge right after her. "Unh, unh, *fuck. Yes!*"

I roared once my climax stole over me, her lush little body draining me of every last drop until there was nothing left. I saw stars behind my eyelids as I lost control of my limbs and collapsed on top of her. It felt like my heart was going to beat out of my chest at any second as I sucked in ragged breaths. For several minutes the only sound to be heard was our labored breathing. I finally came to enough to realize I was probably crushing her, but when I moved to pull away her arms and legs tightened spasmodically.

Instead of disengaging and risking her re-erecting those walls, I looped an arm around her waist and turned us so I was on my back with Lola's small body draped against my chest, my semihard cock slipping from her, causing her to let out a little gasp. I loved that gasp.

Her fingers trailed random patterns along my chest for a few minutes, almost subconsciously as we finished catching our breaths. Finally, Lola stacked her hands on my left pec and rested her chin on top of them, looking up at me with a sated expression. "That was...."

"Out of this fucking world?" I offered, making her grin. "Unbelievable? Earth-shattering?"

"Someone's cocky," she giggled, her grin morphing into a blinding smile.

"Tell me I don't have reason to be after the orgasms I just gave you," I joked back.

She rolled her eyes, but I could see the playfulness dancing in them. "Is dinner ruined?" she asked.

I studied her face as I lifted a hand and brushed strands of hair from her forehead. I didn't think I'd ever get used to just how beautiful she was. "Is my girl hungry?"

Her gaze narrowed into slits, mock-aggravation taking over her face. "Don't call me that. This was just sex."

"Uh-huh."

"It was!" she yelped defiantly.

"If you say so."

"I do!"

I would've argued, but when I wrapped my arms around her, the way her body melted against mine on a contented sigh betrayed her words. I'd let her have that play... for now. I knew I'd win out in the end.

We held each other for a while longer, both of us exhausted from what had just transpired. I was content to fall asleep just as we were, but the sound of her stomach growling let me know I needed to feed her.

"Come on," I coaxed, sitting up and taking her with me. "Let me get rid of this condom and I'll get you fed."

At the mention of food, she hopped from the bed before reaching down, grabbing my shirt from the floor, and slipping it over her head. "I'll meet you in the kitchen," she chirped happily. Then she was gone, leaving me staring after her, the sight of her in my shirt burned on my brain.

Oh yeah, I'd definitely cuff her to my bed if that was what it took.

CHAPTER NINETEEN

LOLA

I'D BEEN SO CONSUMED by my desire for Grayson when he first opened the door that I'd thrown myself at him immediately, not taking in a single thing about the inside of his house. But now that my whorish body had been satiated, I was finally able to focus on my surroundings.

While I lay on Grayson's chest, I'd noticed that there weren't any picture or lamps on his bedside tables. The only thing in the bedroom was the furniture. It was really good quality furniture, but there wasn't much of it, just the bed, two nightstands, and a chest of drawers. As I walked down the long hall into the living area, I noticed that the inside of the house was a complete contradiction to the outside.

Where the yard gave the place a homey, comfortable feeling, the inside was kind of bleak and emotionless, devoid of any color or personal touches. It looked like he'd just moved in and hadn't bought much to fill the space.

The bare walls were painted a plain eggshell white, just a shade darker than the crown molding that edged along the ceiling. The dark hardwood floors were unblemished, but there wasn't so much as an area rug or a runner covering them. A plain brown leather sectional with a matching ottoman sat facing a huge flat-screen TV mounted to the wall. There was a stylish console beneath that held some books. A matching side table sat on the floor on one end of the sectional, but that was it as far as furniture. No pictures along the mantle above the slate fireplace, no photos or art hung on the walls. There wasn't a single thing to speak to Grayson's life or childhood, not even a knickknack.

The barren décor didn't match Grayson's exuberant personality in the slightest. If someone had asked, I would've claimed that a totally different person lived there.

I padded across the bare floors as I continued to wander the expansive house, following the delicious smells to what I hoped was the kitchen. I stepped down two small stairs into what seemed like another place entirely. Unlike the bare space throughout the rest of the house, the kitchen was starkly different. Pale granite lined the countertops, threaded with iridescent grains that glittered beneath the contemporary pendant lights. A large porcelain farmer's sink sat beneath a window with a stunning view of the trees and mountains in the background. In the window were small clay pots of different sizes, each containing a variety of herbs. He had a small herb garden in his kitchen but not a single personal effect anywhere else? That was bizarre, to say the least. A subway tile backsplash cascaded beneath the dark oak cabinets, a pretty white against the dark of the wood. Top-of-the-line appliances were scattered throughout and the counters were lined with cooking utensils. This room was lived in, no doubt about it.

I was jolted from my musings when Grayson stepped up behind me, wrapping his arms around my waist as he buried his nose in my hair. I was so enamored with the space that I hadn't heard him come in. I jumped, startled, and he let loose a deep chuckle that vibrated from his chest into my back.

"Sorry." I could hear the smile in his voice. "Didn't mean to scare you."

I turned in his arms, my own twining around him to return his embrace without my brain giving it much thought. I pushed that realization to the back of my mind. I was too relaxed from sex, too content in just being with him to focus on the scary reality that I was really starting to fall for this guy. That was something I could fixate on and stress about in the privacy of my own home. For now... I was just going to go with the flow. Fighting it was just too damn exhausting.

"How long have you lived here?" I asked, curiosity niggling at me.

"About six years. Why?"

My forehead furrowed in confusion. Six years? That was a long time to live in a house devoid of any personality. "It just... doesn't really seem like you."

"How so?" he asked, releasing me and moving to the oven, hitting the Off button before grabbing an oven mitt and pulling the door open. My mouth watered at the sight of him in nothing but a pair of jeans resting low on his trim waist. God, he was sexy.

As he pulled out a cookie sheet containing two foil packets, I was hit with another wave of delicious smells. I moved to his side and peeked over his shoulder as he tore at the tinfoil on one of the packets. Inside was a perfectly cooked pink salmon filet sprinkled with spices and olive oil, plus slices of sautéed squash and zucchini. It looked heavenly, and my mouth started watering for an entirely different reason.

"Lola...."

I pulled my gaze from the food and looked at Grayson to find him smiling at me. "I asked how my house doesn't seem like me."

"Oh." I shook my head and took a step back, thinking how

best to answer as he moved around the kitchen, pulling plates from a cabinet and utensils from a drawer. "Well, other than the kitchen it's kind of... bland."

"Bland?" he asked, one eyebrow quirking up as he turned from plating the food to look at me.

"Not... bland," I quickly backtracked. "It's a beautiful house, really. It's just... there are no real personal touches anywhere but in here. I guess I just found that kind of surprising. It doesn't look like you've been here for six years. It looks like you just moved in and haven't gotten around to decorating."

"Ah." He nodded in understanding as he handed me our plates and forks before pointing me toward a round, four-seater table nestled in the middle of a large bay window. I set our plates down and took a seat, gazing out into the immaculate backyard.

The curtains and blinds were open to the outside. I could see the backyard butted up to the forest, landscaped just as immaculately as the front. A kidney-shaped pool with an attached Jacuzzi was the main focal point of the space, surrounded on all sides by wicker lounge chairs and patio furniture. A look at the crystal-clear water sent a shiver up my spine. Water and I didn't get along. A bad experience as a child—one of the very rare memories I had of my father—left me scared of any size body of water.

I turned my attention from the pool to Grayson as he joined me at the table, placing a large bowl of salad in the middle and two glasses of red wine by each plate. I scooped out the lettuce, noticing he'd already coated it in a vinaigrette. Man, he was good. I didn't even cook this well, much to my mother's detriment. I was Italian, after all. It was a disappointment she pointed out to me many times in my adult life.

"It might sound trite," he began, "but when I bought it, I

always imagined I'd eventually have a wife who'd put her own touch on the place."

My heart fluttered while my stomach dropped. For a second, I pictured myself putting my stamp on the whole house and was filled with excitement that quickly turned to dread. I wasn't ready for *anything* like that. Not even close. But when I thought about some other, nameless, faceless woman decorating Grayson's home, making it hers, a bitter taste filled my mouth. I was a mess of conflicting emotions.

"That doesn't sound trite," I said quietly, truthfully. Because it didn't, not at all. If I allowed myself to really think about it, it sounded kind of... amazing.

"Maybe not, but it's a naive thought," he responded.

"Why do you say that?" I asked, lifting my fork to my mouth and taking a bite. "Oh God," I groaned. "This is so good! Did you really make this? Be honest. You got takeout and staged it so you could take credit."

He smiled and shook his head, his hair tousled from sex. It was a really good look on him. Hell, *everything* was a good look on him.

"No, I cooked. I love to cook. It's why the kitchen is the only room in the house with a bit of life to it. When I'm home, I spend most of my time in here."

"Damn it," I grumbled around a mouthful of food. "You're making it really hard not to jump you again."

He laughed and took a bite, and I watched in fascination as his jaw worked while he chewed. His throat bobbed on a swallow and I was hit with the desire to lean across the table and lick his neck. I had it bad.

"That's the plan." He winked. "Seduce you with sex and cooking until you can't resist me."

I fake-glowered as I continued shoveling salmon and vegetables into my mouth. The dinner really was delicious.

"So," he started, pulling me from my food-induced euphoria, "tell me something about you."

"What do you want to know?" I asked, wiping my mouth with a napkin and taking a sip of my wine.

"What's your family like? I know you mentioned having a brother, but besides him cheating on your friend, you haven't said much else. Do you two get along?"

"Yeah. In spite of everything, we actually do."

He set his fork down, resting his elbows on the table as he drank some of his wine. "You sound surprised."

"Yeah, well, it was rocky for a long time. After he cheated on Sophia, I hated him for hurting her, for being like our father, but after they broke up, I saw how torn up he was over it. He tried to get her back for a while, but she wasn't having it. When I saw how repentant he was, I realized he wasn't actually a carbon copy of our dad. That bastard never felt bad for hurting my mom... or anyone else. Dominic did."

He studied me for a few moments. "You don't have a good relationship with your father." It wasn't a question. My stomach sank as my mind replayed the conversation I'd had with him on the phone just a few short hours before.

"It's... complicated," I answered. "And not something I really like to talk about."

"Okay." He nodded, thankfully letting the subject drop. "And what about your mom? Are you two close?"

With the topic of my father on the back burner, and the mention of my mom, the tension swirling in my gut began to loosen and I smiled. "Yeah. We're close, more so now that I'm older. I kind of drove her crazy when I was a teenager."

Grayson's smile sent off an explosion of butterflies in my belly. "I can imagine."

"She put me in Catholic school, hoping it would help to ground me," I laughed. "Poor Mom. I think I'm responsible for most of her gray hair. Hers *and* all the sisters at the school. When I graduated, I think they all cried tears of joy that they wouldn't have to deal with me any longer."

His jade eyes glittered with amusement. "I'm sure you weren't that bad."

"Oh, but I was!" I giggled. I took another sip of wine and set the glass down to continue my story. "One of the sisters actually left her order after one of my little pranks during the homecoming dance."

Grayson's eyebrows shot to his hairline. "I didn't think private schools had dances and stuff like that."

"I didn't go to an all-girls school. I think my Mom knew if she did that, I would've been so much worse."

"So what did you do?" he asked, his tone full of curiosity.

"I'd just watched *Carrie* for the first time. I was struck with inspiration at the whole pig's blood scene." He choked on his food as I carried on. "In my defense, I didn't use actual blood. It was corn syrup. And the girl who'd been crowned Homecoming Queen was a real bitch."

His laughter was deep and gravelly, coming straight from his belly. I watched in awe as his head fell back, a smile splitting his handsome face. I loved how I was able to make him laugh wholeheartedly like that. I knew I was screwed when all I could think was that I wanted to be the cause of more of those laughs.

Grayson Lockhart was illegally gorgeous, an amazing cook, *fan-freaking-tastic* in bed, and had a beautiful laugh.

And he liked me. He wanted to *know* me.

As his laughter began to taper off into a chuckle and his green eyes pinned me in place, I came to a frightening realization.

It wasn't just sex. I wanted to know him too.

Shit.

Shithelldamnfuck.

I lowered my gaze back to my plate and started eating with gusto, trying to ignore the way my heart pounded and the blood rushed in my ears.

"Stay with me," he said without a hint of amusement, pulling my focus back to him. The dancing in his eyes was gone as he regarded me intently.

"What?" That one word came out breathless.

"Tonight. I want you to stay with me tonight."

The wise decision would have been to say no, to go home to my own apartment and work to reconstruct my walls. But I'd never been known for making wise decisions. That was why I found myself nodding in acceptance. I *wanted* to stay with him.

For as long as I could.

And that was the problem.

CHAPTER TWENTY

LOLA

IT WAS noon on Saturday and I had finally come out of my Grayson bubble. After agreeing to spend the night with him the evening before, he'd proceeded to keep me up until the early hours of the morning, supplying me with more orgasms than I could count.

I received a wakeup call most women would fantasize about —Gray's head between my legs, under the covers. We finished in the shower, my back against the wall while he pounded into me as the three—yes, *three*—showerheads rained down on us.

Never in my life had sex been so good. *Ever*. Maybe it was because he wouldn't give me control. I'd never had sex where I wasn't the one calling the shots, but after round two, it became abundantly clear that Grayson would never be dominated.

And after I discovered what he could do with his tongue, lips, fingers, cock, etc., I was totally cool with that.

He'd driven me home earlier once I'd been fed bacon and eggs—the bacon sent the last part of my wall that was still standing crumbling to the ground in a massive cloud of dust— and kissed the hell out of me on the steps of my building before making me promise to have lunch with him the following day. I'd blissfully agreed, still floating in my Grayson bubble.

But that was then, and this was now. We'd been apart for two hours, which was apparently just enough time for me to start freaking out. In a panic, I'd called my girls and demanded an impromptu lunch. I needed them to talk me off the ledge. And honestly, no one liked freaking out on their own. That was what friends were for, after all.

We agreed to meet up at a little bistro we all loved in Queen Anne Hill. I decided to wear a pair of my most comfortable heels and walk, hoping the cardio would help work off some of my anxiety.

It was twelve on the dot when I pushed through the door to the bistro. Both my friends were already there, sitting at a little table by the open glass doors that led to the patio.

The second my butt hit the chair Sophia was pushing a mimosa my way. I accepted the drink gratefully and downed the contents in two long gulps.

"Whoa," Daphne said. "Someone's stressed.

"Like you wouldn't believe," I replied, holding my glass out for a refill. Sophia picked up the pitcher and poured.

"Would it have anything to do with this?" Daphne handed me her cell phone. On the screen was a picture of me wrapped around Grayson like a second skin just inside the doorway of his house. I backed out of the photo to see it had been posted on a celebrity gossip site.

"Christ! So much for privacy. How did they get this? It was only last night!"

"You know how fast those vultures work," Sophia chided. "And nothing's private with them."

I handed the phone back to Daphne and dropped my head onto the table with a pained groan. "Hey, look on the bright side. This whole stunt was to repair his public image, right?

Well, it's working. The papers are eating this stuff up." That was Daphne for you, the eternal optimist.

"God, this is bad. This is so bad," I mumbled into the tablecloth.

Sophia's hand on my shoulder pushed, forcing me to sit up straight. "What's going on? Why'd you call us in such a dither?"

I gave her a look. "Dither? Really?"

She shrugged. "I'm trying to use one new word a day."

"And you couldn't have picked a better word than *dither*?" I deadpanned.

"Would you have rather I have used 'tizzy'?"

I curled my lip. She knew I hated that word. It was right up there with "moist" and "Kardashian."

"Can we stay on topic, please?" Daph asked, looking at me. "What's going on?"

The waiter stopped by the table and set out a loaf of French bread and an olive oil dipping sauce. Normally I loved my carbs, but my appetite had run for the hills right around the time my Grayson bubble popped.

"We had sex," I said on a dramatic whisper.

"Who had sex?" Sophia asked.

"Me and Grayson. I went over to his house last night for dinner. You know, the one he bullied me into yesterday?"

Sophia smiled wickedly. "Didn't look like it took too much bullying to me."

"Anyway...." I scowled. "I showed up and he answered the door and I kind of... threw myself at him." I pulled in a much-needed breath. "And we had sex. Like, a lot. And he asked me to stay the night... so I did."

My friends' jaws hung open in shock for several seconds before Daphne came back to her senses. "You had sex?"

"Yes."

"With Grayson?

"Uh-huh."

"A lot?"

"Will you stop repeating everything she just said?" Sophia snapped. "We've already established she had a lot of hot and sweaty sex with Grayson—"

"I didn't say anything about hot and sweaty," I protested.

She gave me a "Bitch, please" look. "Well, wasn't it?"

Damn it. It really was. I rolled my lips between my teeth and bit down, refusing to answer, but the bright crimson blush on my neck and chest gave me away.

Sophia let out a delighted whoop. "I knew it! I knew that guy was going to be killer in the sack. I'm so jealous of you right now."

"Can we please get back on point?" I whined. "This isn't about whether it was hot and sweaty or just lukewarm. It's about the fact that it never, ever, ever should've happened."

A scoff traveled up Sophia's throat. "Okay, Taylor Swift. It *never, ever, ever* should've happened." The bitch actually sang the "never, ever, ever" part.

"It shouldn't have." I glared, somehow refraining from kicking her in the shin beneath the table. "First of all, he's my boss—"

"Your dead-sexy boss who's been chasing after you like a puppy for weeks," Daphne unhelpfully added.

"Secondly, this whole thing was supposed to be for show. It was never supposed to get real."

I hadn't realized just how much I'd given away until my friends turned quiet, their expressions growing concerned and speculative.

"And is it?" Sophia asked softly. "Getting real? For you?"

"It is," I finally admitted after several seconds of silence, in which I stared down at the table, toying with the cutlery. "I have... feelings for him. I know I shouldn't, that it's a *huge* mistake, but I can't help it. I tried to talk myself out of it over and over."

"Honey," Sophia whispered, reaching out to place her hand on mine, "this doesn't have to be a bad thing. He seems like a really good guy. He's not your dad, or—"

Her mouth clamped shut, and I knew exactly what she was thinking. He wasn't my dad... or Dominic. I turned my hand over under hers and twined our fingers together, giving her a comforting squeeze. She'd loved my brother more than anything. She still hadn't gotten over that heartbreak, and it killed me every time I saw the pain in her eyes.

"She's right," Daphne chirped, intentionally cutting through the morose mood that had suddenly enveloped our table. "It wouldn't be fair to paint him with that brush. Especially if he hasn't done anything to warrant your distrust. What if he truly is a good man and he really wants to be with you? Do you really want to risk losing that just because you're scared?"

"How can you say that?" I asked. "You know better than anyone... hell, we *all* know just how bad this could go. All three of us have lived it."

She shrugged and gave me a sad smile, her past still causing pain as well. "We have to let it go at some point, right? I mean, we can't stay bitter forever, can we?"

"Of course we can!" I smacked the table for emphasis. "We even made a pact, remember?"

She rolled her eyes at my dramatics. "That was years ago, Lo. We're in our thirties—"

"Shut your whore mouth," Sophia gasped. "I'm twenty-eight."

"You've been twenty-eight for three years," I teased. "Saying it doesn't make it true."

"As I was saying," Daphne continued with a giggle, "we're getting older. We need to learn how to move on. We offer relationship advice for a living, for Christ's sake. Don't you think it's time we start practicing what we preach?"

Sophia and I hung our heads in shame, knowing she was right but unwilling to admit it out loud.

"Okay," I finally said. "So what do you suggest?"

She gave my question consideration before answering. "Just go with it, I guess."

"That's your brilliant plan?" I scoffed. "Just *go with it*?"

"Yep. Just go with it. And enjoy the hot and sweaty sex in the meantime. If it stays good, Sophia and I will be thrilled for you."

"Yeah," Soph added. "And if it goes bad, we'll help you bury the body and come up with a rock-solid alibi."

It was official. I had the best friends in the world.

CHAPTER TWENTY-ONE

LOLA

I COULDN'T REMEMBER the last time I'd been so nervous. I hadn't even felt this level of anxiety when I finally decided to lose my virginity. And that was really saying something since, in one of his displays of overprotective big brother-ness, Dom had tried to dissuade me from stamping my V-card by informing me that the first time felt similar to being ripped in half with a dull, rusted steak knife.

Talk about colorful imagery. That was something no seventeen-year-old girl ever wanted to hear. Did it stop me? Hell no. It sure as hell scared the shit out of me, but that was still nothing compared to this.

"Stop fidgeting. You've got nothing to worry about." Grayson's right hand left the steering wheel and reached for mine, forcing me to unlock my wringing fingers. There was something about that simple touch that eased my frazzled nerves. It shouldn't have—I never should have allowed him to affect me in such a way—but he did. Instead of getting into a mental struggle with myself over it, I just sat back and released a heavy sigh, trying my best not to fixate on the fact that he kept my hand in his against my thigh.

"Well, I wouldn't be nervous if you hadn't tricked me into agreeing to lunch with your *family*," I pouted from the passenger seat. "I can't believe you used sex and bacon to get your way. That's really low."

He laughed, completely at ease. The stupid jerk didn't have a care in the world. "Relax, baby. They're going to love you."

"You have to say that. They're your family. I've never had a guy bring me home to meet his parents before, so *excuse me* for stressing about it."

"You've never met a boyfriend's parents?" he asked in complete bewilderment.

"First of all," I stated, holding up my index finger, "slow your roll on the 'boyfriend' business. We had sex one time—"

"We had sex four times," he interrupted. "It just happened to be over one twenty-four-hour period."

"Semantics." I waved him off and lifted my middle finger. "And second, I told you, I don't date."

"Not even in high school?"

I snorted and rolled my eyes at the windshield. "Whatever. Everyone knows high school doesn't count."

His thumb began rubbing circles on my wrist right at my pulse. "So what you're telling me is I'm your first." His smile was positively sinful. I wanted to leap across the console and lick him up and down.

"Stop being smug," I warned. "This is a nightmare. I'm having dinner with my boss's boss's boss, who knows I accidentally publicly humiliated his son and am currently in a fake relationship with him to help restore his public image."

"Hate to break it to you, sweetheart, but the relationship stopped being fake the minute you got on your hands and knees and begged to suck my dick."

I pulled in a loud gasp, ignoring the heat pooling between

my legs, and dug my nails into the skin on the back of his hand. "I did *not* beg!"

"Oh you begged, all right," he murmured, completely unfazed that I was currently trying to draw blood. "And I plan on making you do it again tonight."

My head shot to the side just as Grayson rolled his lips between his teeth to hide his smile. "This isn't funny!" I cried at the sight of the amusement laced through his handsome features.

"It kind of is, if you really think about it."

"Argh!" I moved to yank my hand from his but he tightened his grip, preventing my escape. I quickly gave up the struggle, refusing to dwell on the fact that part of my relenting was because I actually *liked* him holding my hand. "I don't do well in stressful situations. Never have. I have a tendency to say completely inappropriate things when I'm uncomfortable, so just be prepared. I'm liable to totally humiliate you *and* get myself fired all at the same time."

His deep chuckle did something funny to my insides. "Don't worry. My nana's going to be there. The woman's seventy-eight years old and thinks her age has earned her the right to say whatever she wants. Odds are even you'll blush at some of the stuff that comes out of her mouth."

I felt my lips pull into a smile at that information. Something told me I was going to get along great with Grayson's nana. "Well at least we don't have to put on an act," I muttered. "Since they already know this whole thing is fake, we don't have to pretend to be something we're not. Thank God for that, right?"

"I told you," he said in a growly voice, "it's not an act anymore. Besides, my father's the only one who had any idea it was a PR stunt in the first place."

"*What!*"

"Look, just calm down, okay—"

The edges of my vision began to blur with red at being told to calm down. "Don't you tell me to calm down, Grayson Lockhart! Just a word of caution—never, *ever* tell an Italian woman in the middle of a full-blown hissy to calm down. Are you really telling me your *entire* family, with the exception of your father, has thought this has been real?"

He shrugged casually, like it was nothing. "It *is* real."

"Maybe now!" I yelped. "But that just started, like, yesterday!"

I could have sworn I heard him mutter, "It's been longer than that," under his breath, but before I could be sure, he continued on. "Truth is, things are always a little tense between my brother and me, have been for as long as I can remember. My father thought it best to keep quiet about anything that could add additional stress on my mother. He's a bit protective when it comes to her. And, well... she's always been a little—" He tipped his head back and forth, as if looking for the right words. "—*exuberant* when it comes to her sons settling down. Dad thought it best she didn't know this was all for show, you know, to prevent any unnecessary upset."

"Are you kidding me?!" I shouted.

I barely had time to process everything he'd just admitted before he swung the car into the driveway of a fancy McMansion. I immediately experienced hardcore house envy. It had a wraparound porch, for crying out loud! On the first *and* second floor. I'd always wanted a house with a wraparound porch.

It was a dream home.

"Wow," I sighed as I stared out the windshield. "This place is beautiful." I turned back to Grayson, my eyes a little wide. "You grew up here?"

"Yep." He grinned, throwing the car into Park. "Broke my collarbone sliding down the banister and everything. My mom remodeled to exactly what she wanted as soon as my brother and I moved out."

"Why wait?" I asked curiously.

He chuckled at a memory before answering. "We were rambunctious kids, had a knack for destroying shit when we were growing up. My mom's trademark phrase was 'See? This is why we can't have nice things!'"

I giggled at his high-pitched tone as I stared back up at the massive house in spite of the nerves. "Why doesn't that surprise me?"

I jumped in my seat at the feel of Grayson's breath on my neck, spinning around to find he'd moved in... *close.* Less than an inch of space separated his lips from mine. "Wh-what are you doing?" I stammered, suddenly feeling too hot all over. Those green eyes of his darkened as the intensity behind them started to grow.

"Living up to my promise to touch you and tease you for as long as it takes." His proximity had effectively muddled my brain, and I barely had a chance to pull in air before he pressed his mouth against mine. It was a gentle, closed-mouth kiss, but it was still powerful enough to sear right through me, instantly making me want more. Everything about him—his touch, his taste, his smell— was more potent than any drug in existence. Just being in his company gave me the most exhilarating high I'd ever experienced.

After what felt like an eternity—but was probably closer to a few seconds—he pulled back. Sorrow at the loss of his lips flooded me as my eyelids fluttered open. I don't know how long I stared at Grayson dazedly before a knock on the driver side window scared me back into reality and caused me to let loose a shrill scream that reverberated through the close confines of the car.

"Christ, Mom," Grayson snarled, sitting up straight and

rubbing at his ringing ear. "Do you have to sneak up like that?" he asked petulantly as he pushed his door open. "You scared the hell out of her. Her scream nearly deafened me."

I followed suit and quickly opened my door, stepping out of the car just as a petite woman with brown hair that was lightly streaked with gray spoke up. "Sorry. So sorry," she replied, but judging by the enthusiastic smile on her face, she wasn't the least bit sorry. "I'm just so excited. You haven't brought a girl-friend home in *forever*!"

It just had to be said—Grayson's mom was *adorable*! Totes adorbs and all that jazz. I wanted to scoop her up and put her in my pocket. Her hair was cut into a short, stylish bob that compli-mented the shape of her face perfectly. She had Grayson's green eyes and had aged *really freaking* well! She hardly looked old enough to have a son Grayson's age. She barely came up to his shoulder, putting her around my height, and her casual yet fash-ionable attire fit her tiny frame to perfection.

Despite the welcoming grin stretched across her delicate, pretty features, I still had an anxious hoard of butterflies swarming around in my belly as I rounded the hood of Grayson's car and extended my hand in greeting.

"Hello, Mrs. Lockhart. It's nice to meet you."

She glanced at my hand and quickly dismissed it, moving in to wrap me in a tight hug instead. I was so stunned by the unex-pected show of affection that my arms remained limp at my sides.

"Please, call me Cybil. I'm so happy to meet you too, Lola. We're thrilled you were able to come today." She released me from the embrace and stepped back, still smiling brightly.

"Oh... uh, well, thank you. I'm happy to be here."

She held me by the arms as she scanned my face. "You're so pretty. Grayson, you didn't mention she was so pretty. The pictures in the papers don't do you justice, darling."

My body warmed and my chest squeezed at the thought of him talking to his family about me. I turned my head to find Grayson rolling his eyes. "Can we at least move this into the house before you start fawning all over her, please?"

Cybil let out a delicate "*Psh*" and hooked her elbow through mine, leading me from the car toward the house. "He's just sensitive because I interrupted him copping a feel. Wouldn't be the first time—"

"Mom! Come on!"

"I can't tell you how many times I had to yell at him to start locking the doors when he was a teenager. All by himself in the bathroom or his bedroom," she muttered thoughtfully. "Who doesn't lock the door when they're doing something like that? I'll tell you what, it got to the point where I spent my days stomping through the house just so I wouldn't open a door and get an eyeful of something no mother should see!"

I choked on my spit trying to hold in my laughter at the thought of a masturbating Grayson being caught by his mom.

"It only got worse when he started dating," she huffed. "Nolan was no help at all. He just gave the boys a box of condoms each and told them to let him know when they needed more. I'll tell you, darling, raising boys is enough to drive you mad."

I smirked over my shoulder and gave a horrified Grayson a wink as we crossed the threshold. "You know, Cybil? I'd just *love* to hear all the stories you have about Grayson growing up."

His face was thunderous as he closed the front door behind him, and it took everything in me not to burst into laughter.

"Glad you could make it," a deep, familiar voice said. I glanced to the side to see Grayson's father joining us in the foyer, a stylish woman in her seventies wielding a cane at his side.

"Thank you for inviting me, Mr. Lockhart." I wondered if I

sounded as skittish as I felt. Even though he and Grayson had so many of the same features, something about the man's commanding presence made me twitchy.

"Nolan, please," he said, offering me his hand.

"Nolan," I repeated, exchanging a firm handshake with him, none of that limp-wrist crap so many women did. *A strong handshake shows strong character.* It was one of the few things I'd believed true from my father.

He released my hand and tucked his into the pocket of his Chinos, and I was suddenly self-conscious about my clammy palms. *God, please don't let me have sweated all over the guy. Please, please, please, please, pretty please. Thank you and amen.*

"Ooh, hoo!" the old lady whistled, using her cane to come closer. She leaned in, inspecting me up close, and beamed, obviously pleased with what she saw.

"I'll hand it to my grandson. What he lacks in brains, he makes up with taste. You're stunning, my girl! Gray went and got himself an exotic *Latina*." She did a saucy little shoulder jiggle and I fell a little bit in love.

"She's Italian, Nana," Grayson replied dryly.

"Even better!" the woman declared, banging her cane on the floor. "She can make me a lasagna!"

"Mom. Please." Nolan had the good grace to look embarrassed, but there was no reason. I loved Nana.

I took the woman's soft, papery hand in mind and leaned in to whisper, "Can I adopt you? You'd fit right in with my family."

She cackled loudly and I caught of whiff of whiskey on her breath. Day drinking too? Nana was totally my kind of chick!

"Honey, I think I'm going to like you just fine."

"The feeling's mutual," I giggled.

Nana took two steps back and did a sweep of me with her eyes. "And child-bearing hips too!" She turned to Grayson, expression serious as can be. "You keep hold of this one, son. She'll carry your babies real good."

"Looks like I'm late to the party," a man called out, drawing everyone's attention. I turned to look at the man moving into the entryway and froze. Not because he looked so much like Grayson, but because of the venom behind his brown eyes as he glared in Grayson's direction.

"Deacon," Grayson muttered, tipping his chin in the man's direction. "Good to see you, brother."

Oh wow. The guy with the obvious chip on his shoulder was Grayson's brother. And it didn't take a genius to see there was some serious animosity between the two of them. Deacon looked like he wanted to smash Grayson like a bug. Grayson's entire body went stiff and alert, like he was just itching for a fight.

"I'm sure it is." Sarcasm dripped from his words as he lifted a tumbler full of amber liquid to his lips and took a healthy drink, eyeing me over the rim. "And who do we have here?"

"This is—"

I stepped forward and offered my hand to Deacon before Gray could do something stupid, like refer to me as his girlfriend. "I'm Lola. Nice to meet you."

He took my hand and, with a mean smirk at his brother, lifted it to his lips and placed a kiss on my knuckles. "Most definitely."

I suppressed a shiver and pulled my hand away. I took a step back into Grayson's chest and he wrapped a protective arm around me. I was suddenly thankful for the security his large frame offered.

I didn't know what was going on between the brothers, but I didn't want to be in the middle of it.

It seemed like we all stood silently, watching the standoff between the two men, just waiting for something the happen.

Then the sound of a woman's voice broke the tension surrounding all of us. "Hey, stranger. It's been a while."

A gorgeous woman with long, lustrous red hair came waltzing into the fray, a bright, blissful smile stretched across her face. I'd never seen such a beautiful woman in all my life. And the way she looked at Grayson made the tiny hairs on the back of my neck stand on end.

"Fiona?" Grayson asked, surprise and joy clear in his tone. "Oh my God, Fee!"

What the what!

CHAPTER TWENTY-TWO

LOLA

FIONA? As in longtime girlfriend *Fiona?*

As Grayson released me to run toward the stunning redhead and sweep her off her feet—literally—in a twirling hug, I was hit with a wave of inferiority.

"Oh my God," he repeated with a laugh as he placed her back on her feet and held her out at arm's length. "I can't believe you're here! It's been forever. How are you? When did you get home?"

Does he really have to sound so excited? Jeez.

"I flew back yesterday. It's so good to see you." She went in for another hug and my muscles locked.

I glanced around my surroundings anxiously. My gaze landed on Deacon and the look of longing on his face as he stared at the woman sucked every ounce of air from my lungs. I suddenly understood all too well why he held a grudge against his brother. He was in love with Fiona.

And Grayson was the one who had her.

From the dreamy look on her face as she prattled on about transferring from Paris and *blah, blah, blah,* it was quite clear her feelings for Gray were far from gone. I felt like an intruder, like I didn't belong there.

"Fee, I want you to meet someone," Grayson said, taking her by the hand and pulling her back into our huddle. They stopped in front of me and he started introductions. "This is Lola," he began.

A sense of possessiveness washed over me, and without thinking, I stepped forward and finished, "His girlfriend. Lovely to meet you."

From the corner of my eye, I saw the shock seep across Grayson's face, but I couldn't find it in me to care. I was too focused on the way *Fiona's* smile lost most of its luster at the sight of me.

"Lovely to meet you too," she responded, her smile turning plastic. "Wow, Gray. I didn't know you were seeing anyone. It's such a... surprise." She swallowed thickly, her throat bobbing up and down. "A very pleasant surprise." If I had to guess, she struggled not to choke on those words.

"Oh yes," Cybil replied cheerfully. "They've been the talk in all the magazines for weeks now. But seeing as you've been in Paris for three years, I'm not surprised you didn't see it. We're all very pleased."

Well, apparently Cybil was Team Lola. That was good to know, at least. And hopefully I had Nana on my side too, what with my child-bearing hips and all. Fiona's frame was more willowy than curvy; she looked like a baby could snap her in half.

Oh man, bitterness and jealousy coursed through me stronger than I'd ever experienced. I hadn't even been this green with envy when I walked in on my college boyfriend drilling my sorority sister.

But seeing Grayson so happy, so excited to see her, left me unsettled and a bit... sad. That was it. I felt sad. Because I didn't think I'd ever come close to being as beautiful and cultured as the woman in front of me. Hell, I'd never even left the continent. She'd *lived* in Paris for a few years.

And to twist the knife even deeper, she and Grayson started rattling off a conversation in French.

I looked at him with wide, bewildered eyes. "You speak French."

"Yeah. French and Spanish." He grinned down at me, looping an arm over my shoulders. "I didn't tell you?"

"No," I replied dryly.

"Yep. And Fee learned too so we could have conversations without anyone knowing what we were talking about."

They both laughed and she reached over to touch his arm. "Oh, that was so much fun, wasn't it?"

I wanted to rip her fingers off and shove them down her throat.

"I'm so glad you two got to catch up," Cybil stated, coming to hook elbows with Fiona. "I'm still angry your mother didn't tell me you were coming home. But no matter, we're just glad to have you here. Let's eat!"

Cybil and Fiona chatted amicably as they headed for the dining room. I stood in place as the others began to pass, chancing another glance in Deacon's direction. He shot me a conciliatory look and the discomfort I felt for him just minutes before began to fade. Now I understood.

"Hey. You okay?" Grayson stepped into my space and placed his hands on my arms, rubbing up and down in a comforting gesture.

"Okay that your long-term ex-girlfriend popped up for a lunch where I'm meeting your family for the first time? Not really," I snapped sarcastically, the words tumbling from my mouth before I could stop them. I really hadn't meant to say that out loud.

He bent his knees so we were closer to eye level. Even in my heels Grayson still towered over me. "Hey now," he said soothingly, tipping my chin up so I was forced to meet his eyes. "It's not like that, I swear. We're just friends. We were friends before we dated, and we stayed friends after we broke up. There's nothing between us. That's all in the past."

I wanted so badly to believe him, but I'd seen the look on her face. "You sure she knows that?" I asked drolly.

"Huh?"

I rolled my eyes and tried to sidestep him. "Never mind. Just forget it."

"Wait a minute." He grabbed my arm and pulled me back before I got very far. "Lola. I promise. There's nothing going on."

"Maybe not for you."

His brows furrowed as he pulled me close. I gave in but left my arms at my sides. "Baby, I'm not following."

"Gah!" I glanced up at the ceiling for divine intervention. "Boys can be such clueless idiots."

"What are you talking about? Come on, talk to me."

I straightened and examined his eyes, searching for any sign of deception, only to come up empty. He really was just a clueless idiot. "Look," I breathed out. "It's nothing, really. Let's just go eat, okay? I don't want to make your mom wait. She likes me so far, and I don't want to mess that up."

"You could never mess that up." He grinned, placing a kiss on my lips. "And you've already gotten Nana's stamp of approval. Trust me, baby, you're golden. But I do have one question." He quirked his eyebrow teasingly. "What was up with that girlfriend stuff, huh? I thought the G-word was along the lines of Voldemort."

"God! I can't even be mad at you for making fun of me because you totally just used a *Harry Potter* reference!"

His face was awash with triumph. "I might've seen the 'I Heart Muggles' coffee mug on your desk the other day. And the 'Dumbledore is my Homeboy' sticker. And the—"

I slapped my hand over his mouth and frowned. "I get it. I have a weakness and you just totally used it against me."

"Hey." He shrugged. "I said I'd get under your skin by any means necessary, didn't I?"

"Yeah, well clearly I underestimated you."

He leaned in, kissing me once more, that time adding just enough tongue to tease and make me want more. "I'll make it up to you tonight. Cross my heart."

With that, he took my hand and led me into the dining room with the rest of his family... and *Fiona*.

<hr>

LUNCH WENT RELATIVELY WELL, all things considered.

Sure, I had to sit through Fiona waxing poetic about her and Grayson's childhood, but I forced myself to grin and bear it. After all, she'd been the one who wanted marriage while he didn't, at least not with her. That had to stand for something, right?

And knowing there was a like soul sitting at the table by way of Deacon kind of helped ease the sting when the two of them started trading inside jokes.

For the most part, I kept a running conversation with Cybil and Nana. I even tried to pull Deacon in a time or two, but he was content to sit and glower at Fiona and Grayson as they chattered and laughed with each other.

Whatever.

The day didn't start going downhill until lunch was over and Nolan declared that we'd all head out to the pool for a game of water volleyball. My blood ran cold at the mention of the pool.

"Oh, uh... I don't... I didn't...." I stumbled over my words, trying to come up with a reasonable excuse. "I don't have a suit!"

"Oh that's all right, darling," Cybil chimed in. "We keep extras in the pool house. I bet there's something in there that would fit you."

"Oh I couldn't," I tried again.

"Please, I insist! As a matter of fact, Fiona is going to borrow one too, aren't you, dear?"

"Absolutely, Cybil. I assume the one I always used is still back there?" Fiona shot me a look, pleased as punch to throw that in my face.

"Sure is. Why don't you take Lola and show her where to find them?"

Damn it. I couldn't say no again without looking ungrateful *and* giving that auburn-headed cow the upper hand, so I followed obediently, jealousy and fear making my steps heavy.

The pool house was exactly what I expected after seeing the Lockharts' immaculate home. It was more of an apartment than anything else.

I followed Fiona into one of the two—yes, *two*—guest rooms where the extra bathing suits were kept. She pulled open a drawer and began fishing around before unearthing a pretty teal halter bikini with wooden rings at the hips and cleavage.

"Just rummage around in there." She pointed, heading toward the bathroom to change. "I'm sure you'll find something in your size." She might have said it with a saccharin smile on her face, but I didn't miss the dig. The bitch was basically calling me fat. I wanted to claw her face off.

"I'm sure I will," I replied just as sweetly, then turned my back on her to begin digging through the drawer. She appeared minutes later in her swimsuit, moving like she was on a catwalk. I had to admit she looked good... even if she *was* flat-chested.

She left me alone to continue my search. I finally found a red two-piece with a black chevron pattern and a bandeau top. For most women with my... *endowments* a bandeau top was a no-no, but I'd been blessed with the Abbatelli genes, which meant my girls sat high and proud.

I slid on the bathing suit and took a quick peek in the mirror. A smug grin tugged at my lips—I looked good. *Take that, Fiona,* I thought, until I remembered exactly *why* I was wearing the damn thing in the first place.

The pool.

The dreaded body of water.

"Shit," I whispered at my reflection as my heart rate spiked. "It's okay," I told Mirror Lola. "You don't have to get in. You can lie on one of the comfy lounge chairs. Far, *far* away from the death trap."

My hands were shaking by the time I exited the pool house. Nolan, Grayson, and Deacon were all in swim trunks, and I might have drooled a bit at the sight of Grayson's yummy abs. Cybil and Nana were sitting at a table under an umbrella, both wearing long, flowing cover-ups.

The guys—and *Fiona*—were already in the pool, setting up the net, so I made my way over to Nana and Cybil, happy to keep them company while the others played.

"Damn, baby!" Grayson whistled in appreciation. "You look *good.*"

I blushed the color of my suit, and couldn't help but feel smug at Fiona's sour expression.

"You really do, darling," Cybil added as I took a seat beside her. "I'd have killed for your curves when I was your age."

Nana snorted. "I'd kill for her curves *now*. I might be old as dirt but I'm not dead yet. I still flaunt what I got."

I laughed and reached for the pitcher of iced tea and an empty glass that were sitting on the table. "I'm pretty sure I want to be you when I grow up, Nana," I laughed as I filled a glass.

"You and everyone else, deary."

Oh yeah. I loved Nana.

I'd just sat back and took a sip when cold droplets of waters splashed onto my shoulders. I let out a squeal as Grayson leaned in behind me and buried his face in my neck. "What are you doing up here? Come get in the water with me. I want you on my team."

I reached up and stroked his cheek, loving the feel of his stubble against my skin. "Oh no you don't, trust me. I'm terrible at sports. But you have fun."

"Please? Just one game?" He pasted a boyish pout on his face. The expression might have worked if I wasn't so deathly afraid of water.

"Really. Besides, if I play, you'll have odd numbers."

"Hurry up, Gray. We're about to start," Fiona hollered over.

"In a sec. I'm just trying to talk Lola into playing," he called back.

"Seriously, Grayson. I'm good here. I'm just going to visit with your mom and Nana for a bit, maybe get some sun."

"Leave her be if she doesn't want to play," Fiona chimed in with her unwanted two cents. "Not everyone is built for sports."

Oh that bitch. I wanted to prove her wrong, but there wasn't a snowball's chance in hell I was getting near that pool.

I was yanked from my anger when Grayson grabbed my hands and began to pull. "Come on, it'll be fun."

"Grayson, no." I began to struggle, jerking my hands as terror had my heart pounding wildly. "Really, please. I don't want to play."

"Just let her go," Fiona added. "We don't need her to win."

I'd have shot her a scathing look if I wasn't so goddamned scared.

"I won't take no for an answer," Grayson said playfully, pulling me closer and closer.

"Please. Stop." My skin was coated in a cold sweat and my whole body began to shake, but he was too busy dragging me to notice the stark fear in my big eyes.

"No one cares if your hair and makeup get messed up. You'll still be beautiful."

"It's not that!" I cried, my voice growing more high-pitched as the water got closer. "Please, *please*. Don't make me—" My protest fell on deaf ears, because he chose that moment to grab me around my waist and throw me into the water... right into the deep end.

My scream was cut off by the rush of water crashing over me, pulling me down, down, down. I thrashed and kicked, desperately trying to swim *up*. When my face broke the surface, I opened my mouth to suck in air and shout for help, only to swallow a mouthful of pool water as I sank back down.

No matter how hard I tried, I just couldn't get my body to cooperate. My chest ached with the need for oxygen, and I had to fight my body's instinctual need to inhale.

It felt like I was down there for an eternity when a hand wrapped around my arm and yanked me to the surface. I sputtered and gasped and clawed at the arm on my waist, terror having taken control of every part of me.

"You're okay. Shh, you're all right."

Fat tears ran down my face as I sobbed and sucked in deep breaths simultaneously. It wasn't until I was safely at the stairs that I realized it was Deacon who'd pulled me out.

"Just calm down, Lola. Breathe. In and out, slowly," he coaxed, but I was still too shaken to listen. I crawled up the cement steps on my hands and knees, scraping them in my rush to get out of the pool. I didn't care about the pain—I just wanted out. *Now!*

"Jesus, baby! What the fuck just happened?" Grayson ran to me, his face pale as he tried to wrap me in his arms. I shoved at him, still crying hysterically.

"I said no, you asshole!" I yelled at the top of my lungs.

"Lola, calm down. It's okay."

He went for me again, but I smacked at his chest with clenched fists.

"It's *not* okay!" I shouted at the top of my lungs. "I can't swim, you bastard!"

With that, I ran on wobbly legs to the pool house, slamming the door behind me as tremors of humiliation and horror racked my body. I could barely see where I was going through the tears flowing from my eyes, but somehow I made it into the bathroom.

And only then, with no one to witness my disgrace, did I sink down and let myself sob uncontrollably.

CHAPTER TWENTY-THREE

GRAYSON

I FELT LIKE A WORLD-CLASS JACKASS. All the work I'd accomplished to destroy those walls of hers was undone with one careless mistake. She'd locked herself in the pool house bathroom for a half hour, crying her eyes out and refusing to let anyone in. The sound of her crying shredded my insides. I couldn't recall the last time I'd ever felt so helpless. The only words she'd spoken to me since she emerged, fully dressed, were a demand that I take her home.

She was still trembling when Mom and Nana had insisted on hugging her goodbye. She remained in a kind of dazed silence as my family bid us farewell, and had stayed quiet the entire ride back to her apartment, no matter how hard I tried to engage her.

"Lola," I attempted again as I pulled the car to a stop in front of her building. "Baby, please talk to me."

"Thanks for the ride," she mumbled, reaching for the door handle.

Okay, that wasn't what I had in mind. I hit the automatic lock on the door to prevent her from opening it. "I'm so fucking sorry. I didn't realize—"

"It doesn't matter," she snapped. "You should have listened the *million* times I begged you to stop, but you didn't. Maybe if you hadn't been so busy playing with your *ex-girlfriend* you'd have noticed I was freaking the fuck out."

"Baby...." I reached for her hand but she pulled it away. "Fiona had nothing to do with this—"

"Whatever. It doesn't matter. Just... unlock the door."

"Not until you talk to me. Why didn't you just tell me?"

"Because it's not something I like talking about!" she barked. "It's embarrassing! I'm a thirty-one-year-old woman who's terrified of water and doesn't know how to swim because of one stupid little episode from my childhood."

"It's not stupid if it still affects you so strongly," I insisted. "Lola, you can talk to me about anything."

That statement got her full attention. Unfortunately, judging from the look on her face and the short bubble of hysterical laughter. "Oh my God, Grayson! We had sex, that's it, and you're acting like it means we're fucking soul mates or something. I've got news for you—that's not how it works."

Anger began clawing at my throat and it took everything I had to swallow it down. "It was more than that and you fucking know it," I growled. "You're pissed at me and I get that. You have every right. But you called yourself my girlfriend—"

"Consider it a moment of weakness, a lapse into insanity. It won't happen again."

I lost the precarious hold I had on my temper and shouted, "That's fucking bullshit!"

"I told you I don't do relationships!" she shot back. "It's not my fault you didn't listen." She yanked on the door handle in aggravation. "Now open this fucking door!"

"Not until you talk to me!"

"You want to talk? Fine, we'll talk."

"Good."

"Instead of trying to fix *my* shit, why don't you concentrate on fixing your own?"

Not good.

"I don't have anything I need to fix. Everything in my life is great. Except the fact that the girl I'm attracted to is crazy!"

She dropped her head back against the headrest and yelped, "Jesus Christ! How could you possibly be this clueless?"

"What—"

"You know what? I'm done. I'm so freaking done. Unlock the door."

"Lola—"

"No! Just open the door!"

Her eyes were wild, flashing with a mixture of emotions I couldn't decipher. Because she looked so close to losing it completely, I decided it best to give her what she wanted now, and revisit the more important things later.

I unlocked the door, stating firmly, "This isn't over."

"Just another thing you're wrong about," she laughed bitterly, as she shoved the door open and stepped out. But before she closed it, she leaned in and offered a parting shot that left me reeling. "Oh, and I hate to burst your bubble of ignorance, but the reason things are bad between you and your brother is because he's in love with Fiona, probably has been for years. That took me all of thirty seconds to figure out. And she's still so desperately in love with you that she doesn't even notice him. So much for not having anything to fix, huh?"

With that, she slammed the door and stomped up the steps into her building.

LOLA

I WAS PISSED. I *hated* how I felt as I walked away from Grayson, but my stupid pride and sense of self-preservation wouldn't allow me to turn around.

Which just pissed me off even more.

"Oh, Ms. Abbatelli, your—"

I held my hand up, palm out, and kept walking. "Not now, Maury. I'm in a shitty mood."

"But—"

I kept moving, feeling more and more bitchy with every step I took. I just wanted to get up to my apartment, wash the stink of chlorine from my skin and hair, and drink myself to sleep.

I counted the floors as the elevator carried me up to my apartment, thankful that no one else got on to slow my ascent. My puffy eyes itched from my pitiful crying jag earlier. My hair was a tangled mass of knots since I'd had nothing to brush it out with after getting it wet. I was sure my streaked mascara and eyeliner made me look like an escaped mental patient. But I didn't care about any of that at the moment. I was too busy drowning in my misery after... well, nearly drowning.

I breathed a sigh of relief when I climbed off the elevator onto my floor, rummaging around in my purse for my keys. I twisted, disengaging the lock, and was so consumed by my own personal pity party that I didn't register the sound of the television or the fact that all the lights in my apartment were on.

That was until a deep voice sounded from behind me, scaring the ever-loving shit out of me.

"Hey, shorty. Where you been all day?"

The blood-curdling scream that came from deep within my belly was fit for a horror movie. I spun around on my gorgeous Alexander Wang studded platform sandals, wielding my huge

Michael Kors tote like a weapon, and smacked the man right in the stomach. He keeled over with a pained "Oomph."

Still screaming like crazy, I lifted my bag high—thankful that I never left home without my wallet, Kindle, makeup bag, phone, travel manicure kit, day planner, and at least three pairs of sunglasses—and brought it down on the back of his head.

"Goddamn it, Lola! Have you lost your mind?"

I was just about to swing again, that time going for the guy's twig and berries, when I recognized the angry voice belonged to none other than my brother.

"Dominic?" I screeched. "Are you crazy?" I continued to shout, arms still extended over my head. "I thought you were a robber! I could have killed you!"

He straightened from his prone position and glared as he rubbed his stomach with one hand and the back of his head with the other.

"Your bag weighs a fucking ton, little sis, but you'd still be screwed if I was a real robber."

"Sweet sister Christian," I breathed, placing a hand on my chest to try and soothe my frantic heart. "You scared the shit out of me. What were you thinking?"

Dom snatched my purse from my hands and dropped it on the table just inside the front door, still scowling at me. "I was thinking I'd surprise my sister with a visit. Didn't Maury tell you I was up here?"

"Oh." I worked my bottom lip between my teeth and shuffled from foot to foot. "I, uh, wasn't really listening to what he was saying."

"Christ, Lola. Really?" He threw his hands up in exasperation and turned around. I followed as he headed for the kitchen. "And you tell Ma not to worry about you living on your own," he grumbled sarcastically as he rummaged through my wine selection. He settled on a nice red blend and started uncorking.

"There's nothing for her to worry about. I'm perfectly safe here by myself."

My brother's look screamed "Bitches be crazy" as he poured wine into two glasses and slid one across the counter top in my direction. "What the hell happened to you? You look like you took a walk through a drive-thru car wash."

It was my turn to glare. "Thanks, asshole. I'll have you know it's been a really shitty day, so if you could refrain from making fun of me, it would be greatly appreciated." I guzzled my wine in a very unladylike manner and wiggled the glass in front of his face for a refill.

He poured me another glass while making that concerned-brother face as he stared at me. "What happened? You get mugged or something?"

"No," I sighed. "Nothing like that. It's a long story."

He rested his back against the counter across from me, crossing his ankles as he sipped his wine. "Well, that's why I came for a visit, shorty, so I can catch up on your life... long stories included. Now tell me why you look like that creepy little girl who climbs out of TV screens and kills people in *The Ring*. Does it have something to do with the guy you're making out with in all the papers?"

I frowned at my brother's smirking face. "God, you're just as bad as Mom."

He ignored me and repeated, "Tell me what happened."

I inhaled a deep breath before sucking down more wine, needing it to help ease my still frazzled nerves. "He took me to meet his parents today."

Dom choked on his wine and started beating on his chest as he coughed. Once he was able to breathe regularly, he looked up at me, his eyes the size of half dollars. "You went to meet his *parents*?"

"Well, you don't have to say it like that," I said flatly.

He let out a laugh of disbelief. "Excuse me for being shocked. You're the one who said you'd rather eat gas station sushi than ever enter into another committed relationship."

"I never said that," I argued, setting my wineglass on the table and crossing my arms over my chest defensively.

"You said *exactly* that."

"Whatever. Are you going to let me finish my story or what?"

His hands went up in surrender. "Sorry, sorry. Continue."

I blew out a puff of air and attempted to run a hand through my hair, but had to stop when I encountered a mess of knots. "So, he took me to meet his parents today and it was...." I paused, trying to find the word to best describe my afternoon before finally settling on "A disaster."

Dominic instantly went into intense big brother mode. Uncrossing his ankles, he moved closer, resting his palms on the counter and leaning in with a stony expression on his face. "What happened? Did that fucker do something to you?"

"No," I huffed, giving my head a minute shake. "God, no. Nothing like that. It was going really well at first...."

"Okay...," he dragged out, prompting me to give him more.

I told him about Fiona's sudden appearance, how seeing them interact twisted a knife in my stomach, how for the first time in my life I'd experienced jealousy so acute it ate at me. I even went into detail about my theory on his brother being in love with Grayson's ex. I spilled it all, opening up to my big brother in a way I never had before. Then I finished by telling him about being tossed into the pool, knowing he was one of only a handful of people who knew how badly something like that would affect me.

"Oh God." He rounded the kitchen counter and pulled me into a big protective hug that infused my limbs with much-needed warmth. "God, shorty. I'm so sorry that happened. You must have been terrified."

"I was, for a little bit, at least," I admitted with a sniffle, burrowing deeper into his strong chest. I hadn't realized until that very moment just how badly I needed the security he offered. "But then I was just embarrassed. I mean, I acted completely insane. In front of *everyone*. It was humiliating."

"Don't even go there," he commanded in a rough, angry tone. "You have nothing to be embarrassed about."

"Easy for you to say. You weren't there to witness my meltdown."

His arms tightened around me. "I didn't need to be. I was there that day, remember?"

I shivered at the recollection of the day he was talking about. I'd only been six years old, but it still sat in my memory clear as day. "Thanks," I whispered, hugging Dominic back just as tightly as he was holding me. "I really needed to hear that." Pulling back, I looked up at my brother and smiled. "Despite you nearly giving me a heart attack, I'm really glad you're here."

He returned my smile and said, "Me too, shorty."

I moved out of his embrace and returned to my wineglass, taking a sip, thinking the discussion was over. I was wrong.

"Now, about the ex...."

I groaned and let my head fall back. "I don't want to talk anymore about her. I hate her. She sucks. Can't we just leave it at that?"

"No, we can't," he informed me, bending at the waist to rest his elbows on the granite countertop. "Because I'm not going to let you hide behind that as an excuse. I know you better than anyone else, and I've never seen you like this."

"Like what?" I asked, trying to come across as sarcastic even as my heart flipped in my chest.

"Like you care. You can't hide it from me, shorty. You

really like this guy. And that terrifies you." I had nothing to say. It was uncanny how correct he was. "From what you said, your guy doesn't have any feelings left for this girl—"

"Yeah, but she's still in love with him," I defended.

"So? That doesn't mean shit and you know it. She might still want him, but if he's done, there's nothing she can do about it. He told you he sees her as nothing more than a friend, and I think you need to trust that. He hasn't given you any reason not to."

I narrowed my eyes at my brother and downed the last of the wine in my glass. "You know, I really don't like you right now."

He chuckled and took a sip from his own glass. "That's because you know I'm right." I didn't respond since the stupid jerk was right; instead, I stuck my tongue out at him. "Ah, now I know I'm right. You only turn into an immature little brat when I'm right."

"Shut up before I kick you out."

His head fell back as he laughed his ass off. "Oh, little sis. I've missed you like crazy."

That worked wonders in warming me back up. "I've missed you too, big brother."

"Good. Now go get a shower. You look like an extra on *The Walking Dead*."

I rolled my eyes and started for my bedroom. "And then you ruin it," I muttered as I walked away.

"Oh, and Lola?"

I turned to look back over my shoulder. "Yeah?"

"Hate to dump this on you now after you had such a shitty day, but I need to warn you about something."

The hairs on my arms stood on end. "Warn me about what?"

The smile that spread across Dominic's face was positively evil. "Mom's coming for a visit in two weeks."

"Son of a bitch. Can this day get any worse?"

My brother's laughter followed me all the way into my bedroom. The prick was enjoying my misery way too damn much.

CHAPTER TWENTY-FOUR

LOLA

IT WAS the Tuesday after the incident at the Lockhart house and I was still avoiding Grayson. I hadn't managed to put my pride aside and seek him out, give him an explanation for my crazy behavior the Sunday before.

I was stubborn... and a coward. I was a stubborn coward. That was the worst. Needless to say, I'd been in a seriously pissy mood the past two days.

We'd just wrapped up our show for the morning, and despite it only being lunchtime, I was ready for the day to be over. Instead of waiting on Sophia and Daphne, I headed out of the studio. We still had to plan out the show for the following day, and there was some research I needed to get through, so I stomped toward my desk, geared up to bury my head in work so I could get the hell out of there and go home to wallow in my misery in peace.

My eyes were cast down at my phone, scrolling through e-mails that needed addressing, and my feet almost came out from under me when I rounded the corner and plowed right into a towering wall of man.

Sure, it was my own fault for not paying attention, but as I'd said, I was in a bad mood. Therefore, I opened my mouth to rip into the asshole who had been stupid enough to get in my way. "Son of a bitch. Watch where you're go—" The words died on my tongue when I looked up to see who I had just run into.

"Ms. Abbatelli."

Fuck my life. "M-Mr. Lockhart. I'm so sorry. It was my fault—"

He held his hand up to silence me. "It's quite all right. And as I said Sunday, please call me Nolan." Even though I'd just acted like a bitch, he was looking down at me with a kind smile on his face, reminding me so much of his son. My heart squeezed painfully.

"Nolan," I repeated, still feeling strange calling him by his first name. "I'm really sorry for running into you, and also for nearly cussing you out."

My heart gave another squeeze at the sound of his chuckle. For Christ's sake, did everything about this man have to remind me of Grayson? It wasn't fair. "That's all right. Better me than another wall, right?"

My eyelids narrowed into slits as I crossed my arms over my chest. "Those glass walls are dangerous," I mumbled.

The corner of his mouth twitched as he fought to hold back his grin. "Of course." Nolan cleared his throat and attempted to school his features into a more serious expression as he asked, "Do you have a free minute to talk?"

I regarded him hesitantly before stating, "That depends. Are you here to fire me? Because if so, I'm really too busy at the moment."

"No, of course not. It's nothing like that."

"Then I'm free now," I said, dropping my arms and lifting my chin, faking an air of professionalism.

"Great. Should we go to your office or—?"

"Oh, um... actually, we can use the conference room if you

need privacy. I have a cubicle." I pointed in the direction of my desk, hidden behind three four-foot-tall partitions.

Nolan's forehead wrinkled in confusion. "You don't have an office?"

"Nope. Just a cubicle."

He shook his head, turned on the heels of his shiny, expensive Italian loafers, and headed toward the conference room; the same one where I'd first made a fool of myself in front of him and his son. I followed behind him in silence, my curiosity mixing with anxiousness as I tried to figure out what he could possibly want to discuss that would require privacy.

The door to the conference room clicked shut, and I suddenly became acutely aware of the fact that I was very much alone with my "boyfriend's" father... that was, if I could even call Grayson my boyfriend, considering how we'd left things last Sunday. Shit, maybe he really *was* going to fire me, and he just lied so I wouldn't put up a fight. If that were the case, he had another thing coming, because I planned to go down kicking and screaming. They were going to have to drag my body out of this office building.

"So, what can I do for you?" I asked with false bravado.

"I just wanted to check on you, make sure you were okay after what happened Sunday. You had quite a scare. Cybil and I have been worried about you."

Well, that was unexpected.

"Oh... uh... I'm fine. Thank you for asking." Embarrassment had my cheeks burning at the reminder of how I'd acted in front of all of them.

"You know...," he started, reaching up to scratch the back of his neck in obvious discomfort. "I know it's not my place... I mean, I'm aware we don't know each other all that well...." His disquiet was contagious, and I began to fidget from foot to foot as he stumbled through what he planned to say. "This may seem forward, but... well, the whole family was quite taken with you, Lola. All of us. I just wanted you to know that if you ever need someone to talk to... I'm here. I know it may seem awkward, giving our professional positions, but—"

"Thank you," I interrupted, wanting to spare him any more awkwardness. The truth was, despite his blundering through that speech, I thoroughly appreciated the gesture. Probably more than he'd ever know.

A small smile of relief spread across Nolan's face. "Yes... good. Well, I just wanted to say that. I've taken up enough of your time. I'll let you get back to it."

He pulled the door open and held it in place, waving an arm out for me to precede him.

I started out only to stop and look over my shoulder when he called my name. "Yes?"

"I know I made a mess of that whole thing, but I meant what I said. If you need to talk, you know where to find me."

I nodded, unable to speak past the swell of emotion clogging my throat. I'd never had any type of fatherly figure; I wasn't sure how to feel in that moment other than overwhelmed.

"He cares about you, you know. A great deal. I know how things started between you and my son, and because of that I understand it may be hard to believe, but it's true. He's been a wreck these past two days."

With that, he strode away, leaving me standing alone in the conference room, my mouth dry as if I'd just swallowed cotton.

"What was that all about?" I looked up to find Sophia and Daphne standing in the doorway with wide eyes. "You didn't get fired, did you?" Sophia, the one who'd voiced the first question, asked. "Because if he did, we'll burn this place to the ground. It's all that asshole's fault anyway."

God, I loved my friends. After I'd told them about the whole disaster, they'd quickly rallied around me, showing unfailing support. I didn't know what I'd do without them.

"No," I giggled, feeling lighter than I had in the past two days. "He didn't fire me, so put the lighter fluid away, psycho. It's all good. He just wanted to make sure I was okay. It was actually... really nice."

"He was checking on you?" Daphne asked skeptically.

"Yeah. Kind of threw me for a loop too. I thought he was going to fire me because of all the shit that went down with me and Grayson."

The skepticism in her eyes gave way to sympathy as she and Sophia moved into the conference room, closing the door behind them. "So you still haven't talked to him?"

I let out a beleaguered sigh and rubbed at my temples. "No."

"You need to," Sophia stated. "For our sake if not your own. You've been walking around with resting bitch face the past two days. Everyone's afraid to talk to you. Even Jerry's too scared, and you know that man can't handle any more stress. Poor guy is only one cheeseburger away from a heart attack."

"I haven't been that bad," I groused defensively. The truth was I had been. I'd snapped at anyone and everyone around me. Poor Maury had taken to ducking behind the lobby desk when he saw me coming off the elevators. And I couldn't even bring myself to tease Bob in the mornings.

"Please!" Sophia scoffed. "This morning you threatened the kid at the pastry kiosk in the lobby. You told him you'd throat-punch him if he didn't get more banana nut muffins."

Okay yeah, I did do that. But there was a perfectly good reason. "Banana nut is the most popular breakfast muffin on the face of the Earth! Not keeping enough in stock is just bad business practice. I taught him a very valuable lesson."

"You scared the shit out of him," Daphne chastised in that motherly tone she sometimes liked to adopt with Sophia and me. "We'll be lucky if he doesn't pack up and move to another building. And you better pray he doesn't. That's the only place I can get a halfway decent cheese Danish."

I held my hands out in surrender. Daphne was ravenous when it came to her Danish. "Okay, okay! I'll apologize to him. Jeez."

"And talk to Grayson," Sophia demanded, concern blanketing her expression. "Seriously, Lo, you've never been like this about a guy before. It's obvious you're hurting. Talk to him."

"All right. I'll talk to him this afternoon," I relented on a whisper. Part of me cringed at the thought of putting my pride aside to go talk to Grayson, but another larger part was thankful that my friends had given me the kick in the ass to do what I'd been wanting to do since I'd walked away from him two days before.

I *missed* him. I couldn't remember the last time I'd actually missed a man. I'd lost faith in them so long ago.

"Great!" Daphne clapped her hands and pulled the door open. "Now let's go eat. I'm starving."

She flitted off without a backward glance. As Sophia moved to follow, I called out her name to stop her. "Yeah?" she asked, casting a glance over her shoulder.

"There's something you should know." I pulled in a deep breath, worried how she'd handle the news I had to share. "Dominic's here."

Her normally cheerful face went blank, just like it did any time his name was mentioned. "What do you mean he's here?" she asked in a flat voice, devoid of any emotion.

"I mean he's in Seattle. He surprised me with a visit."

The only indication that she was unsettled was the rapid rise and fall of her chest. "For how long?"

"I don't know." I cringed at my answer, knowing that certainly wasn't what she'd wanted to hear. "I kind of got the impression it would be a while. He's been complaining about needing a break from our dad for a while. I think he might be here for the next few weeks. I'm so sorry."

She forced a smile that didn't come near her pain-filled eyes. "Nothing for you to be sorry for. He's your brother, Lo. I don't expect you to never talk to him again. Just... make sure I don't have to see him. That's all I ask."

"Deal," I promised, crossing my heart and sticking my hand out for an ironclad pinky promise.

"Thanks," she muttered quietly, mustering up her strength and putting on a brave face. "Let's go before Daphne tracks us down. You know how she gets when she's hungry."

"Don't have to tell me twice." I laughed and threw my arm over my friend's shoulder as the two of us made our way out of the conference room. Knowing I would be seeing Grayson in just a few hours caused my stomach to tangle up in knots. But for now, I'd push all that to the back of my mind and take comfort in spending time with my friends.

CHAPTER TWENTY-FIVE

GRAYSON

I'D BEEN in a foul mood for days now, and the annoying knock on my office door did nothing but make it worse. "Fuck off, Caleb," I barked angrily. I clenched my hands into fists, fighting back the urge to yank the door open and punch my best friend in the face. He'd gotten some sick kind of pleasure from pushing my buttons these past two days, and I wasn't in the mood to deal with more of his shit.

The knock came again. I shot from my desk with a growl and stomped to the door, prepared to break his goddamned nose. The bastard had it coming; he was practically asking for it. "I said *fuck off*, Ca—" The words died on my tongue as soon as I pulled the door open and saw it wasn't him. I sucked in a surprised breath. "Fiona? What are you doing here?"

"Bad time?" she asked with a shy, teasing smile on her face.

"I...." I wanted to say yes, it was a bad time... especially considering everything Lola had said about her still having feelings for me. But despite the discomfort at her unexpected arrival, I couldn't bring myself to turn her away. Feelings or not, Fiona was still a friend. She'd been too much a part of my family for most of my life for me to be rude. I gave my head a clearing shake and stepped out of the way. "No, sorry. Come in. It's not a bad time."

She hesitated for a second before finally moving into my office. Closing the door behind her, I walked back to my desk and sat as she took a seat in one of the leather wingback chairs across from me. The sound of Lola's pain-filled voice from Sunday evening filled my head. Guilt began to niggle at me, and I couldn't shake the feeling that having Fiona there was a betrayal. I tugged at my tie awkwardly, feeling unsettled. I cleared my throat and attempted a casual tone as I asked, "So... what brings you by?"

She looked down and began fiddling with the hem of her skirt. "I wanted... what I mean to say... well... I've been meaning to stop by. After how I treated Lola at your parents'... and what happened with the pool...." She closed her eyes for several seconds as her chest rose with a deep inhale. "Is she... is she all right?"

I blew out a steady stream of air as I sat back in my chair. "She's...." I had no idea how to answer that since the damn infuriating woman had refused to talk to me the past two days. "Honestly, I don't know how she is. She's not really speaking to me at the moment."

Fiona's head shot up, her brown eyes wide. "She's not? But... why? Is this because you threw her in the pool?"

I lifted an arm and massaged the center of my forehead with my fingers, trying to ease the tension building in my skull. "Truthfully, Fee... I think it's because of you." I let out a dry, humorless chuckle as I admitted, "She's got it in her head that there's still something going on between me and you, that you might still have feelings for me. It's ridiculous, and I tried telling her, but she's convinced that...." I trailed off when her cheeks got red and a brief flash of sorrow flitted across her face.

"Would it really be so ridiculous?" she whispered, a sad

smile tipping her lips.

My stomach sank to the floor, my words lodging in my throat. I had no idea what to say. For all the confidence I had when it came to running a business, I was shit when it came to letting a woman down gently. It felt like navigating a minefield —one wrong step and everything would explode.

"Fio—"

She lifted her hand and cut me off. "Look, I know it's stupid. I do. Our relationship ended forever ago, but I can't help it. Every time I'm around you, I remember what it was like when we were together. I...." Her eyes grew glassy as tears welled up. Just the sight of them caused panic to clutch my chest. I never did well with women's tears. Hell, no man did. "I miss you. But I know you don't feel that way about me," she finished, twisting a blade of guilt deep into my gut.

"I'm sorry," I offered pathetically, unable to think of anything to say that would offer the slightest bit of comfort.

She sniffled and waved me off with a small watery laugh. "Don't be sorry. I knew deep down that it was never going to happen. I guess it just took me by surprise to see you with someone else." She fisted her hands together in her lap and looked up at me apologetically. "I... I didn't handle it well. I should have been nicer to Lola. She didn't deserve that."

"I don't know what to say." Again, it was pathetic, but I was treading on dangerous ground. And I was a man, so I was inherently terrible with emotional matters. "I'm sorry that you're hurting. You know I care about you. We'll always be friends, Fee. Nothing will ever change that."

"Good. I'm glad about that." Her smile held less sadness than it had earlier. "And I'm sorry for coming between you and Lola. If there's anything I can do... maybe I could talk to her? Apologize in person and try to explain? I really did like her. She seemed sweet."

"She is sweet," I chuckled, "when she's not busting my balls."

"You need someone like that," Fiona laughed wistfully. "I think that's why it would have never worked out between us. You're the type of guy who needs a woman who can keep up with him."

A lance of hot, sharp pain sliced through my heart as I thought about Lola. "When I'm with her, I feel like I'm the one trying to keep up." The words came out soft, as though I'd spoken them more for myself.

"You really care about her, don't you?"

"I do," I answered with blatant honesty. "Having her freeze me out is fucking killing me."

"Well," she said, coming to a stand. "I'm sure, between the two of us, we can figure out how you can win her back. Why don't we go out for lunch? You can tell me all about Lola and we'll come up with a plan to thaw her out."

I quirked a skeptical brow as I looked up at her. "You sure that's a good idea? I mean, after everything you said—"

"Grayson," she stopped me with a direct tone. "I might have feelings for you, but I'll get over them. You're still my friend. I want you to be happy, and if she's the one who can do that I'll help any way I can." She held her hands out, her features containing genuine honesty. "No ulterior motives, I swear. This is simply two friends having lunch."

"You're on." I stood from my chair and rounded my desk, hopeful for the first time in two days. Maybe Fiona would help me come up with a plan that would get me out of this miserable limbo I'd been stuck in.

I'd gotten a taste of Lola's sinful, fiery sweetness and I wasn't ready to give it up. I wasn't sure if I'd ever be ready. I needed to get her back.

CHAPTER TWENTY-SIX

LOLA

I LET out a dejected sigh as the elevator dinged and the doors slid open to my floor. Lunch with my girls had pumped me up for my impending talk with Grayson, but when I made it to his office and was informed by his assistant that he was out at meetings for the rest of the day, that burgeoning hope fell flat like a week-old balloon.

I just wanted to be alone, put on my "I hate everything" playlist—the one I typically designated for that time of the month—open a bottle of wine, and lie in a hot bath until parts of my body turned pruny. Unfortunately, it looked like I wasn't going to get what I wanted, because the second I pushed through my front door, Dominic was on me in that overbearing, concerned, big-brother way.

"Shit, shorty. Are you okay? I've been worried sick waiting for you to get home. Christ, I'm so sorry."

He pulled me into a hug so tight it was uncomfortable. "Dom," I wheezed with my arms pinned to my sides. "Can't... breathe...."

"Sorry." He quickly let me go but kept hold of my upper arms as he pushed me back and studied my face with a frown marring his own. "You don't look upset. Why don't you look upset?"

"What are you talking about? What's going on? Are you high right now?" I shot up on my tiptoes and peered into his eyes, looking for signs that he was under the influence of something.

"Will you stop?" Dom smacked my hand away from his face when I tried to pull his eyelids open to get a better look. "For fuck's sake. I'm not high, Lo. I'm just worried about you."

My face pinched in confusion as I rested back on my heels. "Why would I be upset?"

I watched, no less befuddled, as realization dawned across his face. "Fuck," he hissed. "You don't know."

"Don't know what?" I asked, my skin prickling with apprehension. "Don't know what, Dominic?" I repeated at a near shout when he didn't answer.

He let out a string of curses while pulling his phone from the back pocket of his jeans. "Here, look at this. A buddy of mine texted it to me about an hour ago."

I snatched the phone from his hand, the breath stolen from my lungs by the picture on the screen. The edges of my vision began to grow fuzzy as a black curtain of pain and fury enveloped me. Then I exploded.

"That mother*fucker*!" I reared back, ready to send Dom's cell phone flying, only to have him thwart my efforts by grabbing my wrist and taking the phone away from me. I needed to break something; that was the only possible thing that could make me feel better. "Give that back, I want to smash it."

"You want to smash something, smash your own phone. I just got this, and I'm not letting you break it because you're pissed."

I huffed indignantly, dropped my purse onto the table by the front door, kicked off my heels, and stomped toward the kitchen. Once I had a full glass of wine in my hand, I began to pace, feeding that rage spiraling around inside of me by picturing the photo collage on my brother's phone in my mind.

A photo collage of Grayson and Fiona hugging and laughing and holding each other's hands while leaning in to each other like they were sharing a secret just between the two of them.

Assholes!

"Shorty—"

"Nothing between them my ass!" I shouted, interrupting my brother. "That lying sonofabitch! He looked me *right in the eye* and told me he didn't have feelings for her! He even had his *assistant* lie to me. She told me he had afternoon meetings."

"Well...," he dragged out. "Maybe—"

I shoved a warning finger in my brother's face. "Don't you dare try and defend him! You thought the exact same as me when you saw that picture. That's why you were so concerned about me. Don't bother denying it."

He held his hands up in acquiescence. "Okay, you're right. I thought the same thing. Those pictures are pretty fucking damning."

"Yeah," I scoffed. "And so is the headline speculating Grayson Lockhart, America's Favorite Bachelor, has thrown over his latest piece of ass for an old flame."

"The article didn't actually refer to you as 'his latest piece of ass.'"

I shot Dominic a killing look and continued pacing. "It called me his latest *fling*. That's not any better, Dom. Just because it wasn't actually typed out doesn't mean that's not what people are thinking. Not only is he a lying, cheating bastard, but he's made me look like an idiot!" I sucked back the entire contents of my glass and moved to refill it. I needed to fuel my anger, hold it tightly, or I ran the risk of being sucked down in a tidal wave of pain. And allowing myself to be hurt by another man in my life just wasn't an option.

But God, it was hard not to succumb to the ache that was filling my chest. Those pictures... the way he was smiling at her. It hurt worse than anything I'd ever experienced, not just because of his betrayal but because of the humiliation he'd subjected me to.

"He's an asshole, shorty," Dominic said, placing his hands on my shoulders to stop my agitated pacing. "He doesn't deserve you."

"I feel so stupid," I whispered, blinking furiously to fight back the tears that were clouding my vision.

Dom took the glass from my hand and placed it on the kitchen counter before wrapping me in his arms. I snuggled into his embrace, letting him take my weight since standing on my own had suddenly become too hard.

He ran a soothing hand over my head and said, "There's nothing for you to feel stupid about. He's the cheating bastard, little sis. He's the one who should feel like an idiot, because no fucking way he'll ever get anyone better than you."

I sniffled and looked up at my big brother, his face wavy thanks to my watery eyes. "I'm glad you're here," I told him softly.

"Me too, shorty." He tucked my hair behind my ear and grinned down at me. "Do you want me to go kick his ass? Because I'll totally do that for you."

I snorted out a laugh and batted at the lone tear that broke free and trailed down my cheek. "Nah. It's a good suggestion, but I'd rather not have to bail you out of jail. I've been saving up for a pair of Jimmy Choos I saw online."

"Okay. But you change your mind, you just let me know."

"Thanks. I will."

With his hands on my shoulders, Dom spun me around and

gave me a gentle shove out of the kitchen. "You go get a shower and I'll make us some dinner. Sound like a plan?"

"Sounds perfect." I started for my bedroom, thinking about how grateful I was to have my brother with me since, as it turned out, I didn't want to be alone after all.

GRAYSON

I LET out a furious curse and threw my phone into the passenger seat as I navigated through the downtown traffic. Lola wasn't answering her goddamned phone, and as I got closer to her building, the anxiety squeezing my chest only grew tighter.

During our lunch, Fiona had helped me plan out the perfect apology, and I was eager to track Lola down and make things right. When I'd gotten back to the office a half hour ago and my assistant informed me that Lola had come by looking for me, I'd thought things were finally starting to look up. That was until Caleb stopped by to show me the latest article written about me on the gossip sites.

Has Grayson Lockhart, America's Favorite Bachelor, thrown over his latest fling for an old flame?

I had no clue who took those pictures of me and Fiona having lunch, but the suggestive angle and the damning headline made it look like something it wasn't. I was going to find the fucker who printed that story and rip his goddamned head off.

But first I had to get to Lola and tell her the truth before she blew everything out of proportion.

I slammed on the brakes and my car skidded to a halt on the rain-slick concrete outside of her apartment building. I left the car running and shoved the door open, startling the poor, unsuspecting valet as I took the stairs into the building two at a time.

"Mr. Lockhart," Lola's doorman sputtered in surprise when I pushed through the glass doors and headed straight for the elevator. "Good evening. Is Ms. Abbatelli expecting you?"

"She is, Maury," I continued, not breaking stride as the lie slipped easily off my tongue.

"O-oh. Okay then," he stuttered as I frantically jabbed at the Up button, willing the elevator to come. I jumped in as soon as the doors opened and pressed the button for her floor. My anxiety-riddled body refused to stop, even in the close confines of the lift, so I paced from side to side until the *ding* alerted me that I'd reached my destination.

I sprinted down the hall and began pounding on her front door like a madman until it finally opened. And the sight that greeted me from across the threshold made my blood run cold.

"Who the fuck are you?" I ground out, clenching my hands into fists so tight my fingernails cut into the skin of my palms. It was either that or tackle the motherfucker who'd just answered Lola's door to the ground and beat him senseless.

The unknown man crossed his arms over his puffed-out chest and scowled. "You've got a lot of fucking nerve showing up here. I suggest you leave before I mess up that pretty face of yours."

I clenched my jaw so tight a sharp pain shot through it. "You could try," I hissed menacingly. I didn't know who this guy was or what the fuck he was doing in Lola's apartment, but I was hoping he'd make the first move so I could happily break every bone in his face. I'd been itching for a fight for days. I needed something, some*one*, to take out all the aggression and anger I'd had pent-up since Lola walked away from me.

"You're a cocky fuck, aren't you?" he chuckled humorlessly. "I can see why she was initially drawn to you."

That comment gave me pause, but only for a moment. "Since you seem to know who I am, maybe you wouldn't mind telling me who the hell you are and why you're in my girlfriend's apartment?"

"*Girlfriend?*" His head dropped back with a roar of laughter. "I don't think so, buddy."

I took a threatening step closer to him. "Listen, you son of a—"

"What's going on?"

I jerked to a stop at the sound of Lola's voice, and the both of us turned in the direction of her voice. At the sight of her in nothing but a thin, flimsy robe with her hair wet from a recent shower, I lost my mind.

"Mother*fucker!*" I growled and then lunged, burying my fist in the asshole's face.

I had to hand it to the guy—he rebounded quickly, landing a jab to my stomach. I vaguely heard Lola yelling at us to stop through the blood pounding in my ears, as the unknown bastard and I continued to fight, taking each other down to the ground.

"God*damn it!*" I snarled in pain when he slammed his elbow into my ribs. I returned with a solid shot to his kidneys, temporarily gaining the upper hand so I could roll the asshole off me.

"You..." *Punch.* "Better..." *Punch.* "Not..." *Punch.* "Have fucking..." *Punch.* "Touched her!"

The sound of a deafening air horn forced us to stop fighting and cover our ears. When I looked up, Lola was standing there, fury painted across her face, with a goddamned air canister in her hand.

"What the fuck, Lola?" the guy gritted out as we both struggled to our feet. "Where the fuck did you get that?"

She shot him a murderous glare while answering, "Mom bought it for me when I went off to college. She thought it would deter rapists."

Wait....

The guy put his fingers to his rapidly swelling cheekbone and winced. "Leave it to Mom to overreact."

"Well it turned out to be pretty handy, didn't it?" she snapped, putting her hands on her hips.

"Wait a second. Your mom...?" I interrupted, looking at the guy. He looked just as bad off as I felt, but as I studied him closer—beneath the swelling—I began to note the obvious similarities to him and Lola.

"This is my brother, asshole!" Lola spit. "Who the hell did you think he was?"

Well shit.

"SHIT," I hissed. Her brother? Well that was just fucking perfect.

"Dominic Abbatelli." He held out his hand. The bizarreness of the situation wasn't lost on me as we quickly shook hands. "Nice to meet you. You've got a pretty decent right hook for a pretty boy."

"Jesus Christ." I lifted my hand to rake it through my hair but thought better of it when the motion sent a stab of pain through my sore ribs.

"What are you doing here?" Lola asked, the venom in her voice drawing my attention back to her.

"I needed to talk to you," I answered quickly.

The sarcastic nature of her laugh, and the fact that it was completely devoid of all humor, twisted my stomach into knots. "And you thought attacking my brother would be a good way of getting my attention? Are you kidding me?"

"I didn't know he was your brother! I thought—"

"What?" she cut in. "You thought what? That I was hooking up with someone else? Wow, talk about being a hypocrite, Grayson. I'm not the cheater here. That would be you."

"Lola, please." I took a step toward her, and at her retreat, Dominic's hand came up to stop me.

"Close enough, my friend. I'm pretty sure my sister doesn't want you anywhere near her right now."

"Look, those pictures... they aren't what you think. I swear." I pleaded with my words as my eyes implored her to see the truth. There was no one else but her. "We were just having a friendly lunch, that's it."

There wasn't a trace of emotion in her voice as she said, "That's not what it looked like to me."

"That's all it was! We talked about you the whole time!"

Her hard facade cracked just then and I caught a glimpse of pain in her eyes. Her brother's hand was unrelenting as I pushed at it, desperate to get to her and hold her and make it better somehow.

"Was that before or after you shoved your tongue down her throat?" she asked acerbically.

"*Fuck!*" I shouted, the pain in my body no longer a concern as I raked my hands through my hair. "That isn't what happened! Lola... fuck, baby, you have to believe me. She wanted to apologize for how she acted. She felt bad for being a bitch and came to make it right."

She crossed her arms over her stomach like she was trying to hold herself up. "Funny how she comes to *you* to apologize for treating *me* poorly."

"It's the truth, I swear."

For three seconds—three lousy seconds—I thought I'd finally busted through that goddamned wall of hers. Lola's eyes flashed with something that gave me hope, and she pulled that full bottom lip of hers between her teeth and bit down.

Then it was all gone. My lungs deflated as those shutters slammed down and her face blanked. "I don't believe you."

That was it. Four words and suddenly my chest felt like it was full of cement.

"Lola—"

"No!" She stepped back, holding herself even tighter as wet hit her eyes, slicing me open. "No. I've allowed too many men in my life to make a fool of me, and I'm not doing it again. Never again. It's time for you to leave."

My jaw ticked as the sound of my pulse thrummed in my ears violently. "I'm not—"

"You need to go," Dominic interrupted, stepping in front of me and blocking my vision of the only woman I wanted.

Christ, how had things gotten so messed up?

I wanted to argue with him, fight again until she was finally forced to hear me, *believe* me. But the look on his face had me swallowing back all my instincts. His expression was one of sympathy mixed with determination. I knew he felt for me, but he also had to take his sister's back.

I let out a ragged breath, hating the fact that I was, once again, letting her get away. But I told myself it wasn't going to be for long. I'd eventually get her back. I just had to give her time.

"We're not finished," I said, my voice jagged and raw. "This isn't over."

"You're wrong," she said on a broken whisper. Then she turned and disappeared down the hall. But not before I saw two tears break free and spill down her cheeks. Walking away from her just then was the hardest fucking thing I'd ever done, but for her peace of mind, it had to be done.

I gave Dominic an abrupt nod and headed for the door, telling myself that this was only temporary, that I'd eventually get her back.

It was the only way I could put one foot in front of the other.

CHAPTER TWENTY-EIGHT

LOLA

A WEEK HAD PASSED since I kicked Grayson out of my apartment, and I'd spent the next several days acting like he didn't exist. I still felt like shit on the inside, but I was determined not to let it show. I pasted a smile on my face and acted as if everything was right in the world of Lola Abbatelli. It was all for show: teasing with Bob as I headed through the lobby each morning, having lunch with my girls like I always did, offering advice to our lovelorn callers as though my own love life wasn't an abysmal joke. But if there was one thing I was good at, it was pretending.

I pretended that the stares from everyone on my floor were all in my imagination, like they weren't all whispering and speculating about what went down between Grayson and me. I pretended that I wasn't missing him every single second of each passing day. I deserved a freaking Academy Award for the performance I was putting on.

Or so I thought.

Apparently, I hadn't been holding it together as well as I thought if the looks Sophia and Daphne were shooting me from across the studio were anything to go by. It was like they were on tenterhooks, just waiting for me to explode as the caller on the line droned on and on about her lying, cheating scum of a boyfriend. Truthfully, she hadn't actually said he was cheating, but I was intuitive like that. I could just tell. And no, it didn't have anything to do with my own lying, cheating scum of a fake boyfriend that made me think that way. I wasn't jaded at all.

At all.

I was merely observant.

Ignoring their concerned stares, I leaned back in my swivel chair and squeezed the hell out of the stress ball in my hands as the caller prattled on about how much she loved her loser boyfriend and didn't want to break up with him. It took everything in me to suppress the desire to roll my eyes.

"Well, Carla, from everything you just told us, I believe the only way for you to know for sure is to come right out and ask him." Dear, sweet Daphne, always the calm, collected voice of reason.

I kind of hated her in that moment.

"You really think so?" Carla asked.

Daphne opened her mouth to respond but I cut her off. I couldn't listen idly by while she led the poor girl down a path of heartbreak.

"Actually, Carla, while I typically agree with my co-hosts on most everything, I have to speak up on this. I think you'd be better off kicking this jerk's ass to the curb."

"Wh-what?" Carla stuttered.

"What are you doing?" Sophia hissed, covering her mic with her hand and shooting lasers from her eyes.

"Yeah," I pressed on. I was on a roll. If my two best friends couldn't speak the truth, then I would. It was up to me to save poor Carla from herself. "Cut your losses and get the hell out of there. It's for the best, trust me. Just because he hasn't cheated with this 'friend' of his yet doesn't mean he isn't going to." I used finger quotes on the word "friend" because it was bullshit. Men and women were never just friends.

"B-b-but—"

"It's a scientific fact that men and women can't be strictly friends—"

"No, it's not," Daphne chimed in. "There's literally no science about that at all."

"Well there should be," I continued, ignoring her and Sophia as they glared furiously. "There are only two categories a man and woman can fall into. They're either *having* sex, or are *about* to have sex. From what you've said, your boyfriend and this friend he *supposedly* grew up with fall into the second category. It's only a matter of time before they're bumping uglies in the bathroom of a diner while you sit at the table, unsuspectingly sipping on your cappuccino, thinking your life is perfect, only to be stuck with the check because they were taking too long and you got tired of waiting so you stupidly paid for both their meals."

"That's... uh... that's very specific," Carla muttered through the line.

"Yeah, it is. And I'm telling you now, don't be that girl. Don't be the idiot who pays for those two assholes to eat. You're better than that, Carla."

The end of my rant was met with total silence from Carla for several seconds as my co-hosts looked on, their jaws hanging open in shock. Finally, Caller Carla began to sputter, "I... this is... I can't... uh... I'm just... I think I'm... I have to go."

The line dropped before anyone could say a word, and a bewildered Jerry knocked on the glass to give us the signal to wrap things up.

Sophia went about closing the show, and I took that as my opportunity to bail out of the studio. Unfortunately, Daphne ran out after me, calling my name.

"What on earth was that?" she yelped, catching my arm and pulling me to a stop.

"What are you talking about? I was just giving the caller advice like always."

Her eyes bugged out. "Sweetheart, that wasn't advice. That was a freaking train wreck. I think it's safe to say you've officially gone off the deep end."

I let out an indelicate snort and waved her off. "I'm totally fine. Never been better. All good here."

Her hand on my elbow slid down and she grabbed my hand, giving it a squeeze. "You're not, honey. Sophia and I have given you space to try and work it out on your own, but you're spiraling. We're here for you, Lola, whenever you decide to talk to us. But in the meantime, I think I have something that'll cheer you up."

She smiled brightly and, using her hold on my hand, began pulling me down the hall in a different direction from my desk.

"What's going on? I asked. "Where are we going?"

I followed after her as she practically skipped through the corridors before coming to a stop in front of a door with our names on the front of it. Daphne threw the door open with a flourish with an excited "*Ta da*! It's our new office! They moved us in here during the show!"

"Isn't this the shit?" Sophia chirped from her place behind her new desk. "Now we don't have to whisper when we want to talk shit about our coworkers!"

The room was bigger than Sam's office. It had been utilized as a small conference space for as long as I'd worked at KTSW, so three desks and all our personal effects fit inside with plenty of room to spare.

"Who did this?" I asked as I set my purse on my desk where all my Harry Potter memorabilia had been neatly organized for me.

"The call came from the big man downstairs." The three of us looked to where Sam was standing in the doorway, leaning against the frame with a cup of coffee in his hand and a smirk on his face.

"Why would he do that?" I asked. "None of the other program hosts have their own offices."

Sam's smirk widened as he slid his eyes in my direction. "Who knew pretending to bang the owner's son would get you an office instead of a cubicle? You should have posed as his arm candy a long time ago."

Red coated my vision as I narrowed my eyes into angry slits. I normally would've brushed off what was most likely meant to be a harmless comment, but my life had been one long, terrifying roller-coaster ride for the past month—one with all the drops that made it feel like your stomach was lodged in your throat and you were seconds from pissing your pants. So instead of ignoring him, I took personal offense. All it took was that one comment to make me lose the tenuous hold on my sanity that I'd been clinging to.

And just like that, I snapped.

———

"THIS FEELS LIKE DÉJÀ VU," Daphne murmured from the corner of her mouth as Grayson, Nolan, and the Human Resources director took their seats.

It was the following morning after I'd temporarily lost my mind, and I found myself sitting at the all-too-familiar conference room table with my best friends on either side of me as I glared at the man across from me. The only silver lining I could think to put on the shit-show that had become my life was the fact that Sam looked like hell. His nose was clearly broken, and two angry purple bruises sat underneath his eyes. I had to find the positive in the situation, because there was no freaking way I was keeping my job after *this*.

A small, sinister smile pulled at my lips at the sight of those shiners. *Serves you right, bastard,* I thought as Stephanie from HR cleared her throat. "Lola," she said on a beleaguered sigh. "You can't go around punching people in the face."

"He deserved it." It certainly wasn't the most mature response, but sometimes adulating was just too hard. I scowled at Sam, trying my best to melt his stupid face off with my eyes; anything to keep from looking at the man at the head of the table who made my stomach flutter and my heart race.

"Unfortunately, 'he deserved it' isn't an argument that's going to help your case. Violence in the workplace is strictly prohibited. It's a breach of contract and grounds for immediate termination."

"That's bullshit!" Sophia shouted.

"But he started it!" Daphne cried.

"Now just wait a minute," Nolan said over everyone else. "We don't have the full story. Let's not be hasty."

"*Hasty!*" Sam spit. "She punched me in the face and broke my goddamned nose!"

I placed my palms on the table and leaned in, reveling in the way he flinched back from me in fear. "I wouldn't have punched you if you hadn't accused me of being Grayson's whore," I gritted out through clenched teeth.

"The hell?" Grayson said, speaking for the first time since he sat down.

"I said no such thing!" Sam objected vehemently.

Sophia's voice was deadpan as she replied, "Well, you certainly alluded to it."

"You called her a whore?"

The fury laced through Grayson's words was too big a draw to ignore. I had no choice but to finally look at him, and what I saw was a man just moments away from re-breaking the nose Sam's doctor had worked to reset.

"I didn't!" Sam replied, shooting nervous eyes around the table's occupants. "I swear!"

"Really?" Daphne asked with sarcastic politeness. "Then what *exactly* did you mean when you said, and I quote, 'Who knew pretending to bang the owner's son would get you an office instead of a cubicle?' Sure sounded like you were calling her a whore to me."

"I-i-it... but... it was a joke!" Sam sputtered as Grayson's face started to turn a concerning shade of red.

From the corner of my eye, I saw Nolan place a staying hand on Grayson's shoulder, preventing his son from leaping over the table and attacking Sam.

"That could be construed as sexual harassment," Stephanie stated. "That is *also* a breach of contract, and grounds for immediate termination."

"Jesus Christ," Nolan muttered, closing his eyes and rubbing at his temples for several seconds. He finally lowered his hands and asked Stephanie, "Could you give us a minute, please?"

A look of relief flitted across her face as she snapped her notebook closed and scuttled from the room.

Nolan's scowl returned to Sam and me once the door closed behind Stephanie's retreating form. "I feel like I'm dealing with teenagers all over again," he scolded, and I couldn't help but feel guilty for my part in the immature actions that had transpired.

"Look, this is ridiculous," he continued. You two have worked together for ten years without a single problem. There has to be a way we can reconcile this situation without losing two of our most important employees. If you can apologize to each other, we can put this behind us, and I'd be willing to look the other way, just this once."

Neither Sam nor I said a word as we stared, waiting for the other to break first.

"Fine," Nolan sighed in frustration. "Looks like I have no other choice."

Panic made my belly clench—or maybe it was the pointy elbow Sophia shoved into my side that did it—but as he began to stand from his seat, I found my mouth dropping open and the apology pouring out. "I'm sorry I punched you in the face," I blurted, my eyes shooting to Sam.

A feeling of contrition washed over me. He really wasn't a bad guy. Nolan had been right; we'd worked amicably for ten years, and there were some days I actually thought of him as a friend—when he wasn't being a douche boss. Things really had gotten out of hand and it was time to put them right. "I shouldn't have hit you, and I'm sorry." I chanced a glance at Grayson from the corner of my eye as I continued. "I've been having a bad couple of weeks and I took my anger out on you. For that, I apologize."

"You're forgiven," he replied with a defiant tilt of his chin. I kicked him in the shin under the table, causing him to grunt before rolling his eyes in defeat. "And I'm sorry too. I honestly didn't mean any offense with what I said, but I see now it was a joke made in poor taste. I apologize."

"See?" Daphne chirped with a tad too much exuberance. "That wasn't so hard. Now we can all pretend none of this ever happened."

"Good." Nolan released a relieved breath and stood up. "I'm glad that's settled." He turned to me with what looked like parental concern. "Now Lola. I know you've been under a great deal of stress recently—"

"*Pfft.*" I crossed my arms over my chest indignantly. "That's an understatement. If it wasn't for this stupid PR stunt, I'd be just fine."

Nolan pushed on like I hadn't spoken. "So I think it would be best if you took the rest of the week off. Take some time for yourself and just decompress."

My back shot straight and my eyes grew huge. "I don't need any time off! I'm perfectly fine!" My job had been my life for ten years. It was the only thing I had to keep me even the slightest bit sane.

"You're a disaster, Lola," he continued, his words harsh but his tone sympathetic. "You punched your superior in the face, for Christ's sake. You're lucky there aren't greater consequences. This is nonnegotiable. You'll take the next three days off or I'm calling Stephanie back in here. Is that understood?"

I fell back in my seat with a pout and mumbled a few choice curse words under my breath before finally relenting. "Yeah, whatever."

"Good," he sighed. "Now, if you'll excuse me, I have grownup work to do." Everyone followed suit and began filing out of the conference room.

I was just two feet from the door when a strong hand gripped me by the elbow and stopped me in place. The door was kicked shut and my back hit the cold wooden surface before I could utter a word in protest. The way he pinned me against the door prevented anyone outside the room from seeing us through the wall of windows, so there was no chance of me waving anyone down for help.

"We need to talk," Grayson rasped, his low voice so close to my ear it caused a shiver to trickle across my skin.

"There's nothing to talk about." I tried to jerk my arm from his hold but his fingers tightened, refusing to release me.

"That's bullshit. You've avoided me for a week and a half, and I'm fucking sick of it. We're clearing this shit up. *Now.*"

I told myself that the way his green eyes flashed with determination didn't make my body hot, but it was a total lie. Every nerve ending in my body prickled with awareness at his touch, even as my eyes shot lasers at his stupid, handsome face. "As far as I'm concerned, everything between us was cleared up the moment those pictures of you and Fiona were posted online."

A masculine growl rumbled from his chest, making my lady parts quiver. "I already told you that wasn't what you thought it was."

"And I already told you I don't care what excuses you make. I know *exactly* what I saw."

His face inched closer to mine as he ground out, "Nothing. *Happened.*"

"I. Don't. *Believe. You,*" I returned.

His fingers clenched around my arm spasmodically before he finally released me and took a step back. My body instantly missed his touch and ached to move closer to him, but I wouldn't allow it. "So that's it?" he asked bitterly. "You're done, just like that?"

"Pretty much." I shrugged, feigning a casual tone even though a little piece of my heart splintered. "For Christ's sake, Grayson, it was sex. Just move on already. You're making a bigger deal out of what happened between us than is necessary."

His nostrils flared slightly and his jaw ticked angrily. "Is that right?"

God, I wanted to touch him, but instead of caving to baser instincts, I kept up the act. "Yep."

As soon as that one lone syllable slipped from my mouth, he pounced, taking me completely by surprise. His lips crashed against mine in a brutal, claiming kiss. My startled gasp was all the invitation he needed. He dominated the kiss from the very start, demanding and taking with each delicious thrust of his tongue.

And just like that, I was lost. All my reserve vanished and I clung to him, willingly ceding all control as his mouth fed from mine. His guttural groan rumbled through his chest and into mine as our hands grabbed and squeezed and ran over every inch of each other, desperate to touch everywhere we could reach. It wasn't enough. It would never be enough. And I knew he felt the same when his hand skated up the inside of my thigh, beneath my skirt, not stopping until he reached the barrier of my soaked panties.

"Christ, Lola," he grunted as a moan escaped my throat.

My head fell back, thumping against the door, and I gasped as he toyed with me through the scrap of lace. "Gray," I panted, grinding my hips into his hands, wanting more, *needing* more.

He trailed open-mouth kisses down the column of my neck and back up, nipping the sensitive skin of my earlobe. "You know," he whispered into my ear as his fingers continued their teasing ministrations, "I knew you were a coward, but I never took you for a liar."

What?

His words yanked me back into reality as he removed his hand from between my legs and took two big steps back. My body trembled with unexpected coldness as his callous words finally penetrated my lust-addled brain.

"I'm not a coward," I snapped, my breath still uneven from everything he'd just put me through.

"You are, Lola. You're so goddamned scared of what you feel for me that you've barricaded yourself behind those fucking walls of yours. Tell me, does it ever get lonely in there?"

That asshole!

"I'm not a coward!" I shouted. "And I'm not the liar here. *You* are!" I jabbed my finger into his rock-hard chest, indignation having snuffed out all the lingering passion I'd felt just moments ago.

"Keep telling yourself that if it helps you sleep better at night."

Planting my hands on my hips, I tipped my chin up and looked down my nose at his as best I could, seeing as the damn man towered over me. "I will... and it does."

He shrugged, seemingly unaffected by everything that had just transpired, which only made me even more furious. "Then I guess you're right," he said drolly, shoving his hands into the pockets of his slacks. "There's really nothing to talk about."

It appeared that I'd won the battle, but if that were truly the case, why did I feel like suddenly crying?

"Guess there's not," I replied, shocked that I was able to pull off sounding so calm and collected when I felt like everything inside of me was being torn to shreds. This was really it. We were well and truly over.

Oh man, that hurts!

I scuttled away from the door as he moved close, reaching for the knob and pulling it open. I needed him to hurry up and leave already so I could run to the ladies' room, lock myself in a stall, and have a good, long cry. But before he disappeared, he glanced back over his shoulder and said one last thing.

"But I should remind you, our little PR charade is far from over."

My back snapped straight, my eyes wide as my gaze shot to him. "Excuse me?"

"You didn't think I'd let you off the hook that easily, did you? As far as the media and everyone else are concerned, you're still very much my girlfriend. I suggest you work on your game face before the gala this weekend. You'll be attending as my date."

Gala? Date? What the ever-loving hell?

The *click* of the door closing behind him echoed as loudly as a gunshot in my head as remembrance dawned. I'd allowed myself to become so carelessly consumed with all things Grayson over the past month that I'd let the most important event of the year slip my mind.

The charity gala at the Seattle Art Museum was one that Bandwidth hosted every year to raise donations for the Wave Foundation. How could I have forgotten? The station had been running commercials advertising it for the past two months.

As hosts of the highest-rated radio show geared toward women, Sophia, Daphne, and I had made it a point to raise as much awareness as possible for the nonprofit that fought to end domestic violence.

The fact that such an important event had slipped my mind just spoke to the tumult that was invading my life.

Each year the three of us held a special event during the gala to increase donations. And this year....

"*Fuck*," I hissed. This year we'd agreed to offer ourselves up for a bachelorette auction, promising the highest bidders a personal one-on-one date.

And I was being forced to go with Grayson... as his date... surrounded by the richest, most established people in Washington.

Could my life possibly get any worse?

CHAPTER TWENTY-NINE

LOLA

YEP. My life could most definitely get worse.

I'd obviously done something to Karma during my thirty-two years of life, because that bitch was currently punishing me. After leaving KTSW on the threat of getting security involved if I didn't go peacefully, I'd gone back to my apartment to start my forced vacation time, only to discover that I had *another* visitor.

I'd opened my front door to the shriek of *"My baby!"* and barely managed to swallow my groan before my mother came charging into the entryway and nearly crushed my ribs in a hug.

"Ma," I wheezed, all the air being squeezed from my lungs as she tightened her embrace. "Need... air...."

She finally unlocked her arms, leaning back to hold me at arm's length so she could study my face. I pasted a fake smile on my face only to have hers crumble in sadness. "Oh, my sweet pea. You look absolutely *awful.*"

My smile fell flat. "Thanks," I deadpanned, dropping my purse on the entry table and kicking off my heels, bringing my mother and me eye to eye. "Just what I needed to hear."

"Oh, you know what I mean." She waved me off and yanked at my arm, leading me toward the living room. "I just meant you look sad. But I'm here now, so no worries. A mother knows how to make everything better."

My brother—the traitor—sat on my sofa, flipping through my TV channels while trying his best to keep from laughing at my plight.

"Speaking of you being here," I stated as she headed for the kitchen and began puttering around. I'd only been gone for five hours max, yet my entire apartment already smelled like an Italian restaurant. "*Why* exactly is that? I thought you weren't coming until Saturday."

She pulled the lid off a Crock-Pot and gave the contents a stir with a large wooden spoon before placing it back down and wiping her hands on a tea towel. As far as I knew, I didn't even *own* a Crock-Pot... or tea towels... or a wooden mixing spoon.

What the...?

I glanced around the kitchen to find several new cooking instruments scattered around the counter tops—instruments I'd never be able to use, seeing as I didn't have the first clue how to cook.

"And where the hell did all this stuff come from?"

"Oh, that sweet man who works in the lobby was kind enough to run out and get me a few necessities when I discovered how lacking your kitchen was. Such a polite gentleman, that one. You know, maybe you should consider dating him!"

My opened and closed several times. "You mean *Maury*? Mom! He's the doorman, not your personal errand boy. And he's at least twenty years older than me!"

"And so complimentary," she continued as if she didn't hear me, a wistful look floating over her face. "A man like that would know how to treat a lady."

Oh, sweet Christ. I didn't even want to think about what that look on her face meant. It was taking everything in me not to gag.

"I'm going to pretend I didn't hear a word you just said and ask again, why are you here four days early?"

"Well, sweetie, when your brother called and told me everything that was happening with that *dreadful* Grayson Lockhart, I knew you needed me, so I changed my flight and got in about two hours ago."

I glanced over my shoulder at Dominic and mouthed, "I'm going to kill you," while dragging my index finger across my neck to show him I was serious. His throat bobbed with a thick, scared swallow before he diverted his gaze back to the TV.

I turned back to my mother, trying to adopt a calm demeanor even though that was mostly impossible where she was concerned. "Ma, you really didn't need to do that. I'm fine."

"Oh please," she scoffed, still puttering around my kitchen like she owned the place. "I'm a mother. I know when my baby girl needs me."

My eyes rolled to the ceiling and I shot up a prayer for patience. That or a *lot* of wine. I was going to need both if I was going to make it through a week *and four days* with my mother under the same roof. She was the boss under whatever roof hung above her head, always had been. Case in point, she'd only been there two hours and already she'd taken control of my kitchen *and* my poor doorman. I was going to owe Maury huge come Christmastime.

I reached for the bottle of wine I'd uncorked the evening before and pulled down a wineglass. "Well, you do... whatever it is you're doing. I'm going to go relax with Dom."

My mother turned to see me pouring a glass and gave my knuckles a warning smack. "Lola Arianna Abbatelli, it's barely noon! You will not start drinking so early in the day. It's undignified."

"A pleasure as always," I muttered dryly, then made my way into the living room, smacking my brother on the back of the head before sitting down next to him. "You asshole," I hissed. "Couldn't give a girl a warning?"

"Hey." He held his hands up in surrender. "I sent you a text forty-five minutes ago. You never responded. And I didn't want to warn you until Ma had the chance to finish preparing the *pasta fagiolo*. You know how much I love that stuff." He rubbed his stomach for emphasis.

My forehead wrinkled as I mumbled, "I never got a text."

Dom shrugged, then lifted the beer bottle in his hand to his lips and took a long pull.

"Ma!" I shouted in the direction of the kitchen. "Why does Dom get to drink but I don't!"

Dom smirked at me, earning another smack on the head as my mom yelled back, "Don't argue with me, Lola Arianna. I'm teaching you to act like a lady!"

"Mom loves me more," he whispered under his breath, smirking once more. I stole the beer from him and downed the rest, then gave him a smirk of my own. No matter how old we got, my brother and I always reverted back to adolescent behavior when we were around each other. It was kind of fun... when he wasn't annoying the shit out of me.

"Why are you home so early?" he asked a few minutes later after returning from the kitchen with a new beer.

I let out a weary sigh and dropped my head to the back of the couch. "They're making me take the rest of the week off, said I needed to de-stress."

"Why? What happened?"

I stayed in the same position, refusing to meet his concerned eyes as I replied, "I punched my boss in the face yesterday and broke his nose."

"You *what*?"

My head shot up and I slapped my hand over his mouth.

"Shh! Don't let Mom hear you," I hissed. "She'll never let me live it down."

Dom regarded me with wide eyes and gave his head a shake. "Holy shit, shorty. You broke your boss's nose?"

"In my defense—"

"You can't start a sentence like that and think it excuses you from anything."

I reached out and gave the skin on the back of his arm a hard pinch, relishing in his grunt of pain before continuing. "*In my defense...* he deserved it. Only reason I didn't get fired is because we were both in the wrong. I walked away with a slap on the wrist and three days' mandatory vacation."

"Could've been worse," Dom grumbled, rubbing at his sore arm. "Christ, maybe they were right. Maybe you do need some time to de-stress.

"That's exactly what I *don't* need," I whined. "I need to keep busy or I'm just going to think about... stuff. Now I've got nothing to keep myself busy with so I don't have to think about stupid Grayson and his stupid good looks and—"

"And how much you miss him?"

I stopped, Dominic effectively taking the wind out of my sails. Seeing my need for it, he passed his beer bottle to me, and I took a pull. "Yeah," I finally whispered. "God, everything's so screwed up."

He reached behind me and pulled me against his side so I could rest my head on his shoulder. "Well, look on the bright side."

"What bright side? There is no bright side here," I murmured, swigging back more beer.

"With Ma here, you'll be so consumed with murderous desires you won't really have any time to think about Grayson. See? Bright side."

I giggled and passed the cold glass bottle back to him. "I

don't know which is worse, the downward spiral my life is on or the fact that Mom's here for a visit."

"Mom, definitely Mom."

I stood from the couch, the beer I'd just drank on an empty stomach giving me a warm, floaty feeling. "Thanks for trying to cheer me up. I'm going to take a nice, long bubble bath. You know, give this whole *relaxing* thing a try."

"I'll holler when the food's ready."

I headed for my bedroom, stopping at the front door to dig through my purse for my cell phone, only to discover it wasn't there.

"Shit," I cursed, realizing I must've left it at the office. I let out a deep breath and continued on to my room. First my bubble bath, then my mother's world-famous pasta fagioli. There was no way I could stay in a bad mood after a long bath and my mom's amazing comfort food sitting in my belly.

I'd worry about my missing phone later.

CHAPTER THIRTY

LOLA

NOT HAVING my phone was like missing an arm. It was an extension of my body. Pathetic, I know, but I was a woman raised in the technological age. I couldn't function without it, so after a few hours of going cold turkey, I was over it. After deciding the best course of action was to wait until most everyone had left for the day, I headed out around eight to go to the office and get it.

The building was locked up for the evening, but I was still able to get in with my security badge. It was eerie how different everything was after the sun had gone down. The lone security guard working the night shift was too entranced by the small television he had set up behind his desk to even notice me, even with the click of my heels echoing like gunshots through the expanse of the otherwise silent lobby. I even did a little jig to see if he'd notice, but there was nothing. He was like a cyborg. Or he slept with his eyes open.

After a short elevator ride, I stepped onto the floor of KTSW and encountered a ghost town. The cleaning crew had already come and gone, so I could thankfully get in and out unnoticed. I hurried through the sea of empty cubicles toward my new office and began shuffling through the paperwork scattered on my desk. "Shit," I whispered, having come up empty. "Where the hell is it?" I yanked open the bottom drawer where I usually stuck my purse, hoping it had fallen out in there.

"Looking for this?"

I let out a startled shriek at the unexpected voice and shot up straight, grabbing the first thing from my desk I could get my hands on—which just so happened to be a stapler—and chucking it in the direction of my office door.

"Ow! Son of a bitch!"

"*Grayson?*" I shouted, my heart nearly beating out of my chest. "What the ever-loving fuck! You scared the shit out of me!"

"Christ," he grunted, reaching up and massaging his forehead where I'd nailed him with the stapler. "Your aim is freakishly good. Am I bleeding?"

I released an indignant huff as my pulse returned to a normal level. Once the shock of his sudden appearance wore off, I was hit with the spike of yearning I encountered every time he was near. The memory of his teasing touch and heated kiss from earlier that morning came rushing back, my skin prickling. My body's reaction, and the way my heart fluttered at the sight of him, set me on edge. I wanted to hate him, so very badly, but I just couldn't. I was hurt, yes, and that pain wasn't getting any better. But the feelings I had for him were so overwhelming, it was a struggle to breathe.

"No, you're not bleeding, you big baby. You're fine. And that's what you get for sneaking up on me. What are you doing here, anyway?" My tone was acerbic as I glared angrily. I tried to convince myself that I didn't find his deliciously disheveled appearance appealing, but it was a lie.

He looked good... *damn* good. His jacket and tie were missing, and the collar of his button-down was open enough to give me a tantalizing peek at his throat. The sleeves of his shirt were folded nearly to his elbows. Despite the slight wrinkle in his clothes, and the fact that he looked like he'd been running his hands through his hair all day long, he still looked freaking amazing. *The bastard.*

In answer to my question, he lifted his right arm, revealing my phone in the palm of his hand. "You left this in the conference room this morning. I was planning on bringing it to you after I finished a few conference calls I had."

"Oh," I mumbled, looking down at my hands, "Uh... well, th-thank you."

"But then I saw you in the lobby as I was heading out."

Uh-oh.

"You saw me?"

At the crooked grin that slowly tilted his lips up, I knew he knew exactly what I was asking. "Yep. Nice dance moves, by the way."

Crap in a handbasket! "The guard was practically catatonic," I defended insolently, crossing my arms over my chest. "I was trying to get his attention."

"Ah, I see." His smile deepened as he took two steps into the room, effectively shrinking the space with his magnetic aura. "Well, it's a shame he missed it. I found it quite entertaining."

"So glad I could amuse you." I glowered at him, trying to hold on to my anger and show I wasn't affected, even though I took two steps back to maintain a safe distance.

"You always amuse me, Lola." His voice was gravelly and deep as he continued to advance. In the dim lights of the office, I could see the hunger darkening his gaze as those green eyes raked up and down my body. "You make me laugh all the time. You drive me crazy. You're all I can think about every second of every day."

"Grayson, don't," I pleaded, taking another handful of steps backward until I hit Daphne's desk. Unable to move any farther, I watched as he closed in on me, my belly tightening with nerves. "I can't do this with you. Please, just—"

"I miss you," he whispered, his palms coming down on the desk by my hips, caging me in. His declaration stole my breath, and a well of emotion clogged my throat as he leaned in, running his nose along the side of mine. "I miss you all the goddamned time. Even when you're standing right in front of me like you are right now. Because I still don't *have you*."

I clenched my eyes shut and swallowed thickly. "This isn't—"

My words were cut off when his mouth slammed down on mine.

There was no slow buildup, nothing soft and gentle leading into the kiss. It ignited the instant his lips touched mine. My brain immediately shut off and my body melted, and I was left with no choice but to follow where he led.

Because he demanded it with that kiss. He commanded my body from the very start, and I was helpless to fight it.

I didn't want to.

His tongue forced its way into my mouth and tangled with mine as his hands squeezed the curve of my ass, pulling me flush against him. I moaned uncontrollably at the feel of his hot, hard arousal against my belly. I was feverish, frenzied in my need to touch and taste him. It was such a visceral want that I could think of nothing else, nothing but his skin against mine.

I pulled at his shirt until it came free of his pants, then snaked my hand up the solid muscles of his back, raking my nails across his flesh as I fought to keep our mouths fused while trying to touch every available inch of him I could get my hands on. I was so consumed that I barely noticed the edge of the desk cutting into my backside as he pressed harder against me.

We were finally forced to break the kiss when oxygen

became necessary. But Grayson didn't go far. He trailed heated, biting kisses down my neck to my collarbone as he yanked the hem of my skirt to my waist. I didn't fight it as his thumbs hooked into the edges of my panties and started pulling them down my thighs; instead, I shimmied my hips to assist, then kicked the useless scrap of lace aside once it pooled at my feet.

Never in my life had I been so frantic for another person. My skin felt two sizes too small as desperation coursed through my blood. I feared I'd splinter into a million tiny pieces any second if I didn't feel him inside of me. The sound of his zipper coming down reverberated through the office like a crack of thunder. Between one breath and the next, he lifted me onto the desk and drove his cock into me, bottoming out in one glorious thrust.

My head fell back on a keening cry as I stretched to accommodate his size. It was bliss and pain and euphoria all at the same time. It was *everything*. It was overwhelming. And I never wanted it to end.

The thought to fight for control, to dominate and take charge of the situation, never once crossed my mind. I simply held on and *felt* as Grayson fucked me hard and fast on the surface of that desk. I could feel myself getting close after just a few punishing thrusts, but I wasn't ready yet. I wanted this to last.

He held me tightly to him, chest to chest, as he manipulated my body more perfectly than anyone ever had. And when my eyelids began to fall closed, he tangled a hand in my mass of hair and yanked, forcing me to keep my eyes on his.

Our faces were mere inches apart, our breaths mingling, and I could see the desperation darkening the beautiful green of his eyes. "Grayson," I breathed, my eyes going wide at the sight of the unconcealed emotion on his face. He'd opened himself so completely for me to see, letting his raw, uncontrollable need for me shine to the surface.

"I need you, Lola," he panted, driving his cock deeper and harder. "Let me have you."

My breath hitched on a painful gasp, fear taking hold because I knew exactly what he was asking, even as every nerve ending in my body pulled tautly and my impending release coiled tighter deep in my belly. I was going to explode, come apart so extraordinarily that I worried there'd be nothing left of me afterward.

"Only you," he grunted, a bead of sweat trailing down his forehead. "It's only you. Don't you see that?"

"Please...." My voice was a plea, but for what, I didn't know. I wanted to give him what he was asking, yet the thought of doing so terrified me.

"Let me have you." The beseeching quality in his voice disappeared with that sharp command.

"Grayson, I'm close." The feeling was so intense I feared it even as my hips moved against his, chasing after the climax I was so scared of.

"Give it to me," he growled, one hand snaking between our bodies. His lithe fingers toyed with my sensitive clit, rubbing hard circles as he drove harder and faster, shaking the desk beneath me. "*Now*, Lola."

And I detonated, crying out unintelligibly as my climax took control and every part of my body clamped down around him. I barely heard his loud, feral roar through the blood rushing in my ears as he followed after me.

My orgasm left me a boneless, panting mess. It felt like ages passed before I was finally able to control my limbs and sit up straight. I unwound my arms from around Grayson's neck, placing my palms on the cool surface at my sides as I fought to gain control of the tumultuous emotions warring inside of me.

Seconds later, Grayson lifted his head from where he'd buried it in the crook of my neck. His fingers traced along my hairline, tucking wayward strands of hair behind my ear as he examined my face. "You okay?" he whispered, concern lacing his words. "Did I hurt you?"

"Yes." His body locked tight, so I quickly amended, "I mean, no, you didn't hurt me. And yes, I'm okay."

He slipped from my body as he took a step back and held my arms, helping me to my feet. I missed the feel of him as soon as I lost it, but that feeling was quickly overlapped when I felt the heat of his release between my thighs.

"Shit," I hissed, my eyes darting down to his fly and back up to meet his gaze. "We didn't use a condom."

"I'm clean," he declared casually, like he was talking about something as innocuous as doing his taxes. "And I know you are too."

I sidestepped him, my movements agitated as I straightened my clothes the best I could. Anxiety began to squeeze my chest and twist my stomach into knots. "I am, but that's beside the point. We didn't even stop to think about protection. That's stupid and irresponsible, Grayson!"

"It'll be fine." He reached for me, but I moved back. His composed demeanor only worked to aggravate me further.

"You can't know that! I'm on the pill, but nothing's guaranteed. That was... that...." I pointed at the desk where we'd all but attacked each other seconds before. "That was reckless! And careless! And... *stupid*!"

"And if something happened because of it, we'll deal. It's not the end of the fucking world, Lola," he gritted, his voice jagged. "If you were to get pregnant, then so be it."

My jaw dropped and my eyes bugged out. "'*So be it*'? Are you... are... are you *insane*?" I sputtered, slightly hysterical. "We can't have a *baby*, Grayson!"

He closed the distance between us in two quick steps, his face only an inch from mine. "Why not? Why would us having a baby be such a bad thing, huh? Personally, I'd be fucking thrilled if you were pregnant. At least that way I'd have *something* to keep you tied to me since you're so goddamned insistent on running away from what's between us."

"Oh my God," I gasped, taking a step away. "You've lost it. Do you hear what you're saying? You can't use a baby to trap someone into being with you, Grayson. That's... that's not... God, that's just so *wrong*."

"*Fuck!*" he shouted, raking his hands through his hair as he began to pace. "That's not what I meant. Christ, this is all coming out wrong."

"Then what did you mean? Explain it to me, because you're starting to freak me *way* the fuck out."

"I just...." He stopped, shaking his head viciously before looking me right in the eye. "I'd take any part of you I could get. Don't you get that? I'm so fucking in love with you that I'd be willing to accept whatever scraps you threw my way. I'd never trap you into being with me if you got pregnant, but I'm not going to lie and tell you that the thought of having you in my life for the next eighteen years, even if the connection is through another person, doesn't hold a certain appeal."

I was stunned, speechless. The ground beneath my feet could've begun to quake and crack and I wouldn't have been able to move or take my eyes off him. I couldn't process what he'd just said, but at the same time I couldn't stop replaying his words.

He said he loves me.

He said he loves me!

Holy shit!

"I—you—I... you can't—"

"Don't tell me I don't love you," he barked. "Don't."

"We've... it's... you've barely known me over a month!" I shouted, throwing my hands out, because I couldn't force my brain to wrap around what he was saying.

Grayson was on me in a second, his large, rough hands cupping my cheeks as he stared down at me. His green eyes held so much sincerity it stole my breath. "You're all I think about when I'm awake. You consume my dreams when I sleep. I want to be near you all the time. And before you say it, it's not just about the sex, even though I've never had better—*never*. It's more than that. I want to make you laugh just so I can hear it. I listen to your show every goddamned day because I miss the sound of your voice. When you're around, the need to touch you is so fucking overwhelming it makes my skin crawl. I want to make you happy. I want to be the one to make it better when you're sad. I want to fight with you and make up with you. I want *everything*, and I want it with you. Only you. *Only. You.* So don't tell me I don't love you, because that's a goddamned lie. What I feel for you in the short time I've known you is more than I *ever* felt for Fiona in the four fucking years we were together."

"I...." I had no words. Not a single one, because everything he'd just described was *exactly* what I felt every minute of every day.

Oh God.

I loved him.

I was *in* love with him. Crazy, stupid, irrational love.

And he loved me too.

And I couldn't get my mouth to form words! *Speak, Lola! Say something, anything!*

I just stared at him, unable to process everything going on in my head. It wasn't until he began tucking his shirt back into his pants that I was able to unfreeze.

"Wh-what are you doing?"

"I'm leaving," he answered flatly. "I've said everything I needed to say. I know you well enough to know that fighting you anymore would be pointless."

"But—"

"You need time to think," he stated, finally looking up to meet my gaze. "If I push you anymore tonight, you'll shut down completely, so I'm giving you what you need. I'm going to leave and let you have your space. But know this." He was back in front of me, his hands on either side of my neck, his thumbs rubbing soothing circles beneath my jaw. "I'm not letting you go. I love you. And despite what you say, I know you have feelings for me. You wouldn't have been so hurt about those lies in the papers if you didn't."

"Gray—"

"Go home, baby. Get some sleep." He'd cut me off again. It was really starting to piss me off.

I narrowed my eyes to angry slits. I wasn't sure what I was going to say, but I knew I at least wanted to say *something*. "Will you just—"

He silenced me with a quick kiss, not letting me get a word in edgewise. He finally released his hold, taking a step back and reaching into the pocket of his pants. "Here. Don't want you to forget this." Grayson took my hand and placed my cell phone in my palm. "I'll pick you up Saturday for the gala."

Then he turned and left, leaving me all alone in the dark, quiet office with kiss-bruised lips and an aching heart.

CHAPTER THIRTY-ONE

LOLA

IT TOOK nothing short of selling my soul, but I'd somehow successfully managed to talk Dominic into getting our mother out of my house under the guise of shopping so I could have Daphne and Sophia over and we could all get ready for the gala together. I needed my girls. I needed to talk about absolutely *everything* that had happened in our office three days ago—with the exception of admitting we did the dirty on Daphne's desk—and pick apart every word he'd said... like women always do.

I went into great detail about the earth-moving sex while Daphne did my hair. I talked through, analyzed, overanalyzed, and picked apart his words while Sophia worked on my makeup. By the time we were all glitzed out, I'd been talking for three hours and still felt no closer to settled than when I started.

I was a freaking mess!

"I don't know what to do," I admitted on a pathetic cry. I wanted to throw myself down on my bed all dramatically like one of those damsels in the movies, but I was afraid doing so would ruin my hair. And if I did that, Daphne would surely kill me dead.

"Well," Sophia started, leaning in to the mirror above my

dresser to apply her red lipstick, "the way I see it, there's really nothing you *can* do."

"How do you mean?" I asked, as I pulled my gown from the garment bag and took a second to admire it before slipping it on. It was the best gown *ever*—a sleeveless, black bandage Herve Leger gown by Max Azria with intricate beading, a wide V-neck and rounded back, and a kickass fringe hem. It hugged every one of my curves from chest to midthigh, then flared out with embellished strips of fabric all the way to the floor. It was flapper-meets-classic. It cost me some serious cake, but I loved it more than any article of clothing or pair of shoes I'd ever owned.

Sophia turned to eye me as I slid the dress up over my hips. "Babe, isn't it obvious?"

I shot her a look, sliding my arms through the inch-wide shoulder straps. "If it was, would I be asking?"

Daphne let out a small giggle, and I turned to look at her as she pulled up the side zip of her one-shouldered crepe gown in a stunning coral that looked beautiful with her blonde hair and light coloring. "Lo, you're totally in love with the guy, and from everything you just told us, he's crazy about you. What Sophia means is there's nothing you can do because fighting what you feel for him is pointless. You're miserable without him. Might as well face facts and just accept it."

Sophia nodded sagely while capping her lipstick and dropping it into the beaded gold clutch that matched her white, Grecian-style gown. "Can you honestly tell me you've been behaving like a functioning adult these past couple of weeks?" I opened my mouth, ready to defend myself, but she wasn't finished. "You've cried yourself sick, eaten more ice cream than is healthy, snapped at anyone who looked at you cross-eyed, and got yourself suspended for breaking your boss's nose, for Christ's sake! That is not behaving like a sane member of society, honey."

"I was not suspended." Yes, that was what came out of my mouth. "It was a mandatory paid vacation."

Sophia rolled her eyes and sat down on the edge of the bed, her voice soft as she said, "You love him, Lola, just admit it. It's not bad, and it doesn't make you weak."

"Wouldn't you rather be happy than keep going like you've been?" Daphne asked compassionately.

I looked down at my hands. My fingers were clasped together so tightly my knuckles had turned white. "Yes," I answered on a whisper.

Sophia stood and came toward me, placing her hands on my shoulders. "Then stop fighting it. Stop fighting *him*. You love each other. That's all that matters for now. Quit waiting for something bad to happen and let yourself enjoy it."

My eyes grew watery, hot tears blurring my vision.

"Oh, no you don't," Daphne cried out in warning. "Don't you dare cry. You'll ruin your makeup. Then I'll start crying and ruin mine. And we all look hot, so don't screw that up."

I got control of my tears by laughing. That was just one of the many reasons I loved my girls—they had my back no matter what. I sucked in a fortifying breath and walked to the full-length mirror in the corner of my bedroom. My hair was pulled back and slightly teased, pinned up at the crown of my head. Thick, glossy curls hung around my shoulders and down my back. My eye shadow was smoky, the eyeliner winged, creating the perfect cat-eye look. She was right, I looked hot. We *all* did. Messing this up would be a travesty.

I spun around, prepared to thank my two best friends for everything, when my cell phone trilled from my bedside table.

"Answer it," Sophia hissed when I stood frozen to the spot.

That snapped me out of my self-induced panic and I rushed to the phone, sliding my finger across the screen and holding it to my ear. "Hello?"

"Ms. Abbatelli, Mr. Lockhart is here for you."

Rabid butterflies took flight in my belly and my hands began to tremble. "Okay. Thanks, Maury. I'll be right down."

"Yes, ma'am."

"Wait!" I shouted into the receiver before he could hang up. "How... how does he look?"

"Uh... pardon?" Maury asked.

"Does he look angry? Like, is he scowling? Or is he smiling happily? Or maybe stoic? Do you think he looks more stoic or pensive? It'll probably be one of those two."

"I—" Poor Maury, I really was a handful for the poor guy. "I don't think I'm a good judge of—"

"For Christ's sake, Maury! It's either stoic or pensive. Pick one of the two! I need to know what I'm walking into here."

A rustling sound came through the line, and then Grayson's deep, velvety voice filled my ear. "I look eager, baby. Will you cut poor Maury some slack and get your sexy ass down here already?"

My heart did a trillion backflips in my chest at the sound of his voice. True to his word, he'd stepped back and given me space. I hadn't heard from him since our encounter in my office, and I missed him. I missed him fiercely.

"It's not nice to eavesdrop on other people's conversations," I muttered lamely... because what I said was definitely lame.

His chuckle rumbled in my ears, sending tiny bolts of lightning straight to my core. "Are you coming down, or am I going to have to come up and get you?"

His words were a sinfully delicious threat, painting an erotic picture in my head of what would happen if he were forced to come up. I almost asked him to come get me when a throat cleared from behind me, pulling me from my sensual daydreaming and reminding me that I wasn't alone.

"I'll come down," I spouted quickly. "Give me just a sec."

I ended the call and dropped my phone into the black wristlet lying on my bed before turning back to my friends and taking several deep breaths. "He's here."

Daphne snorted and Sophia rolled her eyes before saying, "Well no shit. I couldn't have guessed."

"Oh God," I sputtered, the beginning dregs of panic clawing at my stomach. "I love him. *Shit!* I love Grayson. Oh God. Oh no."

"Don't panic." Daphne rushed to me and helped me sit on the edge of the bed, forcing my head between my knees. "Slow, deep breaths. It's all good. Think about all your favorite fashion designers, and the smell of Starbucks in the morning, and attending Hogwarts.

That did the trick. "Okay," I said on an exhale as I sat up. "That's good. I'm good. All better now."

"Good," Sophia chirped, grabbing my hands and pulling me up. She shoved my wristlet at me, took me by the shoulders, and spun me around. "Now get moving. We'll lock up." With a slap on my ass, she sent me on my way.

I kept my eyes closed and counted silently in my head the whole elevator ride down to keep myself calm. When the *ding* alerted me to my arrival on the ground floor, I inhaled deeply and stepped onto the glinting marble floor on shaky legs.

I kept my eyes on my feet as I took three careful steps, so I didn't immediately see Grayson's expression when he caught his first glimpse of me in my amazing dress.

"Holy fuck." At the sound of his pained exclamation, I jerked to a stop and my focus shot up. All the wind whooshed from my lungs at the sight of him. *Holy fuck* was right. I'd drooled over Grayson in a suit. I'd jumped him the first time I saw him in jeans and a tee. But nothing... *nothing* could have prepared me for what he looked like in a tuxedo.

"Sweet Christ on a cracker," I muttered under my breath.

His chest expanded as he pulled in a breath. "Wow, baby. You look...."

"Like sex on a stick," I whispered.

Grayson's face broke into a blinding smile that only made me want to climb him like a tree even more. "Yeah. Exactly."

What? I gave my head a cursory shake to clear the lustful haze. "No... I mean thank you, but I was talking about you. You look... just... *whoa.*"

"The feeling's mutual, Lola. That dress is made for sin."

I stared at him for several seconds, wondering if I could take a running leap and launch myself at him without tripping and falling on my face in the middle of the lobby. The desire to touch him was almost too much to bear. But before I could put my plan into action, a throat cleared, pulling our attention to the front desk where Maury stood, looking increasingly uncomfortable with each passing second.

I couldn't help the short giggle that erupted from my chest. Poor Maury.

"You ready, gorgeous?"

I turned my eyes back to Grayson and instantly melted. Last month, last week... hell, even three days ago, I would've said no. But standing there now with his hand extended out to me, my chest warmed, my heart felt light, and I knew... I was totally ready.

I was in love with Grayson Lockhart. And what was more, I believed him when he said he loved me.

"Grayson," I said, placing my hand in his. "I need to tell you—"

He gave me a little tug and began leading me from my building to the waiting town car. "Tell me in the car. We don't want to be late."

His driver was standing at the rear passenger door as we

descended the steps to the sidewalk. I grinned widely at his familiar face. "Hey, Tommy. How's it hanging?"

He rolled his eyes heavenward, but I could tell he was trying to suppress a smile. He tipped his chin down with a crooked smirk. "Miss Lola. Lovely to see you again."

"Right back 'atcha." I gave his shoulder a playful smack as he opened the door for us, then climbed into the back seat, sliding over to make room on the supple leather bench for Grayson.

"You're rather chummy with Thomas," Grayson said with a smile as the door shut, closing us in the tiny space together. The subtle smell of his cologne filled my nostrils, overpowering all my other senses. *Would it be too much to lean over and lick him?*

"He's a cool dude," I answered while trying to stamp out the sudden wave of unquenchable lust.

Thomas returned to the driver seat, and within seconds we were on our way.

I was staring out the window, watching the cityscape as it passed, when I felt Grayson's warm breath on the bare skin of my shoulder.

"So... what was it you needed to tell me?"

I turned my head, surprised to find he'd moved so close without me noticing. Less than two inches separated his body from mine. If I leaned in just a bit, I'd be able to taste his lips.

"Lola...."

I hadn't realized I was staring, my mind having drifted off, until I heard him say my name. "Huh?"

"You said you needed to tell me something."

I did? God, it was so hard to think straight when he was so close. All my brain could compute was *want, need, here, now, mine, all mine.* I closed my eyes and shook my head in the hopes of getting my thoughts in order. "Oh... right."

"So what is it?"

"I...." Then, like the coward I was, I totally chickened out. "I forgot."

"You forgot?"

I pasted a self-deprecating smile on my face. "Yeah, sorry. Maybe it'll come back to me later."

His expression dropped into a frown, and I could've sworn I saw disappointment lingering in his jade eyes. "Yeah... maybe."

He slid back over to his side of the bench and turned his attention out the window, leaving me to stew in my own miserable self-loathing.

CHAPTER THIRTY-TWO

LOLA

GRAYSON'S DEMEANOR didn't improve much once we arrived at the Seattle Art Museum, but to his credit, even though I could tell he was unhappy about our exchange in the car, he didn't let it show outwardly. He smiled for the cameras that lined both sides of the carpeted entrance while holding me close, in what would appear to onlookers to be a loving embrace. He offered polite greetings and kind words to those who stopped us on the way to the ballroom.

He even placed his hand on the small of my back, leaned in, and asked if I wanted a glass of champagne once we made it into the ballroom. When I nodded, he moved off toward one of the two bars that lined the far walls of the spacious room to retrieve my drink.

"Oh, Lola. Darling, I'm so happy to see you!"

I spun on my heels, the fringe of my skirt swinging out in a glittering whirl of jet-black beads. "Cybil, hi."

Grayson's mother grabbed me by the forearms and leaned in to place a kiss on my cheek. "You look absolutely stunning."

"Thank you, so do you." I smiled sweetly, Cybil's presence helping to calm my rapidly fraying nerves.

I didn't realize I'd been joined by anyone else until another person spoke up. "You do look lovely, dear. That dress is something else. I think I want one of my own." I laughed at Grayson's nana. I really did adore that woman.

"How about I let you borrow this one?"

"Oh, you're on. I think I could pull it off. I might be old, but I've still got it."

"Oh that you do, Nana. Most definitely."

I felt his presence seconds before he spoke. "Mother. Nana." Grayson stopped close to my side and handed me a crystal champagne flute before leaning in to place a kiss to his mother's and grandmother's cheeks. Once he stood tall, his arm looped around my waist, pulling me into his side. I didn't even try to stop myself from nuzzling even closer.

I knew my actions caught him off guard because his entire body went stiff for a moment before that arm around me tightened. I looked up at him, trying my best to tell him with my eyes that I was right where I wanted to be.

I must have pulled it off, because the wall he'd placed between us in the car suddenly fell and he returned my smile with one so full of love it took my breath away.

"Aren't you two just adorable," Cybil sighed, pulling my gaze back in her direction.

"Where are Dad and Deacon?" Grayson asked, stealthily moving the conversation in another direction.

"Oh, they're milling about somewhere." Cybil waved her hand at her side. "Probably at the bar. You know how your father feels about these black-tie events."

"And he's not wrong," Nana grumbled. "I think I'll join them. I'm in need of a whiskey." Nana turned and started in the direction of the bar, her cane tapping silently on the carpeted floor as she went in search of libations. I couldn't help but think that an inebriated Nana would certainly liven up the evening.

Just then, Sophia and Daphne came waltzing into the ballroom. Having spotted me the moment they entered, they made a beeline to our little huddle. I made quick introductions between Cybil and my friends.

Hearing their names, Cybil's entire face brightened.

"It's so nice to meet you. I'm such a fan of your show."

Dear Lord, his mother listens to our show? I gave a bug-eyed look to my girls, who were trying their best to stifle their laughter.

"Thanks," Sophia offered. "Glad you enjoy it."

"Oh, I do! That segment you did on vibrators was rather enlightening."

"Jesus Christ," Grayson grunted as I choked on air. My friends laughed as Cybil scowled at her son.

"Grayson! Language."

"Well excuse me, Mom, but what the hell do you expect? I don't need to hear that shit."

"I'll have you know your father's still as amorous as ever. That doesn't die in a relationship just because you get older."

He let out a slow *"Fuck"* and looked down at me. "Are my ears bleeding? They feel like they're bleeding. I think I might need to go to the hospital."

"So dramatic," his mother admonished. "Anyway. Lola, darling, I just wanted to tell you that I think what you and your friends are doing tonight is admirable. I saw the program. There's no doubt you'll raise a ridiculous amount of money for such a good cause."

"Wait... what?"

It was my turn to go stiff at Grayson's question. Once again, I'd completely forgotten. I looked to Sophia and Daphne for help, but they were too busy enjoying the show to engage. The traitors.

"They're doing a bachelorette auction tonight," Cybil

offered. "They've agreed to offer themselves up for a date to the highest bidders. Isn't it a wonderful idea?"

The dark look he gave me said he thought the idea was anything *but* wonderful.

Seemingly unaware of the thundercloud that had suddenly taken residence over our little gathering, Cybil turned to my friends and said, "You know, there are a few gentlemen here tonight with some pretty thick wallets. Why don't I take you ladies around and make introductions? Help drum up excitement before the auction starts?"

"What a wonderful idea," Daphne chirped, hooking her elbow through Cybil's.

"Definitely," Sophia added with a side-eye look in my direction. "Let's do that right now. Grayson, you'll keep Lola company, won't you?"

I was going to murder her in her sleep.

"You don't need to worry about that," he replied with a gruff, unhappy rumble.

Uh-oh.

The three of them scuttled off, leaving me to my doom. A quick peek through my lashes showed he was *not* happy. "Gray—"

"You think that maybe you should've mentioned you're offering yourself up as a date for money tonight?"

Yep, *so* not happy.

"Honestly, I totally forgot about the auction until your mother mentioned it."

"Christ, Lola," he grunted. It was then that I noticed he was holding a tumbler of amber-colored liquid. He lifted the glass to his lips and downed the entire thing in one short swallow.

"It's really not a big deal."

He let go of my waist and turned to face me full-on with a

menacing glare. "Other men are going to be bidding on you, Lola. How the fuck is that not a big deal?"

"It's for charity?" I offered quietly.

"Not helping. And don't be cute when I'm pissed off."

I took that as an opening and stepped close, pressing our chests together as I smiled demurely. "You think I'm cute?"

"You know you are. Don't change the subject." He was still scowling, but I could see his hold on his anger was beginning to slip.

I opened my mouth to speak when a familiar, unwelcome voice spoke from beside us.

"Hey, shorty."

My head dropped back. "You've *got* to be kidding me!" I snapped at the ceiling, in search of divine intervention.

It didn't come.

I straightened my head and narrowed my eyes at my brother. I had to hand it to him, he looked good in a tux, but... *WTF!* "What are you doing here? How are you here?"

"I bought a ticket," he replied with a smug grin. "You aren't the only one in the family who's loaded, you know."

"Please, God, tell me you don't have Ma with you." Because that would be fucking *perfect*.

"No. Turns out she had a date with that doorman of yours. When I left, she was humming a Frank Sinatra song and getting dolled up."

Fuck my life.

I chose to ignore the fact that my mom getting close to Maury did *not* mean good things and asked, "*Why* are you here?"

Dominic had the good sense to look contrite, but that didn't matter for shit when he responded with "Look, I know you're going to be pissed, but—"

"No!" I snapped, shoving my index finger in his face. "No. Don't you even go there, Dom."

"I have to, Lo," he answered earnestly. "I have to at least try."

"What's going on?" From the corner of my eye, I could see Grayson's head bouncing back and forth between my brother and me, but I refused to take my eyes off Dominic.

"You don't have to try anything. This is neither the time nor the place, Dom. Sophia doesn't want to see you."

"*Ohhhh*" came Grayson's mutter of understanding. He remembered me telling him about Sophia and my brother dating. He also remembered that it hadn't ended well.

"Listen, I'm not going to make a scene, I swear," my brother said beseechingly. "I won't approach her if I think it'll make trouble. I just... I have to see her, shorty. I can't be in the same city and pretend she isn't here. I tried."

"Gah!" I tugged at the hair on the sides of my head before throwing my hands up. "Could this night possibly get any worse?"

Then I heard her voice. It was like Karma was laughing directly in my face, saying, "Sucks to be you!"

"Hi, Lola."

I turned woodenly, my gaze landing on the auburn-haired stunner.

Fiona.

Ladies and gentlemen, welcome to the seventh circle of hell.

CHAPTER THIRTY-THREE

LOLA

I'D HAVE GIVEN anything for a hole to open up beneath my feet and suck me down into a dark abyss. Anything. Even my favorite Kate Spade handbag. The very same one I'd gotten into a knock-down, drag-out fight with some soccer mom bitch for last year during a Black Friday sale.

No such luck.

"I like your dress. It's beautiful."

It took me several seconds for my brain to engage and actually comprehend what she'd just said.

"Uh... thank you." She sounded so sincere, but I wasn't buying it. I examined her expression like someone would stare at a slide beneath a microscope, looking for any signs of manipulation. I found none. Instead of sneering or shooting me scathing looks like she had that afternoon at the Lockharts', she was looking back at me with what appeared to be such stark remorse in her eyes that some of the ice in my veins actually began to thaw. "You... look really nice too." The compliment felt awkward on my tongue, especially considering how I'd felt about this woman the past few weeks, but it felt like the right thing to do.

She smiled genuinely at me, her gaze bouncing between Grayson and me before she spoke again. "Could I...?" She fidgeted nervously for a moment. "I'm sorry to interrupt, but... do you think I could speak with you for just a minute?"

Grayson's arm wrapped around my waist in what could only be described as a protective hold. His arm was like a steel band tied around me, pulling my back flush with his chest.

"I don't think that's such a good idea, Fee," he spoke for me.

Unlike some women who would've found the possessive gesture to be insulting, I found it kind of swoon-worthy, albeit slightly annoying. I was more than capable of answering for myself, after all.

Her eyes traveled back to Grayson, but only for a second, and it was then that I realized she wasn't staring up at him with the same lovesick adoration in her eyes. "I'll only take a moment. Please."

I peeked up at him to see a concerned frown marring his handsome face. "It's fine," I whispered, placing my hands on his arm around my waist and giving it a reassuring squeeze. His jade eyes flickered with uncertainty and... fear? I wasn't certain, but whatever the emotion behind his gaze, it warmed me to my very core. "Really. I'll be okay."

"Lola," he growled warningly, causing me to roll my eyes.

Spinning around in his hold, I grabbed the lapels of his jacket and brought his face closer to mine.

"You and I need to have a conversation. Not right now, but later tonight. There are some things I need to tell you, but right now I'm asking you to trust me when I say I'll. Be. Fine. Can you do that?"

He closed his eyes and inhaled briefly, and when he opened them again, so much love was shining down at me it made my knees weak. *God, I love this man.* "Okay," he whispered, "but only if you promise to come back to me when you're done."

Yep... totally swoon-worthy.

"I promise."

"I mean it, Lola. I'll track you down if I have to."

Standing on the tiptoes of my killer heels, I placed a gentle kiss to his lips and looked him right in the eye as I declared, "You won't have to. You have my word."

That seemed to placate him because his arm loosened, allowing me to walk away.

Fiona and I moved silently through the ballroom and through a set of French doors that led to a quiet, empty terrace away from prying eyes. I wasn't sure what she had to say to me, but I knew that, whatever it was, it was best said in private.

White fairy lights wrapped around the scrolled iron railing, providing enough light against the dark backdrop of the starlit sky for me to see her face clearly. I stood with my arms crossed over my chest and waited for her to speak first. When she finally did, her words took me by complete surprise.

"I'm so sorry, Lola."

"You... *huh?*"

"I'm sorry," she repeated, stepping up to the railing and leaning her hip against it. "I treated you terribly when we first met, and I had no right. I was just... I was jealous. Grayson never looked at me the way he looked at you, and I handled it poorly. You didn't deserve that."

I was trying not to swallow my tongue as shock whipped through me. "...Thank you."

"And I want you to know, those pictures that were posted were totally out of context, I swear."

Just the mention of the photos sent a spike of pain through my chest. I had to close my eyes for a second and breathe through it. "He said—"

"We talked about you the entire time," she interrupted. "He was so desperate to make things right after the pool. He spent the entire lunch asking me what he should do to get you to forgive him."

"I didn't know," I whispered, placing my hand against my chest and unconsciously rubbing at the ache behind my breastbone. "He told me it wasn't what I thought, but I didn't realize..." *that he'd been telling the truth.* God, I was such an asshole.

Fiona surprised me by moving closer and taking my hands in hers. "He loves you, Lola. In a way I've never seen in all the years I've known him. I'll admit that it stung, seeing him look at you in a way I never experienced," she said, a sad smile tilting her lips, "but I shouldn't have taken that out on you. I think I confused what I feel for him now with what we used to have. Does that make sense? I still care for him greatly, and he's one of my best friends. But I've been gone for so long, and seeing him again... I think it was more nostalgia than love." She spoke quickly, like she was trying to talk through everything going on in her head. "He's been a part of my life for so long, and seeing him with you, I felt threatened that I might lose him."

"Fiona," I started, cutting through her rambling, "I'd never do that." I gave her hands a squeeze, hoping she could see my candor. "I know you two were friends before, and that you remained that way after you broke up. He told me the history. He's important to you, and you're important to him too. I'm not going to lie, knowing you two...." I trailed off, struggling to say the words. "It'll take some adjusting for me, knowing you two were together, but if there really are no deep-seated feelings lingering, then I don't see why we can't all move past it."

"There aren't. I promise. Like I said, I just got wrapped up in the past. I'm not that girl, Lola. I know it may be hard for you to believe, considering how we met, but I'd never purposefully try to sabotage a relationship. All I want is for Gray to be happy. And you make him happy."

"He makes me happy too," I responded with a smile.

"Do you think... is there any way you could forgive me? Maybe we could start over? I'd like us to be friends."

"I'd really like that," I found myself answering honestly.

Her relief was palpable, and when she released my hands and took a step back, she looked like a massive weight had just fallen from her shoulders. She extended her hand outward. "Hi. I'm Fiona Prentice, an old friend of Gray's. It's nice to meet you."

I took it with a small laugh and gave it a quick shake. "I'm Lola Abbatelli. Nice to meet you too."

For the first time in weeks, I felt light, happy, like everything was going to be all right.

"So, friends?" she asked.

"Friends," I replied. I suddenly wanted to tell her about Deacon, about the fact that he was in love with her, but something held me back. It wasn't my place, and my gut told me that those two were going to have to find their way to each other on their own. But I was comforted by the fact that I'd be able to sit back and enjoy as everything played out. And with the way Deacon had looked at her with such acute longing, I had no doubt it eventually would; I just had to hope she was smart enough to see what was standing in front of her when the time came.

"I guess we should be getting back. Gray's liable to have a heart attack if I keep you much longer."

She took a step toward the doors, but then something dawned on me. It might not be my place to intervene with her and Deacon, but that didn't mean I couldn't give them a little nudge in the right direction. "Wait." I grabbed her arm, staying her movement. "I need a favor."

"Sure. Whatever you need."

Oh... this was going to be so good. I couldn't *wait*.

CHAPTER THIRTY-FOUR

I WAS GOING out of my mind, ready to jump out of my skin. If Lola wasn't back in the next three fucking seconds, I was going after her. I wanted to trust Fiona not to ruin things for me, but my foundation with Lola had been rocky from day one and it was hard to believe she wouldn't get spooked again. I saw something in her eyes just before she wandered off that gave me hope. I just wasn't sure if I could believe it—not yet, anyway.

It wasn't until I saw the two of them enter from the terrace, smiling at each other, that I was able to breathe a sigh of relief. Unfortunately, that relief was short-lived.

"You've got to be fucking kidding me," Dominic growled from my side. I turned to find him scowling at something across the ballroom, the muscle in his jaw ticking like crazy.

"What?"

"This has got to be a fucking joke."

Before I could question his sudden outburst, Lola slid up against me, linking her arms through mine. "Hi." She smiled up at me brilliantly, stealing my breath and making my cock twitch. Christ, she was beautiful.

"Hey," I said softly, leaning down to bring our faces closer. "Everything good?"

"Everything's perfect." She planted her lips against mine and I couldn't help but agree. The outward display of affection on her part was unexpected, but no less welcome. I was sure I'd never get enough of this woman.

"Shorty," Dominic butted in, pulling us from the moment. "I hate to break up the love-fest but...." He lifted his chin in the direction he'd been scowling, and Lola and I followed his gaze. A man in or near his sixties was walking our way. The cut of his tux screamed *money*. But the bleached-blonde on his arm who'd been nipped and tucked past anything a plastic surgeon should ever have agreed to, and the blatant arrogance on his face, alerted me to the fact that, while he might be rich, he certainly lacked class.

"Oh my God." Lola sucked in a sharp breath, and I felt her go so stiff it was a wonder she didn't break into a million pieces.

"Who is that?" I asked, not liking the way the light dimmed from her amber eyes one bit.

"My father," she exhaled.

Fuck. I knew from everything she'd told me that she and her father didn't have a good relationship. I also knew from the sudden shift in her demeanor from happy to upset that seeing him was a complete surprise... and not a welcomed one.

"I'll take care of this," Dominic growled before stalking off in the man's direction.

"Hey," I whispered, using my free hand to tip her chin up. The pain in her eyes tore me in two. "Talk to me, baby. What's happening in your head right now?"

"I don't like him," she said, sounding sad and broken. "He's not a nice man. He's a cheat and a liar, but it's worse than just that," she said, her voice near frantic. "When I was five, he took me and Dominic to the pool in our building. It's one of the only memories I have of him doing anything even remotely fatherly with us. I didn't know how to swim, and I was too frightened to get off the steps, and I guess that annoyed him. He said I was too old to be scared, and that I was acting like a baby. So he picked me up and threw me into the deep end."

Rage blanketed my vision with a red film as she spoke. Her voice trembled with stark fear as she recalled the memory.

"I was terrified. I couldn't keep my head above water. Dominic started to swim to me to pull me up, but my dad yelled at him, telling him it was the only way I could learn. I finally managed to kick my way to the edge and pull myself up. Dominic was so mad," she whispered. "I remember thinking he was going to punch him, but instead, he just grabbed me by the hand and took me back to our apartment. I couldn't stop crying. I'd been so scared, and all my father could talk about was how I'd been weak, how I embarrassed him by making such a ridiculous scene."

My chest tightened painfully as I pulled her into my arms, trying to ward off the trembles that were racking her body. "That's why you're scared of water."

"Yeah. I know it's stupid. I should be over it by now—"

"It's not stupid," I growled. "Your father was a first-class prick for doing that to you. It's not your fault. It's his."

"He... he called me when he saw our picture in the papers. He never calls me unless he wants something. But he saw that I was with you and thought he could use me to try and get closer to you and your father. I told him never to call me again, but I guess that's why he's here now. He has an investment firm. He wants to use your family's name to his company's advantage. I told him no. I swear, Gray—"

"Hey, hey." I reached up and ran my knuckles along her jaw in an effort to soothe her. "It's okay. I believe you."

"I can't believe he's here."

"I can." I cupped her cheek, needing to feel her skin against mine in any possible way. "Lola, I've known men like him my whole life. Money-hungry leeches who ride other people's coattails to the top are a dime a dozen. You don't need to worry about keeping him away from my father or me. Trust me, we're more than capable of handling assholes like that."

She opened her mouth to speak but was interrupted by a man's voice. "Ah, there's my baby girl."

The fake cadence in his tone set me on edge, and it took everything in my power not to knock the old man's teeth down his throat when he pulled Lola from my side and planted a kiss on each of her cheeks. It took a real piece of shit to use his own child to further his career goals.

"Just as beautiful as I remember. You remember Chelsea, right?" he said by way of introduction to the woman on his arm, but that was all the attention he granted her. It was clear she was nothing more than a trophy, and judging by the diamonds glittering on her neck and ears, she was more than okay being an older man's arm candy.

"Dad," Dominic gritted out, coming to stop at the man's side. "I told you, now's not the time."

"Nonsense!" the man declared on a chuckle. "A father should always take an interest in the man in his daughter's life." He turned from Lola, blatantly dismissing her, and extended his hand to me. "Roberto Abbatelli. It's a pleasure to meet you, son."

I looked down at his hand like it was a piece of flaming trash. "I know who you are."

Oblivious to the venom in my tone, or simply not caring, he lifted the hand I ignored and patted me on the shoulder. "I was so glad to find out my girl caught the eye of an esteemed man such as yourself. It speaks well of her character that she was able to land a shark among so many fish. But then, her beauty is enough to catch any man's attention, am I right?"

Chelsea stared off into space with a blank, bored look on her face, as though she was used to hearing the man she'd tied herself to speak so low of women. It spoke volumes to the kind of man Roberto Abbatelli was.

"Jesus, Dad," Dominic grunted at the same time Lola spoke up with a furious "*Seriously?*"

"Sweetheart, why don't you take Chelsea to powder your nose, or whatever it is you women do, while I talk business with your man?"

"I'm sorry," she bit out sarcastically. "Did I fall asleep and wake up in the nineteen-fucking-fifties? Did you *really* just say that to me?" She was going to blow. That fiery spirit of hers I'd come to love and admire so much had been brought to the surface at her father's chauvinistic comment, and I feared her head was just seconds away from exploding all over the room. I needed to intervene before she did something that warranted the police being called... or worse, landed her old man in the hospital. Not that he wouldn't have deserved it.

"Leave," I said, drawing everyone in our small circle's attention with just that one sharp command.

"Excuse me?" Roberto chuckled again.

"I said leave. I have no desire to talk business or anything else with you. Your daughter doesn't want you here, so you need to go."

The old man sputtered indignantly, his face growing red with embarrassment. "Why... you can't be serious."

"I most certainly am. You've been in my presence for all of two minutes and managed to belittle your daughter and make an ass out of yourself in that short amount of time. If Lola hadn't already made me aware of what a slimy motherfucker you were, your actions would have made it abundantly clear. I know exactly what you were hoping to gain by approaching me, and I'm more than glad to inform you that I'll do business with a spineless, dickless piece of shit such as yourself over my cold, dead, rotting fucking body. Now if you'll excuse me, dinner is about to be served, so I need to get my girl to her seat. She's impossible to deal with when she's hungry."

Without so much as a backward glance, I led Lola away from her father and to our reserved seats.

"That was...." She trailed off as I pulled her chair out for her. "I am *so* turned on right now," she leaned in and whispered once I sat down next to her.

"Man." Dominic came up behind me and clapped me on the shoulder with a laugh. "That was fucking outstanding!" He turned to Lola. "Let the record show that I totally approve, shorty. You've got a good one here."

"So noted." She grinned. "Now get your ass away from our table before Sophia sees you."

He offered his sister another smile and took off just seconds before Daphne and Sophia joined us. Caleb followed next, taking the empty chair to Daphne's right, and proceeded to try and engage her in conversation. It was obvious to everyone watching that she wasn't the slightest bit interested, which only made him work that much harder. He'd been fixated on the blonde since he first laid eyes on her down in the studio more than a month before.

My mother and father, Nana, Deacon, and Fiona rounded out the rest of our table. Dinner was surprisingly enjoyable, everyone laughing and chatting amicably. Even Lola and Fiona tipped their heads together, whispering and laughing at certain points. The anxiety that had been knotting my gut for the past two weeks finally started to dissipate, and I felt calm and relaxed for the first time.

That was until the MC got up on stage and announced that it was time to start the bachelorette auction.

"Fuck me," I muttered into my glass of whiskey.

"It'll be fine," Lola leaned in and whispered with a smile.

"How the hell is it going to be fine? I'm probably going to go broke tonight just trying to keep you away from all the other motherfuckers in this room."

She giggled happily and gave me a quick kiss before standing from her chair. "Trust me?"

I let out a disgruntled sigh, but nodded. No matter what, I trusted her. I just hoped she didn't mind dating a poor man, because I had a feeling bidding on Lola Abbatelli was going to drain my bank account substantially.

CHAPTER THIRTY-FIVE

LOLA

"GOOD EVENING, LADIES AND GENTLEMEN." I smiled past the mic in my hand at the large crowd, making a conscious effort to avoid eye contact with Grayson. I was afraid I'd lose my nerve and chicken out again if I looked into his eyes. And I couldn't do that to him. I couldn't do that to *us*.

I'd already made the girls aware of the change in plans. Now all that was left was to make the announcement. I couldn't remember the last time I'd been so nervous. Public speaking was my *thing*. But standing there on the small stage as the ballroom fell quiet, I was a jittery mess.

"Thank you all so much for coming out tonight to help support the Wave Foundation. As you all know from previous years, I, along with the other ladies of *Girl Talk*, like to do our bit to raise even more money for this cause. And this year is no different. After deliberating about what we could do to make everyone reach *even further* into their wallets, we finally came up with the perfect idea. What better way to raise money than a bachelorette auction, right?"

The crowd clapped and applauded excitedly, clearly loving the idea that Sophia, Daphne, and I had come up with, just as we'd hoped. "We decided that we'd auction ourselves off for a date to the highest bidder—now, hold on," I said over the playful laughter and cheers. "It's just *a date*, so don't get too excited," I teased, earning more chuckles.

"But after we came up with this brilliant idea, something changed," I continued, finally finding the courage to look in Grayson's direction. "See that *devastatingly* handsome man sitting right over there?" I pointed at him, drawing the entire room's attention his way, silently reveling in the way his cheeks tinged pink under everyone's scrutiny. "Well, we came up with the plan for the bachelorette auction before I ever met him. But now that I've had a chance get to know him..." *Here goes nothing.* "...and fall in crazy stupid love with him, I decided it wouldn't be right to offer up something that was no longer mine to give."

I ignored the surprised gasps and "awes" of the crowd and kept my focus trained on Grayson's shocked face. "Because the truth is, I belong to him completely. And it wouldn't be fair to him. But to make up for the fact that I unexpectedly—and somewhat unwillingly, at times—gave my heart to that sexy man shortly after publicly humiliating him on the radio"—more laughter—"I've enlisted the help of a friend to take my place, and I'm certain you'll all be thrilled with my choice."

My eyes inadvertently went to Deacon as I announced, "So please welcome the beautiful Fiona Prentice to the stage." I didn't miss the way his jaw dropped open, or the way lust clouded his vision as he watched Fiona make her way up the steps to where I stood next to my two best friends. "Gentlemen, get your checkbooks ready. And let the auction begin!"

With that, I handed the mic back over to the MC and made my way off the stage on shaky legs. Grayson was standing there as soon as I cleared the last step.

"Gray—" Before I could get another word out, his mouth

was on mine, his tongue invading in a soul-destroying kiss that rendered my knees completely ineffective. Luckily, he was holding me tightly against him so he took my weight instead of letting me fall to the floor.

He ripped his lips from mine before I was ready. "Did you mean it?" he panted, his voice rough and jagged.

"I'm in love with you," I said as an answer. "I've been in love with you for a long time. I just wouldn't let myself believe it."

"Christ, baby," he grunted, dropping his forehead against mine and tangling his fingers in my hair. "You have no idea what you've just done. There's no fucking way I'm ever letting you go now."

I wrapped my fingers around his wrists, holding his hands in place as I nuzzled into his touch. "Well I'd hope not, seeing as I just publicly declared my love for you. It would be humiliating if you did, and then I'd have to kill you. Can you imagine the PR the company would have to do?" I bugged my eyes out comically. "Talk about a disaster."

He chuckled deeply, then declared, "God, I love you so much."

"I love you too," I replied, a huge smile splitting my face in two. "But there's still one last hurdle we have to jump before we have our cheesy, clichéd happily ever after."

"I took an online quiz that said I'd belong to Ravenclaw, so if you're worried I'd end up in Slytherin, it's not a problem."

My mouth dropped open in complete shock. "God, I don't think I've ever wanted you more than I do right now. You're going to get *so* lucky tonight."

He let out a deep belly laugh that made my insides all melty. "Good to know my research on Harry Potter is such a turn-on for you."

"While I'm thrilled you'd go to such great lengths to prove your devotion to me, that's not the hurdle I was talking about."

"Whatever it is, we'll get through it."

I pulled back and gave him a skeptical frown. "You say that now... but you haven't met my mother."

If there was ever a statement more deserving of ominous background music, I hadn't heard it. But he didn't seem fazed in the slightest.

Poor guy. He didn't have a clue what he was in for.

EPILOGUE

GRAYSON

THREE MONTHS later

"BABY, will you just relax? You're starting to drive me crazy."

Lola stood from where she'd been hunched over, dusting the bookshelves for the millionth time that day, and gave me a look that said she was trying to set me on fire with her eyes.

"You could help, you know," she harrumphed, propping her hands on her luscious hips. "It *is* your house, after all."

"Ah, ah, ah," I *tsked*, standing from the sectional and setting my beer bottle down on the side table before closing the space between us. "It's *our* house now, baby." I took her hips in my hands and pulled her against me. The feel of her tits pressing into my chest caused my dick to stir.

"Silly me. How could I forget," she breathed, burrowing closer. Her light-brown eyes darkened with want as the dust cloth fell from her hand and her fingers came up the trace my abs beneath my T-shirt. We couldn't get enough of each other. Since we'd started our cohabitation, we'd spent every single free second we had tearing each other's clothes off. It was fucking bliss.

Despite her reservations, it had taken me no time at all to win her mother over. Moms loved me, after all. Then it took approximately a week after the gala to convince her to move in with me. Which, in hindsight, worked out perfectly, since her mother and Maury had hit it off so well they'd run off to Vegas and eloped. Her mom was living in Lola's old apartment with her new husband.

Now Lola's stuff mingled with mine, creating a warm, comfortable feel in a house that had once been devoid of personality. She breathed life into the place—she breathed life into *me*. She'd done what I'd always hoped for and turned my house into a home.

"I know something that'll relieve some of your stress," I growled, nuzzling the crook of her neck and biting at her tantalizing skin.

She let out a low hum that made my cock stand at full attention. "That sounds—wait... no." She gave me a hard shove that sent me back a step. "Stop trying to distract me with your sexy body! We've got too much to do and everyone will be here in—" She looked at the clock hanging on the living room wall and her eyes went wide. "—*three hours!*"

"Baby." I hunched down and caught her eyes. "Calm down, okay? The house is spotless. You've been cleaning it for the past two days. There's literally nothing left to clean. You're cleaning cleanness. You need to relax. It's not like we don't already know each other's families."

Her face fell into a sexy little pout. Jesus, even her pout got me hard. "I know, I'm sorry. I'm just nervous. This is the first time our families are meeting. And your people are so great and mine are kind of nuts, and I'm scared it's going to go wrong."

"Everyone's going to get along great. You'll see."

Her frown didn't lessen as her fingers toyed with the cotton of my shirt. "You say that now, but don't come crying to me when a *West Side Story*-style brawl breaks out in your living room. My mother's certifiable, and Nana's squirrely. I don't trust her with that cane."

I laughed and leaned in planting a kiss on her lips. "Sometimes your imagination frightens me."

"As it should." She nodded seriously. "But I'm being real here. What if something happens and my brother punches you again? It could totally happen."

"He's not going to punch me," I assured her. "Besides, I'm his boss now, so he's too busy trying to make a good impression to even *think* about punching me."

"This is true," she muttered to my shirt.

That was just another of the many changes that had occurred in the past few months. After the showdown between me and their father at the gala, Dominic had decided it was time to cut the last of the strings that held him to an unhealthy relationship, quitting his job with his father. He'd pulled up his roots and moved from New York to Seattle, officially becoming an employee of Bandwidth Communications a month back, much to Sophia's detriment.

There had been a lot of adjustment on everyone's part, but everything seemed to be going well, and life was moving at its regularly set pace no matter what. And for the first time ever, Lola and I were hosting a dinner at *our* house—catered, of course, since my girl couldn't cook for shit—so our families could finally meet. I'd never felt so happy in my life. I just needed to get my woman to loosen up and get onboard the happy train with me.

"Do you love me?" I asked, leaning down and nipping her bottom lip.

"Yes," she sighed dreamily, tilting her head back so I knew

she wanted my attention on her neck. I was glad to give her whatever she wanted, placing open-mouth kisses along her throat to her collarbone. "Do you love me?"

"Baby, I think I've loved you since the minute you shot me down in line at Starbucks. You were just slow on the uptake."

She giggled and leaned in even closer. "It was the dress," she teased.

"Oh, it was definitely the dress," I agreed, my voice dipping low. "That dress is burned into my fucking brain. But it was also the woman *in* that dress."

She stood on her tiptoes, her lips sliding along mine as she spoke. "My man is *so* getting lucky tonight."

And just like that... life got even better.

The End

Read on for an excerpt from
Tempting Sophia a steamy romantic comedy
coming soon

Unedited and subject to change

TEMPTING SOPHIA EXCERPT

PROLOGUE - SOPHIA

Growing up as the only daughter of a single father who was a career firefighter hadn't always been the easiest. My mother, in her infinite wisdom, had decided that parenthood just wasn't for her shortly after giving birth to me and bailed. Dad had done his best after she took off, but as the years passed it became glaringly obvious that raising a little girl on his own was seriously uncharted territory. I loved him to death, but he didn't know the first thing about females, and there was no denying that a lack of female influence had seriously impacted my behavior as a child.

When I got my very first period I came home freaking out that my internal organs had ruptured and I was bleeding to death. After blanching white as a sheet and locking himself in his study for a good thirty minutes, my dad came out with a stack of printed papers, slapped them down on the kitchen table, and told me to read every page word for word. That was how I'd learned about the dreaded menstrual cycle.

When I sprouted boobs seemingly over night, going from an almost non-existent A cup to a full C, he'd tried locking me in my room until I agreed to wearing a sports bra two sizes too small *and* duct taping those puppies down. Was his reaction slightly overboard? Yes. But I was his baby girl, and he just couldn't deal with me growing into a woman.

And let's not even talk about my first foray into dating. I still had nightmares about that. It was bad. And when I say that I mean in the sense that word spread and no boy in my high school would come within thirty yards of me for fear of losing a beloved appendage.

But all of that was beside the point. The point was this, my life would have been much less complicated if I'd had a woman schooling me on how to behave like a lady, or the types of boys to steer clear of once I got older.

Case and point: In elementary and middle school I was more of a tomboy than a girly girl. The other girls in my class liked to make fun of me, but having a father who was the very definition of a man's man had taught me a few useful skills. Instead of being hurt at the teasing and name-calling I handled it like a guy would. Meaning I got myself suspended for a week for cutting one of Lucy Alexander's pigtails off in retaliation.

It wasn't until I reached high school that I really started to become interested in boys. Well, one boy in particular.

Dominic Abbatelli, the older brother of one of my best friends, and the most gorgeous man to ever walk the planet.

He was four years older than me, and already out of high school by my freshman year. But that didn't stop me from falling, and falling hard. I wanted him to look at me the same way he looked at all the other girls I saw him around town with. I wanted that passionate, sinfully heated gaze of his directed at me. *I* wanted to be the one he shared those secret looks that spoke of naught things with. I wanted to catch his attention. So I enlisted the help of his sister Lola to take me from tomboy to glam. I gave up all my boyish ways, the sports bras, ducts tape, and sneakers, and embraced all things girly like my life depended on it. Makeup, clothing, hair, shoes...you name it, I went all out to catch his eye.

I thought my father was going to have a heart attack the first time he saw me in a skirt.

I spent the next few years mooning after my best friend's older brother like a lovesick puppy, and I'd finally started to give up hope until one day shortly after my graduation, he finally noticed me.

It was one of the best nights of my entire life that led to a handful of blissfully happy years. That was, until I surprised my boyfriend during a long weekend by returning home from Seattle. I hadn't seen him in well over a month. The separation was taking a serious toll on both of us, causing petty fights and stupid arguments, and I wanted to make things better. I was missing him like crazy, so I spent what meager savings I had on a plane ticket back to New York.

And what did I get for all my troubles?

Well, I got to walk in on the love of my life giving the business to a chick who *was not me* while he had her bent over the back of the couch.

It wasn't one of my finest moments, but I was thankful some

of my father's lessons came back to me right then, because the only reason I was able to walk away from a nearly four year relationship was because I'd left one of them with a bloody nose and the other with a huge bald spot.

After that fun little experience I decided that it was my lot in life to save other women from a fate such as mine.

That was how my two best girlfriends and I came to be three of the most popular women in Washington and the surrounding states.

We learned from past experiences and doled out relationship advice on the top rated talk radio show geared toward women, aptly named *Girl Talk*. We did our parts for the sisterhood in the hopes of saving as many broken hearts as possible.

And I discovered that it was much easier and a lot less messy to keep a handful of men on my hook as random bed partners than it was to *ever* get into another relationship.

Don't get me wrong, I never judge other women based on their relationship choices, but I'd been there, done that, and gotten the cheap-ass t-shirt. I didn't need to take that trip again.

Besides, I had great friends, a killer job, and an income that most men would envy. My life lacked for nothing.

No way in hell was I letting a man barge into my world and complicate the bliss I'd created.

I was just fine on my own.

Chapter 1

Sophia

What had I been thinking, letting Daphne and Lola talk me into doing a bachelorette auction? Sure, it was for charity, and the money would go toward a worthwhile cause. But as I stood on that stage with a bright spotlight shining down on me as the MC talked me up to potential bidders, I couldn't help but feel like a slab of meat being picked over by hungry vultures.

I tried not to roll my eyes as the lanky guy in an ill-fitting tux spouted off my winning attributes like I was a prized show-pony —most of which weren't even correct. "The beautiful Sophia loved long walks on the beach..." *Wrong. I* hate *sand with a passion, and seagulls could go to Hell for all I care.* "...horseback riding..." *The hell I do. Horses scare the shit out of me. No animal should be that tall.*"...and spending her free time with family and friends." *Well at least that moron got one thing right.*

I pasted a plastic smile on my face as I tried my best to see the faces in the crowd with that god-forsaken spotlight blinding me "Let's start the bidding. Shall we? Can I get—?"

"Ten thousand dollars," I vaguely familiar voice called out.

"Fifteen," someone else spoke. And just like that the bidding was off, but I was too busy trying to place the first voice to pay attention.

"Twenty!"

"Twenty-five!"

"Thirty!"

The man's voice countered every bid, and I found myself squinting in the direction it came from.

"Forty!"

"Forty-five!"

As the bidding continued I shoveled through my memory bank, trying to place where I'd heard that voice before. Obviously the dude wasn't hurting for money, but something about his tone seemed determined.

"Fifty thousand!" another man said.

Then...

"One hundred thousand dollars!" *What in the sweet hell?* Gasps rang out through the room as my skin started to prickle.

"Going once...going twice...*Sold!* Sir, why don't you join us up here on the stage? Let's give this charitable gentleman a round of applause!" The MC cried into the microphone. Everyone clapped at the guy who'd just won a date with me for a whopping hundred grand while my insides began to knot and the tiny hairs on my arms stood on end.

Then it dawned on me. All I could think as the guy with a familiar voice got closer was *nonononono*...because I knew, I just *knew* who that voice belonged to. But it wasn't possible. Was it? I mean, Lola would have said something.

The second his foot hit the first step the spotlight shifted off of me and onto him my entire body froze, my lungs seized, and all the blood drained from my face.

The MC's voice sounded like it was coming from deep inside a tunnel as he asked for his name. His response echoed inside my head like a gong.

"Dominic Abbatelli."

Fuck. My. Life.

"Well, congratulations Dominic! Thanks to your generosity, you'll be going on a date with this beautiful woman right here!" All of a sudden the MC's jubilance grated on my every nerve. I wanted to punch him in the throat as his hand hit the center of my back and pushed me off to the side with Dominic in order to continue the auction.

The plastic smile remained on my face as I allowed Dom to lead me down the stairs. And the only reason I let him was because my legs were so shaky I feared I'd fall if left to walk on my own.

Once I was on the ground at the side of the stage I quickly put distance between us, shaking off his touch like it burned me. "What the hell are you doing here?" I hiss out of the side of my mouth.

"Careful, Butterfly. Pull back your claws. People are still watching."

Emotions were a funny thing, really. I never would have thought I'd want to cause someone bodily harm at the exact time I wanted to burst into a deluge of tears. But there I was, clenching my fists to keep from throttling ex while my eyes stung at the sound of my nickname on his tongue.

I hadn't heard that name is years. I should have been over it, but hearing him call me butterfly again after almost a decade still caused a lump to form in my throat. Memories were fickle like that. They'd sat stagnant in the back of my mind for so long I'd nearly forgotten about them, but with just that one word they were shoved to the forefront of my brain. It played like a video clip in my head: me standing in Dominic's bathroom, leaned over the sink as I brushed mascara on my lashes; him leaning against the door jam with a content smile on his face as he watched.

"Why don't we just stay in tonight?" he asked, his eyes hungrily skating along my body clad only in panties and a bra.

"Because we're going out! You promised to take me dancing. I want to see those famous Abattelli moves, " I teased, blowing him a kiss in the mirror.

"My little butterfly," he said softly, coming to stand directly behind me. "Always flitting around, never content to stay in one place for long."

His arms wrapped around me, and I shoved the mascara wand inside the tube and turned to place my hands on his shoulders. "That's just not true."

"It's not?"

"Nope." I shook my head, standing on my tiptoes to place a kiss on his lips. "I'll always be content wherever I am as long as you're there with me."

God, I hated that nickname even while another part of me treasured it. He crowded my space, forcing me to keep moving. I gave a sidelong look at Lola's table, hoping to burn her alive with my eyes, but she wasn't there.

Not surprising, really. She'd been having an on-again off-again relationship with a man named Grayson Lockhart, a guy who just so happened to be our boss's boss's boss, for the past several weeks. She'd been falling for with him even though she denied it every step of the way, but seeing as she'd just stood up on that exact same stage minutes before and professed her love to him, the two of them were probably getting it on in a coat closet or something at that very moment. I was going to murder her so dead the next time I saw her. The least she could have done was warn me that her big brother had crashed the charity event our station sponsored every single year.

She had some serious explaining to do. And a whole lot of groveling.

"Oh, no. No way. Unh unh." I shook my head and attempted to dig my heels in when I caught sight of where he was leading us. The French doors loomed ominously before me, leading out to a terrace far from the rest of the party. No way was I allowing myself to be trapped on an empty, dark terrace, with nothing but the romantic view of the lake glowing in the moonlight as stars filled the sky. Nope. That chick-flick romance bullshit was *not* happening.

"Keep walking, Butterfly," he whispered in my ear, sending a spark of electricity across my skin. "I won't hesitate to throw you over my shoulder and carry you if I have to."

The son of a bitch wasn't lying either. I could hear it in his voice. And if that wasn't enough to make me comply, the fact that he'd done the very thing he'd just threatened more than once during our relationship would have done it.

I let out an aggrieved huff and crossed my arms over my chest as we came to the doors. Dominic kept a hand firmly on my back as he swung one of them open and pushed me through.

He followed behind me and closed us away from the rest of the partygoers. As if that wasn't bad enough, he stood with his legs planted slightly apart between the glass doors and me like a goddamned security guard, making it impossible for me to get away.

A shiver from the chilly night wind worked its way through my body as Dominic and I engaged in a sort of standoff with one another. Finally, the way he regarded me with those deep amber eyes I'd once loved so much became too much to bear, and I had to look away. I focused on the stone facing of the wall just over his shoulder while I rubbed at my arms to ward off the cold. "Why are you still here?" I finally found the courage to ask, even if I wasn't strong enough to voice my question while looking at him. He'd come to Seattle to visit Lola, but his vacation didn't seem to have an end date anywhere in sight. "Shouldn't you be back in New York by now?"

Dominic scratched at his stubble-covered jawline before moving to the railing and leaning down to rest his elbows on the metal surface. The move brought him closer to me and allowed the moonlight to highlight his stupidly handsome face. My heart rate kicked up as his square, solid features came into better view. *Stupid heart.*

"I've been reevaluating a lot of things lately," he said in a quiet voice. "Figured it would be best if I stuck around while I worked through some things."

The ominous statement did little to alleviate my nerves. "Best for whom, exactly? Because I don't think your sister's going to be thrilled with having you crash at her place for an indefinite amount of time."

He stood tall and turned his head in my direction. Those intense eyes hit me once again only this time the swirling storm of emotion inside of them stole my breath. "I'm not going back to Manhattan."

"What are you talking about?" I whispered as panic began twisting at my insides.

"I'm staying here. In Seattle."

My head jerked back like I'd just been hit. "Are you kidding me?" I whispered venomously. Hadn't he already caused me enough pain? He'd already broken my heart once before. It had taken me years and thousands of miles of distance to get myself back on my feet, and now he was telling me that I no longer had the comfort of a continent between us to keep me safe? "You're *such* a bastard!" I snapped, dropping my arms to my sides. My entire body went rigid as I began to seethe. "This is *my* city, Dominic! Mine! Your life's supposed to be on the other side of the country *far* away from me!"

"I'm staying for you!" he barked, moving close and getting in my face.

I reared back on one heel, the spike teetering precariously as my eyes went round. "*What?*" I screeched incredulously. Then the shock quickly gave way to laughter of disbelief "How can you possibly be staying for me? Oh my God, Dom! I don't *want* you here! Don't you get it? I stayed in Seattle to get the hell *away* from you!"

"I fucked up," he ground out, his tone so ragged it sounded like he'd swallowed glass. "I fucked up and I lost you." He surprised me by reaching up and taking my face gently between both his hands. I was so stunned by the action that I couldn't move. "But I'll make it right, Butterfly—"

"Don't call me that," I bit out, forcing down the swell of tears in my throat. "*Don't.*" I tried to pull away but his fingers tangled in my hair, keeping me in place.

"I'll make it right," he repeated. "I'm going to win you back if it's the last fucking thing I do."

"*Have you lost your mind?*" I yelled into the quiet night. "There's no making it right! I caught you fucking another woman, Dom! It'll be a cold day in Hell before you win me back!"

"You broke up with me!" he shouted, throwing his hands into the air.

It was the exact same fight we'd had countless times after that night. And just like all those years ago, hearing him say that made me murderous. "It was a fight," I growled, my teeth clenched painfully tight. "We got into a *fight*!"

"Yeah, a fight that ended with you saying that maybe we shouldn't be together before hanging up on me."

"Oh, my god!" I breathed with a touch of hysteria as I ran my hands through my hair. "I'm not doing this. I'm not having this same fucking argument with you again. It didn't matter ten years ago and it matters even less today. This is over."

I moved to sidestep him and get the hell out of there when his hand clasped on my elbow and jerked me back with such force I spun around and landed against his rock-solid chest. Before I could utter a word his mouth came down on mine in a kiss so unexpected, so consuming that my body, heart, and mind had no choice but the reciprocate. By the time he pulled back my lips felt swollen and bruised. I could barely catch my breath, and the ground felt shaky beneath my feet.

I couldn't form a single coherent thought as he trailed his fingertips along my hairline down to my jaw.

"That was just the beginning," he said softly.

Then, just like that, he disappeared back into the ballroom, leaving my world completely shaken and turned upside down.

That motherfucker!

I seethed as I tossed my vibrator to the side. My chest rose and fell with exertion, but despite the self-induced orgasm I'd just had my body still wasn't satisfied.

And it was all that bastard's fault!

If he hadn't kissed me like his life depended on it... like *my* life depended on it, I wouldn't have been in such a state.

"Ugh!" I shouted into the darkness of my bedroom. I balled my fists and gave my mattress a few punches for good measure, but it was pointless. I knew better. There was no cure for the frustration—sexual and otherwise—that was coursing in my blood. I called it the Dom Affect. It was how I got any time I was subjected to Dominic Abbatelli's presence.

Which was why I'd spent the better part of a decade far, far away from him.

Knowing sleep was useless I climbed from my bed, readjusted my PJs, and stomped from my bedroom into the kitchen for a much-needed glass of wine. When all else failed I could always count on getting stupid drunk.

I'd just finished filling up my glass and took my first sip when my cellphone started to ring. I plunked my glass down and walked over to where I had it plugged in on the kitchen counter, glaring at the name on the screen.

I accepted the call but didn't get a word out before Lola started in. "On a scale from one the low fat ice cream, how much do you hate me right now?"

"My anger doesn't even register on that scale," I answered menacingly. "You've got a lot of nerve calling me after the stunt you pulled tonight."

"I'm sorry!" Lola cried through the line. "I'm so, so sorry, honey. I didn't know he was going to be there until he showed up. I swear! Then Fiona wanted to talk and my dad showed and the auction..." she rambled. "It was just one big clusterfuck of an evening."

"Well it seemed to have ended well enough for you," I dead-panned. "You got the man and I got blindsided."

She sighed heavily in my ear. "You're right. None of that's an excuse. I should have told you he was there."

That was the thing with my relationship with Lola. No matter what she did, I couldn't stay mad at her. The woman didn't have a conniving bone in her body when it came to her friends, so I knew she hadn't truly meant any harm.

I blew out a loud puff of air as I headed back to my wine. "I forgive you," I grumbled sullenly. "But I'm still mad. You're brother...he just *the worst!*" I declared.

"I know." Lola spoke in an appeasing, yet slightly sarcastic tone. "He's terrible. We should totally stone him or key his car or something."

I let out a very unladylike snort of laughter. "Don't make me laugh when I'm mad at you."

"Sorry," she replied, not sounding the least bit sorry. "So, are we good?"

"We're good."

I could hear the relief in her voice when she continued. "Good. And it's just a while longer. Soon he'll be back in New York and you can go back to pretending he doesn't exist."

I paused with the wineglass halfway to my mouth. "But, he said he's moving here."

"*What?*" she shrieked so loud I had to pull the phone from my ear with a wince. "When the hell did he say that?"

"He told me tonight."

"What else did he tell you?"

I was suddenly bone tired at the thought of relaying the events of the evening. I let out a weary sigh and sat my glass down, only half finished. "Can we talk about this tomorrow? I really don't want to get into it again tonight. And don't you have a new hotty boyfriend you're supposed to be riding like a cowgirl anyway?"

She let out a loud laugh. "I'm calling between rounds. Grayson had to replenish his fluids."

"'Lalalalalala!" I shouted, twisting my face in disgust even though she couldn't see me. "I don't need to hear that!" Especially considering how my traitorous body had been behaving since that stupid kiss. "I'm hanging up now."

"All right, but we're talking tomorrow. I want to know everything."

We said our goodbyes and I disconnected. I set the phone next to my discarded glass of wine and trudged back to my bedroom. Exhaustion from the night's events had officially worn my body out. Unfortunately my mind refused to shut off, and I spent the next several hours tossing and turning.

When I finally did drift to sleep my dreams were plagued with all things Dominic.

The man was like a virus, there was just no getting rid of him.

Read More Now

Enticing Daphne

IT'S easy to stop believing in happily ever afters when the man you thought you'd spend the rest of your life with abandons you right before your wedding day. After that disastrous event I decided that commitment was for suckers. I was young, successful, and in the prime of my life.

I didn't need a man to make me happy.

Then an unexpected blast from the past came waltzing into my studio and decided I was a challenge he was more than willing to accept. The only problem is that he doesn't remember he's met me before.

He's the ultimate playboy, determined to stop at nothing until he entices the hell out of me. But if Caleb McMannus thinks he can lure me in with his sinful looks and silver tongue, then he's... probably right.

Charming Fiona

AS I CHILD, I believed in true love and fairytales. I convinced myself that there was one special man out there, made just for me. All I had to do was wait, and one day he would appear. Then I grew up and discovered the ugly truth.

Disney movies were full of crap.

Relationships took work. People made mistakes. And sometimes, you didn't see what was standing right in front of you until it was too late.

Deacon Lockhart was my best friend. And then I lost him. But now I finally have a chance to make things right, and this time I refuse to screw it up. With every smoldering look and wicked word, he charms the hell out of me... and I'm pretty sure I'll never get enough.

Click here for more info

DISCOVER OTHER BOOKS BY JESSICA

THE PICKING UP THE PIECES SERIES:

Picking up the Pieces

Rising from the Ashes

Pushing the Boundaries

Worth the Wait

THE COLORS NOVELS:

Scattered Colors

Shrinking Violet

Love Hate Relationship

Wildflower

THE LOCKLAINE BOYS (a LOVE HATE RELATIONSHIP spinoff):

Fire & Ice

Opposites Attract

Almost Perfect

THE PEMBROOKE SERIES (a WILDFLOWER spinoff):

Sweet Sunshine

Coming Full Circle

A Broken Soul

ABOUT THE AUTHOR

Born and raised around Houston, Jessica is a self proclaimed caffeine addict, connoisseur of inexpensive wine, and the worst driver in the state of Texas. In addition to being all of these things, she's first and foremost a wife and mom.

Growing up, she shared her mom and grandmother's love of reading. But where they leaned toward murder mysteries, Jessica was obsessed with all things romance.

When she's not nose deep in her next manuscript, you can usually find her with her kindle in hand.

Connect with Jessica now
Website: www.authorjessicaprince.com
Jessica's Princesses Reader Group
Newsletter
Facebook
Twitter
Instagram
authorjessicaprince@gmail.com